They knew exactly what they wanted from each other

Deck pulled Callie close and kissed her. Heat and relief surged through him. It was the same and different at once. Familiar and new. Just as strong, but more certain.

How the hell had this happened? Deck was foggy on exactly what had led to him holding Callie in his arms, taking her soft mouth, but he wasn't sorry. He'd started it. He knew that. Something about seeing her again, the past so fresh between them.

He'd meant to comfort her, but had lost control, and now her breasts were pressed against his chest, his cock was hard against her belly, and her sweet tongue was in hot pursuit of his own.

He took her ass in both hands, yanking her tight against him. She moaned, trembling as she had all those years ago, but she wrapped her legs around his waist, telling him what she wanted. He felt the hot drive to be inside her, making her come, coming himself.

"Deck," she said, pulling back. "What are we doing?"

He tried to halt the free fall. "You want to stop?"

"Maybe we should." She bit her lip, shivered. "But I don't want to."

Blaze

Dear Reader,

This book means a lot to me. It's about the healing power of love. Like Callie, I lost my mother at too young an age. Also like her, I tend to run from emotion, instead of facing it head-on. And, as Callie's high school counselor wisely noted, *what you resist, persists.*

When she comes home to rescue her father's guest ranch, Callie faces her fear that she's guarded her heart so well she no longer has the capacity for deep love. With Deck's help, she works through that and emerges more open and loving because of it.

Though Deck stayed in town, he, too, put his emotions on hold. Callie helps him open up and risk his heart for a great and healing love.

This book is also about coming home. A city girl who moved a lot, I've wondered what it would be like to return to the same small town you grew up in to see people who've known you forever. That could be as comforting as a warm fire in winter or as suffocating as a down pillow over the face. Callie feels a little of both.

I like the way Callie and Deck work their lives out in the story. I hope you do, too.

All my best,

Dawn

P.S. I'd love to hear your thoughts. Write me at dawn@dawnatkins.com. For news, visit www.dawnatkins.com.

Still Irresistible

DAWN ATKINS

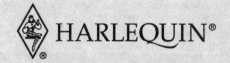

HARLEQUIN®

TORONTO • NEW YORK • LONDON
AMSTERDAM • PARIS • SYDNEY • HAMBURG
STOCKHOLM • ATHENS • TOKYO • MILAN • MADRID
PRAGUE • WARSAW • BUDAPEST • AUCKLAND

Recycling programs
for this product may
not exist in your area.

ISBN-13: 978-0-373-79460-7
ISBN-10:   0-373-79460-6

STILL IRRESISTIBLE

Copyright © 2009 by Daphne Atkeson.

ABOUT THE AUTHOR

This is award-winning Harlequin Blaze author Dawn Atkins's twenty-third published romance novel. Known for her funny, spicy romances with a touch of mystery, she's won a Golden Quill Award for Best Sexy Romance and has been a several-times *Romantic Times BOOKreviews* Reviewers' Choice Award finalist for Best Blaze, as well as a finalist for a *Romantic Times BOOKreviews* Career Achievement Award for Best Love and Laughter. With her husband and son she lives in Arizona, where—like Callie Cummings, the heroine of this book—she loves the desert. Unlike Callie, she gets ve-r-r-ry nervous around horses.

Books by Dawn Atkins

HARLEQUIN BLAZE

*Forbidden Fantasies
**Doing It…Better!
†Sex on the Beach

To my grandfather, who never wanted his illness to keep me from my "book work," and to the Valley of the Sun Hospice, true angels, who made his passing heaven.

Acknowledgments

Eternal gratitude to Joe Collins, paramedic, firefighter and all-around answer man, and to ranch woman and author Susan Yarina, who saved my writerly life. Any factual or procedural errors in their areas of expertise are completely my own.

1

AN IRRITATED WHINNY DREW Callie Cummings's gaze to the barn, where a cowboy was backing a reluctant horse into the corral with a tight grip on its halter.

Callie caught her breath. It was Deck. She would have recognized that butt blindfolded.

Providing she could touch it.

Touch it. An automatic ping of lust passed through her. And why not? What woman with blood in her veins wouldn't respond to Declan O'Neill and his fabulous behind?

But she wasn't here to appreciate Deck's backside. Or his front side, for that matter, which also delivered. She was here to turn her father's failing dude ranch into a desert spa.

A daunting task for a Manhattan event planner, but Callie was determined to succeed.

She had no choice. Her father was counting on her. When he'd said he was afraid he'd have to sell, he'd sounded so heartbroken it had been like losing her mother all over again.

Callie stood poised on the bottom porch step with her bag. Eleven years hadn't reduced the tension between her and Deck. By unspoken agreement, they avoided each other during her frequent trips home. She could pretend she hadn't seen him and go in, but Deck was ranch foreman and they had to work together. Better to get the first awkward conversation over with.

Plunge into the hard part, that was Callie's way.

Dropping her bag, Callie took a steadying breath and marched toward the corral, her heart as jumpy as the horse

Deck was wrangling, her feet wobbly in the kitten heels perfect for travel, but dangerously flimsy for the rocky desert ground.

You're not in Manhattan anymore.

For better or worse, she was home. The Arizona sun, warm enough that January was high season, toasted Callie's scalp and arms. The familiar smells—horse and creosote, hay and wood—made her both homesick and miserable. She missed the place and she dreaded it, too. Mixed memories. Always.

Reaching the corral, she leaned on the fence, trying to look casual, taking Deck in. Tall and lanky with broad shoulders and long legs, he had an animal grace that used to make her melt just watching him walk.

He had all the good-cowboy traits—honor, loyalty, strength, stoicism, skill—and none of the bad. He didn't chew tobacco or drink or cheat or gamble or act crudely or have bad hygiene. He smelled of Irish Spring and leather and cedar and sunshine. And the only thing ratty about him was his ancient Stetson, but that looked classy.

That was old news. Eleven years old.

Bound by the shared tragedy of losing a parent, they'd fallen into each other's arms for six incredible weeks their senior year.

"Hey, Deck," she called. Too late, she saw she'd snagged her silk sleeve on the rough wood and frowned.

"This is no place for silk, Callie. Or anything white." The crinkles at the edges of his sky-blue eyes deepened with humor. He looked rugged and knowing. And he was laughing at her.

Her cheeks warmed. "I just got here. Give me a minute to get grimy and start smelling like manure." She hoped she'd sounded amused, not snotty. She never got it right around him.

He just looked at her. What was in his eyes? Disapproval? Superiority? He hadn't been that way back then. Maybe she'd only assumed she'd understood him. The one thing they'd had in common was grief and need, after all. Now Deck seemed more guarded. On the other hand, when you had history, everything could mean something or nothing at all.

Deck's expression shifted like clouds in changeable weather, but remained unreadable. She felt another sexual zing.

Did he feel anything? Anything at all?

The horse whinnied and pulled back on the reins.

"You training a new horse?" she asked, glad for an excuse to break an eye lock that felt like arm wrestling.

"Yeah. This is Brandy. Cal bought her for his lady friend. I've been working her for a while." He ran his hand down the neck of the restless horse, who gave a ferocious snort. "Brandy's still too spirited for a beginner."

Her father's lady friend, his first since Callie's mother died, was Dahlia Mitford, whom Callie would meet for the first time today. She felt responsible for the woman, since she'd paid for the dating service, then prodded her father into using it. He'd hit the jackpot right out of the chute.

"Spirited? She looks demon-eyed with rage."

"She just needs a rider she can trust, don't you, girl?" Deck's voice seemed to send ripples of relaxation down the horse's body. He'd had the same effect on Callie those first awful days when she'd been frantic with sorrow, wild to escape her own skin.

Deck had saved her. Deck understood her pain, accepted it, having lost his dad to a brain aneurysm after a fall from a horse six months before her own mother's car wreck.

"So I hear you're sprucing up the place," Deck said, not looking at her, but slowing his hand on the horse, listening.

"That's understating it a bit."

"What do you mean?" His gaze lifted to hers.

"We'll be making some changes."

"Like what?"

"This and that." She didn't want to get into the details right off the bat, but he clearly wanted more. "Updating the ranch house, adding a room annex, more casitas, adding amenities—a pool, a spa, tennis courts. We're renaming it Rancho de Descanso."

"Rest Ranch? Is that a joke? The Triple C is a working cattle ranch."

The ranch had been named for her and her parents—Calvin, Colleen and Calissa—but those days were done. "We're capitalizing on the trend toward experiential vacations with luxury. Desert getaways are hot—the good kind of hot."

"People come here to run cattle, to learn to rope and ride, to enjoy the desert, not to get facials and mud baths."

"Tastes change. We can't afford to get left behind." Wait until he heard she would be selling off the cattle.

"Sure, the place needs paint," he continued. "And I'll rebuild the porch as soon as Cal signs off on the supplies. I've been after him to buy some ads, since we run empty some weeks, but there's no need to turn the place inside out."

"Paint and ads won't cut it, Deck. This is high season and we've only got eight guests. We can handle thirty."

"Cal know about this?" he demanded.

Anger stung her cheeks. How dare he talk to her as if she were a kid taking the pickup without permission?

"We haven't gone over the details, but he trusts me. He asked for my help."

Deck paused. When he spoke his voice was softer, oil on troubled water. "Sorry. It's just that he's been tough to pin down on ranch issues lately, so I'm not sure what he wants."

"What do you mean?"

"He's gone a lot. Out of town. Not available. Frankly, if he'd been paying more attention, the ranch wouldn't be in the shape it's in and—" He stopped himself. "Sorry. I'm just the foreman, not the boss."

"Exactly. And you haven't seen the books." The spreadsheet was a study in red. "The only place we haven't lost money is on the guests. I'm doing what has to be done. Be assured of that."

She'd sounded pompous and that wouldn't improve their rapport. "We can talk about all this later, Deck. For now, I can sure use your help." She managed a smile. The man knew the ranch as well as she knew her Brooklyn apartment. "I'll talk to Dad."

"That would be wise."

If she'd had hackles, they'd be on end and she'd be growling. Deck was so damn sure he was right, as if he'd already separated the chaff from the wheat, the worthwhile from the waste, and she should bow before his wisdom.

She opened her mouth to say, *And who named you the Great and Powerful Oz?* but was saved from making things worse by someone calling her name.

She turned. From the porch, a thin woman in a tie-dyed dress motioned wildly for her to come. "You're here! Come in!" Had to be Dahlia. Callie was startled to notice how young she looked. Her father hadn't mentioned that. "Get out of the sun before you wrinkle!" she called.

Callie waved.

"Watch out for her teas," Deck said. "If she gives you a choice, take peppermint. The rest are nasty." His eyes lit with the mischief she'd loved back then, like he'd let her in on a great secret. He tilted his hat, dove gray and worn, but perfect on his head. "Good to have you back."

Instantly, she remembered that August night, her last before leaving for college. *"Don't go, Callie."* His voice had been rough with emotion. *"Stay with me."* He'd been drunk, but his words seemed dredged from somewhere deep.

Did he remember? Or had he washed it from his mind? Probably. You had to protect yourself. Certainly he'd learned that, too. They'd had the lesson young, after all.

"Thanks, Deck," she said. "It's good to be back." Sort of. She turned to go, feeling his eyes on her as she walked away. She tried not to wiggle on her flimsy heels.

The man was still sexy as hell. He made her nervous. He made her mad. He made her want him.

She hated that.

She turned her attention to Dahlia, who was dragging Callie's suitcase up the porch stairs, while two guests looked on from the porch.

Callie rushed over. "I've got it. Thank you." She had to yank the bag free of Dahlia's grip. At the top, Callie nodded at the man and woman playing cards and drinking lemonade in faded wicker chairs.

Those would have to go. Callie would replace all the furniture and redo the porch for sure. A glance at the log facade told her she was right. A new stain and fresh trim in something trendy—say, umber?—would do just fine.

The pots of flowers on either side of the door were new and bright. Dahlia's touch, she'd bet. The woman created beauty products and ointments from desert plants. Callie had said she'd consider them for the ranch's new spa.

Once they were inside, Dahlia yanked Callie into a bruising hug, then looked her over with bird-bright eyes. "I'm so, *so* glad to meet you." She smelled pleasantly herbal. If that was a sample of her creams, Callie liked it so far.

"I'm glad to meet you, too, Dahlia."

"You're as lovely as your pictures." Dahlia examined her face like an aesthetician with the blackhead remover. "I have the remedy for the bags under your eyes. In fact…" She hurried to the registration counter to grab a large cellophane-wrapped basket, which she thrust into Callie's arms.

"My gift to you. One of everything. Face cream, body lotion, shampoo, conditioner, masque." She tapped each jar or tube as she named it. "I can't wait to work with you."

"I'll try them out and we'll go from there. And my dad…?"

"Catching his siesta. He gets so weary." Her father was a youthful fifty. She'd made him sound like a fragile old man. Close up, Dahlia looked midthirties, not *that* much younger. "I have tea steeping for us." Dahlia gestured toward the tucked-away Cummings family kitchen.

"Let me put my things away and check on Dad," Callie

said, starting for the stairs with the overloaded basket of Dahlia's Desert Delights. She shifted her suitcase to one side so a couple and their young daughter could head down the stairs. They were chatting happily. When Callie was finished, the place would be lively with guests year-round.

DECK HELD his shit-eating grin in case Callie glanced his way again. She thought he was a smug asshole. No point in disappointing her. She wiggled away in her all-wrong outfit, her heels so fragile they'd snap in a knothole. She was too busy wrestling Dahlia for her bag to look back.

No surprise.

Meanwhile, Deck still reeled from the brain buzz and flood of lust he got whenever he saw her. When the ranch house door closed, he rested his forehead against Brandy's neck and blew out a breath.

What was it about her? No other woman gave him the thud in the chest, the hot knot in his gut, the below-belt ache. She was the first, the one that got away. Maybe that was it.

All she had to do was say his name, and his pulse kicked like a riled horse. Then he never failed to act like a dick. Which was why he avoided her when she was home. At least he hadn't let on how much he still wanted her.

Did she still want him? Unlikely. She got nervous and defensive around him, but Callie never looked back. She'd left Abrazo for Manhattan like she'd staged a prison break.

Brandy whinnied, so he led her a few yards into the corral with a firm hand, talking low. "Easy, girl. Settle. Steady does it." No way would the horse be ready for the sunset ride Cal had planned with Dahlia and Callie.

Deck usually bought all the horses for the Triple C, but Cal hadn't asked his advice on this spirited filly, which would be perfect for Callie, if she hadn't stopped riding back in seventh grade. Her horse, Lucky, died and broke her heart, though she would never admit that was the reason.

He trotted Brandy around the corral until she managed an easy lope, beginning to trust him. He led her out of the corral, closed the gate and took her for a quick ride across the rolling pasture before he brought her back to her stall and rewarded her with some oats. "Wish I could stay, but I have business inside," he said with a sigh.

He had to tell Cal Brandy wasn't ready, which meant another run-in with Callie. Deck needed to remind Cal of the planning and zoning hearing tonight, too—they both sat on the commission.

Taylor Loft, the police chief, was buttonholing commissioners to push through a tax exemption that coincidentally would save him thousands, since he'd started moonlighting as a developer. His father had been a decent chief, but Loft was a manipulative opportunist, who pissed Deck off every time he ran into him.

Because Callie went back to him? Could Deck be that small? With Callie around, he wasn't sure of anything.

"Wish me luck, girl," he said to Brandy, patting her rump before he headed toward the ranch house.

Instead of Callie and her dad, he found Dahlia alone in the Cummingses' kitchen. "Cal around?" he asked.

"Callie went upstairs to get him. She just got here."

"Yeah. I spoke to her. I can come back." He turned away.

"No. No. Let me get you some tea."

"No thanks, I'm just—" The woman looked so nervous and desperate, he said, "Sure. Half a cup, I guess."

She handed it to him.

Praying for peppermint, he took a sip. Score. "Very nice."

"Sit, sit," she said, eager to entertain someone, it seemed. "So you saw Callie already? She's such a pretty girl."

"She is that," he said, sitting across the table from her. Which only made her more annoying.

"Calvin is so happy to see her."

"I imagine he would be." Since his heart scare, Cal seemed

to miss his daughter more. He should have told Callie he was in the hospital, Deck thought. She would have rushed out, screw the big party he claimed she had to manage. Callie was a good person at heart, despite her silly job. She called her father every week and visited every few months.

"I hope she'll take the pressure off Calvin."

"I'm sure she will." Ironically enough, that had been Deck's intention when he'd decided to buy the ranch. He'd figured Cal wanted out, and the Lazy J money was just gathering dust in the bank. The very afternoon he stepped into Cal's office to make an offer, the man announced Callie was coming home to fix up the place, his grin as big as his face.

Too late. Deck had moved too late. Now Callie's hare-brained scheme could wreck the Triple C. Maybe if he treaded lightly, she'd figure that out and hightail her pretty ass back to New York where she belonged, and he could take over after all.

Deck was a patient man. He would wait and see. Animals took time. Crops, too. Biology didn't turn on a dime. Every worthwhile thing took its own sweet time.

The clock ticked loudly in the silence. Deck sipped. Dahlia stared and fidgeted. Where the hell was Cal? "So, uh, I took Brandy out again, but I don't think she's quite ready for a new rider."

"She's not? Oh, that's too bad. Thank you, anyway." But the woman looked faint with relief. She had no interest in the ranch, from what Deck had seen. She'd distracted the hell out of Cal, dragging him to Tucson whenever a health-food restaurant invented something new with tofu. He'd been late with bills, slow on repairs and like molasses with decisions.

As a result, the Triple C was in trouble, according to Callie. Deck should have spoken up sooner. "I should be going." He stood. "If you could just tell Cal about Brandy for me? And could you remind him of the meeting—"

"He'll be here any second, I'm sure. So…you've known

Callie a long time?" She must be nervous about whatever Callie and Cal were saying about her upstairs.

"Since we were kids, yeah. We went to school together." But they ran in different circles. Callie had been a star in tiny Abrazo. He didn't blame her for wanting to swim in a bigger pond. Once he'd gotten past the tequila-soaked shame of that August night, he'd wished her well.

Except for one thing. She'd felt *sorry* for him. That still burned. No one pitied Declan O'Neill. Losing his father had been hard, but he'd worked the ranch the way his dad would have and watched over his mother until she got her footing again. He'd gotten past that bad time when he'd almost cashed it in. He never thought about that. The memory froze him stiff.

"We're lucky she could leave her company for so long to come out here. She does such exciting work. Parties with celebrities and socialites and big companies…"

"So I hear." From what he could tell, Callie spent her days sampling cakes, choosing dance bands and turning goldfish bowls into centerpieces.

"She's really made something of herself." Dahlia beamed.

"Seems that way." He had no doubt she was good. Callie was a sight to see on full throttle. But party planning?

Truth be told, Deck expected more of her. She'd been a firebrand in high school, smart and funny, full of ideas, impatient to fix any injustice. He figured she'd head a corporation, work for a cause. Hell, go into politics.

Maybe he'd just built her up in his mind.

She thought less of him, too, no doubt. To her, he'd gotten stuck in a hick town, spending his days babysitting cattle, his nights in a trailer, his life a pure waste.

She was wrong. There was solace in hard work and reward in the tangible outcomes of his efforts—a healthy herd, well-managed pastures, well-trained horses, spirited and smart.

Nothing wrong with that.

Still, Callie made him think of missed chances and open

horizons. Seeing her made that sliver of restlessness he'd felt lately itch like a horsefly bite.

That was a pure trap. The grass always seemed greener in the next pasture, until you got there and found the same goat heads and dry patches you'd thought you'd escaped.

The truth was that he and Callie plain rubbed each other the wrong way.

They sure as hell used to rub each other right.

"Yes? Is something funny?" Dahlia asked.

"Uh, no." He didn't expect to be laughing anytime soon.

"Maybe I'll go up and see what's keeping them." Before she left, she poured him more tea.

What could Deck do but drink it?

2

STARTING DOWN THE HALL of the owner's quarters, Callie noticed her father's bedroom door ajar, so she set down her bag and the basket and tapped before leaning in. "Dad?"

"Huh?" Her father sat up on the bed. "Uh… Oh, sweetheart, you're here…good deal." He sounded groggy.

"Are you okay, Dad?"

"Just waking up." He pushed out of bed to hug her, then regarded her warmly. "You're a sight for sore eyes. Seeing you in the doorway, you looked just like Colleen when we first met."

"I'm glad," she said, happy to resemble her mother, though the reminder made her ache. "I miss her, too, Dad." Tears made her nose sting. How stupid.

"What you resist persists." The school counselor kept saying that whenever Callie tried to escape her probing questions. She'd itched to get away. *Run, run, get out* was her mantra. Leaving for college had been the first moment of true relief.

She lunged in for another hug, noticing that instead of the usual Old Spice, her father smelled of eucalyptus and menthol. "Are you wearing liniment?"

"It's an ointment for arthritis Dahlia cooked up."

"You have arthritis?"

"I'm a little stiff in the mornings is all. It's nothing. I think herbs are fine for teas and face goop, but for curing? Not so much. It makes Dahlia happy, so I use it."

"That's kind of you." She felt the same way he did about herbal remedies.

"It's so good to have you back," he said, looking her over tenderly. "When you're here, the place feels right again."

She stiffened. What an odd thing to say. He never talked like that. Five months after her mother's death, he'd insisted Callie go to New York University as planned, even when she claimed she wasn't ready, which was a lie. She'd been worried about him living all alone. Her father would not hear of it. It was her mother's dream for her daughter, and he would be busy working the ranch. She belonged in college, period. She had her own life, and her independence made him proud.

"Is something wrong, Dad?" she asked gently.

"Not at all. I'm just sentimental these days." He waved away her concern. "I hate to drag you away from your business, but I really appreciate your taking the place to hand."

"I'm happy to do it, Dad. My partner can pick up the slack while I'm gone." Stefan owed her the favor, after all.

For being a cheating rat.

But that was another story.

"I'll expand my expertise, too, so that's good for my career. I'm anxious to dig in. I've got two contractors giving bids—tomorrow and the day after."

"Whoa, now. Give yourself some time to relax, huh?"

"I saw the spreadsheets, Dad," she gently reminded him. "We're drowning in debt. Valhalla Investments expects quick action, too. We have to watch the timing for travel calendars for our launch. The pieces are like dominoes. Everything has to click into place. No time to lay back or slow down."

She was armed with research, a plan, funding and a consultant known worldwide for her resort makeovers. She'd declared the ranch makeover "cookbook"—mostly marketing and promotion, which Callie knew cold—and would be a phone call away. What Callie couldn't learn, she'd hire experts to do.

"We'll see how it goes, huh?" her father said. "Maybe you'll stay to run the place."

She caught her breath. He had to be joking. "Very funny,

Dad." Not in a million years. Her plan was to get in, get out, not get tangled up in memory and emotion. This was like any assignment, just longer range. She'd be here four to six months, but she'd keep her head and be fine.

"I know you have a lot going on in New York." This new wistfulness tugged at Callie. He always swore he was busy and happy. She tracked him closely, but she had the feeling he sometimes put on a show for her benefit.

"Come on, you two! Tea's getting cold!" Dahlia sang to them from the base of the stairs.

"Be right down," her father called, then spoke to Callie. "She's worried you won't like her. She's been reading books about stepkids and losing a parent and what all."

"She doesn't need to do that. If you like her, I'll like her." She was determined to.

"I'm sure it's tough to see me with another woman."

"You're forgetting I was the one who got you dating."

"But now it's real. That's got to feel strange. You know that no one could replace your mother, right?"

"Of course not."

"I love her, Callie. I was asleep and Dahlia woke me up. Thank God you both hounded me."

"She hounded you?"

"After our date, she kept calling until I answered the phone to get it over with. And here I am. I'm so glad she wouldn't take no for an answer."

"Sounds like she stalked you." She laughed, but the idea gave her a twinge of worry.

"That's what it took to shake me out of my trance. I had to see that I wouldn't find another Colleen, but that I didn't have to be alone, either." He did look happy, if a little bewildered.

Her father led her down the stairs toward Dahlia, who waited with a huge and nervous smile. "Here they come, father and daughter. Just look at the two of you, together at last."

The woman was enthusiastic. Callie had to give her that, though Callie felt worn out and they'd barely met.

"You look so much alike," Dahlia said, looking from one to the other. "You have your father's eyes, Calissa."

Calissa. Only her mother called her by her full name. It hit her ear all wrong. "Thank you. And I go by Callie," she said gently. Besides, everyone said Callie was the spitting image of her mother, not her father.

She did not need to be so effusive. Callie was grateful Dahlia had rescued her father from a loneliness he hadn't admitted to himself, let alone to Callie. Thanks to Dahlia, once the ranch was back on track, Callie could return to New York without the constant worry that her father was sad and alone.

Dahlia led them to the kitchen where Callie was startled to see Deck rise from the table. What was he doing here? She wasn't ready for another encounter.

"I wanted to fill you in on Brandy, Cal."

Her father turned to Callie. "I thought we'd all go for a trail ride before supper. She good for the ride?" he asked Deck.

"Afraid not. Not for a new rider, anyway."

"That's a shame." Her father turned to Dahlia. "I guess you'll have to ride another horse tonight, darlin'."

"Why don't you three go ahead? I don't have the right clothes here and I have dinner to prepare."

"Your lentil soup just needs to simmer, doesn't it?"

"There are side dishes. Lots and lots to do. You three go on and have fun." She sounded nervous.

"I'll stay and help you," her father said. "Guess it's just you two this time." He nodded from Deck to Callie.

"You game?" Deck asked her with a smart-ass grin. "Or have you been in the city too long?"

"I can ride a horse, Deck," she said, rising to his bait. She hadn't ridden since seventh grade and wasn't interested in starting up again. Certainly not with Deck, not as sexually jumpy as he made her feel. "I need a tour of the ranch. It might as well be on horseback."

"Will an hour give you enough time to get grimy and start smelling like manure?"

"What?" Cal asked. Dahlia laughed uneasily.

"A half hour is more than enough, Deck."

Mischief gleamed in the man's eyes, as if he'd won a battle she hadn't known she was in.

"Maybe you can help Callie take it down a notch," her father said. "She's still got that horns-down, mad-charge New York way about her."

"I don't think Callie wants to take it down a notch," Deck replied.

"Would you two please not talk like I'm not here," she said, trying to act amused instead of annoyed. "I know exactly what notch I'm on and how long I want to be there." What the hell was she saying?

"I'll meet you in the corral in an hour." Deck tipped his hat to her. "Cal, we need you at the zoning meeting tonight. The vote will be tight."

"Sure thing. I'll be there."

"'Night then," Deck said and turned to leave.

Callie took in his departing backside, the jeans molded to his ass, one pocket worn from his wallet. His boots made his walk loose and slow and he'd grown broader. Eleven years ago, he'd been a boy. Now he was all man.

"Callie?"

"Huh?" She jerked her head to Dahlia, who must have said something to her she missed.

"I said, honey in your tea?"

"Sure, sure," she said, sitting down, gathering her wits.

Dahlia handed her a mug and Callie caught a whiff of peppermint. The good tea, according to Deck. With honey, it wasn't half-bad. He'd been right about that.

"Anyway, I'm *so* glad you're taking this pressure from

your father's shoulders," Dahlia said to Callie. She squeezed Callie's father's hand on the table. "This place has aged him."

"Is that true, Dad?" Callie asked. "Is the ranch too much for you?" Had he hidden that from her, too?

"The Triple C will always be home. I need time for more now, that's all." He patted Dahlia's hand and the woman blushed. "Dahlia's getting me out and about. We'd like to travel—see Europe and India. I've been stuck in a rut." He looked into Dahlia's eyes and she looked back in an equally moony way.

Callie glanced down, embarrassed. She sipped her tea, aware of the tingle of alarm fighting to get through the syrupy sweetness of the scene. Was she just a cynical New Yorker? She so wanted her father to be happy and well. She set her mug down with a clunk. The love birds startled and looked her way.

"So…" Dahlia said brightly, "Rancho de Descanso…what a great concept. As soon as you have your logo, we can make up labels with 'Exclusive from Dahlia's Desert Delights' for the products. Do you have the design yet?"

"A graphics team is working on it right now, but—"

"Just let me know. We'll want compatible designs and—"

"Let's not overwhelm her, Dahlia," her father said, putting his arm around Dahlia's shoulder. "She barely got here."

"I'm sorry. I'm just *so* thrilled."

"Did you put in the flower pots outside?" Callie said to shift topics before the woman offered her a facial. "They really brighten up the entrance."

"Yes. Some herbs I need for my tinctures and teas. My own garden is jammed to the netting."

"What are the purple and pink flowers shaped like bells?"

"Those are foxglove. The small white ones are sweet woodruff. Both have healing uses. Western medicine relies on synthetic compounds to an alarming degree. It's such a shame to ignore nature's bounty."

"I suppose it can seem that way." She smiled, then caught her father's gaze. They were both humoring Dahlia. "I should get upstairs and unpack and change, I guess, since I'm going for a ride." She sighed.

"Rosalie put extra towels in your bathroom and a blanket for your bed," her father said. "Holler if you need anything."

At the second-floor landing, she paused to look down at the spectacular great room, where a middle-aged man read a paperback novel from the small ranch library.

Her mother's classic taste stood the test of time. Raw beams and stone fireplaces were popular in the newer guest ranches. Callie would replace the worn furniture and add some contemporary art, but her mother's choice of Navajo rugs, Tohono O'odham baskets and exquisite wood pieces still looked great. She'd keep the kerosene lighting, too, as a rustic touch.

Upstairs, Callie entered the pink-princess glory of her room with the usual knot in her chest. Her mother had been happy to create the girlie oasis of canopy bed and French provincial furniture Callie wanted. She never let Callie suffer for their choice to live in the boondocks.

The room was full of mementos—riding trophies, dried corsages, cheerleading photos and awards. The bureau still held the prom shot of her and Taylor—who'd recently gotten divorced, her father had mentioned. She could turn the room into a true guest room, but she knew her father would be upset by the change.

She picked up the candid of her mother and her at that last Halloween party. They were dressed as witches and they had their heads together laughing.

A bottomless ache came over Callie, making her sink to the bed. She hated this. It had been eleven years. *Get over it.*

Her mother could always find a reason to celebrate. She hosted parties and town events like crazy. Until the last one. Her mother had been returning from Phoenix, her car jammed with stuff for Callie's eighteenth birthday bash, when she fell asleep on a lonely stretch of I-10.

As if that horror hadn't been enough, Callie had read the

newspaper story, where a witness vividly described the highway littered with foil banners, crepe paper, appetizers and paper plates. "It looked like a party had exploded on the road." The words and the picture they drew remained branded in Callie's brain.

To spare Callie's feelings, they'd held the funeral two days after her birthday, but it hadn't helped. She'd ignored her birthday ever after, avoided the subject with friends. No one knew, and she liked it that way.

Callie slipped the photo into the drawer—no point torturing herself—and opened her suitcase on the bed. Throwing open her closet door, she surveyed the fashion mistakes she'd left when she headed for college, including the ridiculously slutty dress Taylor had bought—sequined fake snakeskin she'd managed to only wear once. Her old jeans were there and the never-worn Stetson her dad had bought her to try to coax her back into riding.

Glancing at her watch, she decided to unpack later. Instead, she'd make a couple of quick calls. The first was to touch base with Finn Markham, head of Valhalla Investments, the company funding the resort, pinning down his visit to the property. She wanted to talk to him about possibly buying the riverside acres. The proceeds would offer a financial margin in case they took too long to turn the revenue corner. Raw land wasn't as valuable as developed land, but it was an option worth considering.

Getting voice mail, she left a message, then took a calming breath before punching in the number to Be There Events, the company she and Stefan had built together.

"Hello, Callie," he answered gravely. "How *are* you?"

"I'm great. Ready to dig in," she said cheerfully, irritated by the drama in his tone. "How's it going there?"

"The usual craziness. We miss you."

Oh, lighten up. She was the injured party, but Stefan was the one who'd been moping around ever since. So much for easy, simple sex. They both lived for their work, so hooking up had been easy. But not simple three years later, when she learned Stefan was sleeping with a model from one of their events.

"Do you have questions?" she asked. "Everything clear?"

"Your notes are great. An idiot could handle this. And I sure qualify as one of those."

"Don't, Stefan. It's over and done. I told you no hard feelings." Not many feelings at all, she'd realized, which appalled her. When he'd confessed the affair, she'd been…numb.

Her pride was wounded, sure, but her heart was undamaged. It reminded her of the time she fell off Lucky when she was ten. She'd hit the ground and braced for agonizing pain. It never came. She'd been jarred, slightly bruised, but otherwise fine. She got up and rode off, virtually unscathed.

"It means nothing," Stefan had said of the affair.

Then why do it? She knew why. What they had together wasn't enough. For either of them, it turned out. She'd initiated the breakup. Stefan protested, but hollowly. He seemed to be reading the lines from the script for *Cheating Lover, the Play.*

She'd been too troubled to act her part. Even before Stefan, she'd been a no-strings girl, but now she feared she'd been protecting her heart so long, it had lost function. The heart was a muscle, after all. Without proper use, it could atrophy, become crippled.

She'd realized to her shock that she might not have the capacity for a lifelong love.

"What else can I do to help you?" Stefan said.

"Hold down the fort. That's plenty for now." When she got back they would talk. Before the breakup, she'd decided it was time to move on. She loved events, but Stefan wanted more publicity and marketing projects. She'd decided to follow up on the open invitation from Ogden, Rush & Tillman, a high-profile PR firm, to launch their special-events division, handily bounding several rungs up the success ladder.

She was finished with Be There Events. When a thing was

over, you left. That was her philosophy. Never get stale, never get stuck. Done is done.

That was why she loved New York. There was always a place to go, a leap to risk, a challenge to meet. The affair had come at a good time, all things considered. Though she would have rather not discovered the crippled-heart part.

Finished with the phone, she saw she had time for a quick shower. She tied her hair back to keep it dry and stepped under the hot stream, letting the water uncoil her tension. Too bad she had to gear up for the horseback ride with Deck. She pictured his flashing grin, the knowing light in his blue eyes, the perfect curve of his ass, his big hands and where they might wander if he were here right now…mmmm.

Later, girl. She'd brought her ultrafancy vibrator—a gift from her girlfriends after the breakup—to handle her carnal needs for the next few months. If only she and Deck didn't have a history. A mindless affair would be the perfect relief from the stress of the monumental work ahead.

Nothing with Deck could ever be mindless, she knew, though her body kept insisting she give it a try.

Forget it. Her focus was on the ranch. The construction in-timidated her, but her consultant had pointed out it was like any project. You made a plan, hired good people, watched the dollars and the details and it all worked out. Tomorrow she'd begin with a meeting with the first contractor.

Tonight she had to get through a sunset ride with Deck.

3

THE SUN HAD STREAKED the sky with color when Callie marched down the porch, her red leather boots clicking sharply against the wooden steps, the fringe on her matching jacket swinging free. She'd only worn this once to a Western-themed client event and wanted to get some use out of it. She'd dressed for wow factor, wanting to off-balance Deck a bit.

Beneath the jacket, she wore a white scoop-necked stretch top. On her head was her Stetson, bright white, spanking new.

Her stone-washed jeans hugged her hips and legs so tightly she could barely draw breath.

A mistake, she realized, standing on the porch. She had to get her legs up and over the barrel of a horse's rib cage. Bad move. She turned to go change, but Deck called her name.

She'd just make these jeans work like the rest of her plan. She would ease into the ranch changes, break the news about selling off the livestock, and hope she could keep Deck on the team through the changeover.

When she got close enough, Deck deliberately thumbed his hat high up his forehead and whistled. *"Niiice,"* he said, "though I wouldn't waltz in front of any bulls in all that red if I were you."

Terrific. He was making fun of her.

"Those pants look downright painful." He ran his eyes down her length, making her aware that he was a man and she was in skintight jeans that hugged her ass and pinched her sex—which got worse the longer he looked her over. "How do you even move?"

"I manage," she said, lifting her chin.

"Don't get me wrong. I'm not complaining," Deck said, his low tone and lazy gaze telling her the answer to her earlier question. Yeah, he still found her attractive. Arousal rolled through her. At least she wasn't alone.

She climbed stiffly up the fence to sit on the top slat, acting as casually as she could manage. She'd have to drop onto her horse from up here. Throwing a leg up and over would snap a femur, she was sure. Deck tracked her every move.

Brandy gave an irritated snort. "Easy, girl." Deck ran a hand down the horse's neck. "I'll ride Brandy, don't worry."

"I'm not worried." She was glad not to have to manage a horse so fresh to the saddle until she saw the horse Deck had chosen for her. Gray and swaybacked, with a low-hanging head and white hairs around its eyes and lips, the poor beast looked dead on its hooves. "*This* is my horse? He's ancient."

"Wiley's older, but he's steady and even tempered, which is what we need."

"You think I need an old, slow horse?" she said testily.

"*Brandy* needs an old, slow horse." He shook his head, smiling. Gotcha. Why was she like this around him? "Now if you want more of a challenge, be my guest…" He gestured at Brandy.

"I don't want to interfere with your training."

"It wouldn't be a problem," he said, not fooled by her fib. She hated that he saw right through her. Mostly because she couldn't return the favor.

She scooted along the fence closer to the sagging spine of her horse. Reading her movements, Deck steered Wiley nearer. She dropped into the saddle, her jeans straining as her legs spread over Wiley's ribs. She accepted the reins from Deck, then urged Wiley into a walk to get back her seat.

Deck opened the gate, then untied Brandy. "You ready for a ride, girl?" he murmured in a hypnotic tone, smoothing the horse with his broad palm, masterful and gentle, as if he understood each twitch of muscle, twist of tendon. "You are ready, aren't you, girl?" He was wooing the horse. "You want a ride, don't you? You want it, huh? Yeah, you do."

Please stop. The words were making her hot. Any second, she'd blurt, "Yes! Yes I want it. I want it *bad.*"

Finally Deck swung smoothly onto Brandy's back. The horse went still, reared, staggered backward, then lurched around the corral.

Callie tried to turn Wiley out of the way, but Brandy was too fast and banged into her horse's rump. Wiley lunged forward, throwing Callie onto his neck. Her hat flew off and her pubic bone slammed into the saddle pommel. She yelped as pain burned through her.

"You okay?" Deck called, more worried about her than the rearing, spinning beast beneath him.

"I'm fine," she choked out, needing to rub her bruised spot, but not wanting to do it in front of Deck.

"Hold tight. We'll be back after we burn off some energy." Deck leaned over Brandy's neck and she took off out of the gate in a streak of shining muscle. Deck gave the horse her head, and they flew west across the field, making Callie's heart lift at the beauty of horse and rider silhouetted against the changing colors of the sunset sky.

A horse running full out was an amazing sight. It was the fire, the energy, the way the creature's whole being seemed focused on the run, like its heart would burst with the joy of it. Callie's chest tightened. How had she forgotten this wonder?

Horse and rider were small in the distance when they finally swung back her way. By the time they reached the gate, Deck had Brandy in a relaxed lope and guided her effortlessly into the corral. Near the far fence, he leaned down to scoop up Callie's Stetson, easy as a rodeo star. He returned to settle it on her head. His gaze took a lazy trip down her body, making her want to wiggle in the saddle. "You all set?"

She nodded. Soon they were on their way, riding in silence

at first. Clouds to the west glowed pink, orange and purple. The air held a slight chill, and a light breeze carried the green scent of the Rio Feliz their way.

"We can go faster if you want," she said. "I'm okay."

"Slow and easy is fine." He looked at her. "You were never much for taking your time."

Her mind flashed on their frantic nights in each other's arms. She swallowed hard. "Not usually, no."

"If you rush, you miss things."

"If you *don't* rush, you miss things."

He chuckled. "Ah, but when you slow down you catch all the details. You take it all in, enjoy every second, every inch."

God, was he talking about sex? Or was she just fixated? She got that shivery feeling again. It didn't help that the seam of her jeans rubbed her crotch with each roll of Wiley's hind-quarters. She shifted her weight to ease the itch.

"You okay?" Deck asked.

"I'm fine. Why?" She jerked her gaze to his.

"You seem…wiggly." He swallowed and she realized her movements had aroused him. Good. It was no fun suffering alone.

"Just adjusting so I won't be sore later."

"Wouldn't want that," he said, pushing his hat harder onto his head. "Maybe hit the hot springs after. Good for sore muscles."

And making love, she remembered. They'd been together at the springs and it had been warm and intimate and healing. "I'll have to try that." Her voice came out so husky she had to clear her throat. "Brandy seems more settled."

"Getting there."

"Dahlia sure was relieved not to have to ride with us."

"True." Deck chuckled. "She's not much on the ranch."

"What do you think of her?"

He shot his gaze to hers. "Cal's fond of her."

"And…"

"I don't know her well," he said, clearly choosing his words with care. "She keeps him…busy."

"I found her kind of overwhelming, but she was nervous about meeting me. You were right about the peppermint tea, by the way. Her other teas are nasty?"

"Oh, yeah. She gave me one that was supposed to be good for my organs. Shriveled my tongue and I couldn't taste for a day."

"But did it help your organs?" Too late, she realized how he might take that.

"They survived." He shot her that wicked half smile again. "I'm sure she means well. Cal seems happy enough."

"He does. And kind of…dazed."

"Maybe that's how love works. Like a punch in the solar plexus you never catch your breath from. What do I know?"

Did that mean he'd never been in love, either?

They'd reached a barbed wire fence, beyond which she saw dozens of cattle, brown and black, most bent to chew the grass. Several rested under the roof of a ramada, others drank from a water trough beneath a slowly turning windmill. She used to ride out to check the herd with her father. She'd loved the huge eyes, the patient faces, the slow grind of their jaws on grass.

Tell him you're selling them all. She opened her mouth to break the news, but an animal bellowed loudly. They both looked over to see a bull mount a cow, which staggered under the weight, but didn't move away.

"Ah, romance," Deck said.

"Is that what you call it?"

"No?" he asked. "Maybe that's my problem with women." She laughed. "You have problems? I find that hard to believe."

"I do all right, I guess."

"No one special?" None of her business, but she had to ask.

"Not really. How about you?"

"We broke up a couple months back. He's my business partner, actually."

"Ouch. That's got to be awkward."

"Not as much as you'd think." And that still bothered her. "So how many head do we have?"

"Couple hundred, mostly black Angus, a few red. A decent number of wild Corriente from Mexico. They do well with drought. Not nearly enough cow-calf pairs, though."

"The supplemental feed costs are through the roof, Deck."

"That'll be offset by the alfalfa we'll plant. The real problem is the herd is down. Like I said, your dad's been hard to pin down. We had a chance at a bunch of steers and some pairs, but I couldn't get his okay on the buy."

Just as well, since we'll be selling….

Deck dismounted to open the gate and she saw they'd be heading to the top of the hill over the river. She'd tell him there, when they stopped.

As they climbed, Brandy bucked and lunged and back-tracked, though Deck patiently worked with her, training her as they traveled. Wiley conserved his energy with a slow, steady pace. She'd missed this, Callie realized, enjoying the slow roll of the horse beneath her. She'd loved even more the wind in her face on a full run, riding the surge of the horse's lope. She used to feel part of Lucky, running free and feeling so alive.

They'd reached a wider section of trail so they could be side by side. "You enjoying yourself?" Deck asked.

"Yeah," she said softly.

"You look good on a horse."

"I can't believe how long it's been."

"You stopped after Lucky died."

"It was middle school and there was too much happening in school and with my friends in town. I got bored."

"You rode that horse everywhere," Deck mused. "I couldn't believe you painted his hoofs pink with little daisies. And put glitter on his hide. Talk about humiliation."

"Come on. Lucky didn't mind."

"You charmed him. But then you charmed everyone." He smiled at her the way he had, as if he'd never met anyone like her, as if he couldn't get enough of her.

"I can't believe you remember that."

"Of course." He held her gaze, telling her he remembered that and a whole lot more.

She shivered, feeling a rush of memory herself. Deck had made her feel special. And safe. Something she'd needed after her mother's death, when the world seemed an unpredictable and dangerous place. She'd depended on Deck, on his arms, his kisses, his comfort.

Until he decided it was over. That had stung. She'd bounced back a bit and suggested they hang out in town, get a Coke at Ruby's with her friends a few times. He'd declined, saying he had chores. A few days later he said they should end it. She was back to normal and it was time. He acted like he'd been doing her a *favor*.

Hurt and angry, she went back to her friends, to Taylor, who'd missed her terribly, and Deck went back to managing the ranch, and that was that. She'd be off to college soon anyway, what was the point in dragging it out?

All the same, the memories stuck. To this day, the smell of cedar blocks in her sweater drawer made her miss him.

Now they reached the top of the hill and she saw the Triple C spread out at her feet. Ahead lay the river, a lazy *S* curve lined by cottonwoods. Her heart lifted with pride. "It's so beautiful," she breathed.

"Yeah," he said. "It is."

Her father had worked and loved every acre for thirty years. She would make sure he kept it if it killed her. "I hope we don't have to sell off this section," she said, speaking before she'd thought through her words.

"What?" Deck turned to her abruptly. Brandy snorted.

"The river makes these acres attractive to developers. They'd be perfect for ranchettes."

"We need these acres for grazing, not to mention deed and density restrictions and water rights. This is a desert, Callie."

"I don't want to sell if we don't have to, but it's an option. This is the future, Deck. In the last decade, half the guest ranches in the country have been sold off and developed. The land's too valuable to leave raw."

He looked at her, his cheek muscle ticking like a bomb about to blow. "We'd have to cut the herd."

"About that…" She took a deep breath. "I plan to sell the livestock as soon as it's feasible. I'll need you to track the sales so we can maximize our profit."

"You're selling the cattle." The words hung dead in the air.

"We've been losing money, especially with the drought. Our only hope is turning the ranch into a resort."

He stared at her, so she kept talking. "I know you took the foreman job to help Dad and I'm very grateful to you for that."

Supposedly, he'd been at loose ends after selling his family's horse ranch after his mother remarried and moved to California, but she knew he'd acted out of kindness.

"If you wanted to leave, I wouldn't blame you." She stopped. "Of course, we'd love to keep you through the changeover. If you wanted to become the field manager after that, that would be wonderful. We'll add trail horses, of course. You'd work more with guests and manage more staff, coordinate the recreational activities and things like that."

"I'm a rancher, Callie, not some guy with a whistle and a volleyball net." His voice was low.

"It's totally up to you. If you decide to leave, just give us time to find and train your replacement." She held her breath, waiting for his reaction.

He looked out toward the horizon for a long silent moment. Finally he turned to her, Brandy shifting impatiently beneath him. "It's your land. Cal's and yours. You can do with it what you want. As to my plans, I'll let you know."

"Good." That was that. The worst was over. Deck wasn't

happy, but now he knew the situation and could make his decision.

She took him in. Silhouetted by the glowing sunset sky, he looked like a painting of the last cowboy—noble, proud, connected to the land, full of dignity and strength.

And so sexy. She shivered.

"You cold?" he asked.

"Not really. No." She wasn't about to explain. "But the light's fading. We should get back."

Without another word, they turned their horses and headed downhill. Poor Wiley snorted and sagged as his tired knees took on the gentle slope. In the distance the ranch house glowed a golden welcome from the big picture windows. Smaller lights lit the few guest rooms in use.

That would all change. She'd build a new two-story wing of guest rooms and five new casitas. Besides updating the ranch house and old casitas, she'd landscape ten more acres around the ranch, put in a pool and a tennis court, not to mention the four-star spa. She would work her magic as quickly as she could, then escape.

At the base of the hill, Deck turned to the east, taking a different trail back—the one to the hot springs. She wanted to say *Not now, not with you,* but what excuse could she give?

Soon they rounded the bend to the main pool, five feet across, edged by large stones. Farther on, there were two smaller pools, one set away from the others, marked as private for the family's use. In the summer, the entire area was bright with the red, orange and yellow of desert wildflowers.

"Remember this?" he asked her.

"Of course," she said, meeting his gaze, heat like a hot wire between them. She looked down to the water, settling herself. Wiley shifted beneath her, reacting to her tension. "Is the water level constant? The heat? Is it mucky at all?"

"It's the same, Callie," he said. "Still deep, still nature's hot surprise."

"That's good to hear."

She was flooded with the memory of stripping in the night chill of early spring, slipping through the steam to meet Deck, naked and waiting for her. Sheltered by the rough stones, up to their necks in the water, breathing in the earthy smell, they'd seemed like the first man and woman in the garden.

That was so long ago. Wiley side-stepped, picking up her distress. "We'll improve this, of course." She had to stick to the task before her, not get lost in nostalgia or regret.

"Huh?"

"We need concrete steps and a handrail, for one thing. For safety and convenience."

"You want to turn it into some Holiday Inn hot tub?"

"I've studied hot springs all over the Southwest. This is the norm, Deck."

"It's fine the way it is. Natural and beautiful."

"It'll be that, but better. I want to dig out the smaller pools. Maybe open up a fourth where the water slides down the rocks?" She pointed. "Fence it off so guests can reserve it for clothing-optional soaks."

His expression made her decide not to mention the massage ramada, changing room and meditation garden she planned.

"They're your springs," Deck said wearily.

She could explain her reasoning, but what was the point? Deck loved the ranch as it was. She wouldn't change his mind any more than he could change hers.

So, she simply turned Wiley toward home.

Catching sight of the barn, the tired horse lunged into a lope. Callie tightened her body and leaned forward, enjoying the free feeling and the speed for a few lovely moments.

Making the corral a few yards before Deck, Callie started to dismount to open the gate, praying her jeans had stretched out enough to allow her to do so with dignity. She was halfway down when Brandy arrived. She must have nipped Wiley's hindquarters, because her horse whinnied and barreled forward. Callie landed on her butt in the dirt, biting her tongue and bruising her rear.

Deck was off Brandy in an instant to help her. "You okay?"

"I'b vine," she managed, over her burning tongue. She grabbed her hat, pushed to her feet, then shoved the hat down hard, not allowing herself even a grimace from the pain. She moved for the gate, but her legs had that first-ride stiffness and she stumbled a bit.

Deck caught her arm, then brushed the dust from the back of her jeans. It was an innocent Eagle Scout gesture, but his hand was on her and he stood so close that the cedar, leather, sunshine smell of him made her go weak in the knees.

She stepped back to collect herself. "Thanks. I'm fine. Really." She moved as if to loosen the saddle.

"I'll put up the horses. Go on to supper," Deck said, his voice rough, telling her he'd been affected, too.

"Okay, then. Thanks. Again." She backed up, then bumped into the fence, flustered by the moment.

"I'll see you tomorrow," he said, his gaze not letting go.

"Tomorrow. Sure." She turned to walk away. Was he watching her? What was he thinking? And why did it matter?

He thought her plan was nuts. He was wrong and she intended to prove it to him. If he would just stop being so damned sexy all the time. And smelling so good. And the touching had to stop. Absolutely.

In fact, if she didn't need his ranch expertise, she'd be half-glad if he decided not to stay at all.

4

DECK SLAPPED his gesso-loaded brush in big aimless strokes across the solitary rider he'd painted, covering it up for good. The piece was as wrong as Callie was about the ranch. She planned to turn the Triple C into a place where the guests bitched if the ice came cubed instead of crushed.

Deck itched to take the place in hand, fine tune the operation, start raising certified organic beef, despite the tough requirements. The challenge appealed to him.

He could buy a spread elsewhere, but Deck loved the Triple C, knew every acre of it like home. He might still have a crack at it—if Callie and Cal decided they'd had enough.

Tastes change, she'd said, like he was some rube lost in the past. He knew all about change. People left, they died, they disappeared behind their eyes, as his mother had done for months after his pop passed. Deck stuck with what he could count on.

If Callie went through with her scheme, Deck had to leave. He wouldn't strand her or Cal, of course, but as soon as he could see his way clear, he was out of there. Maybe it was a good thing. Maybe every man nearing thirty needed a shake-up, regardless of how well situated he was.

Deck finished the primer coat on the canvas, then left the brush to soak. He scrubbed his hands, his thick ranch calluses stained with a rainbow of acrylic colors. The same hands that dug post holes and wrestled steers to the ground could dab a hair's width of light on a saguaro spine. He liked that.

He'd been painting more lately, getting lost in the work

until his shoulders ached and his vision blurred. He had the urge to stay busy. He wasn't sure why.

Painting had been a refuge since that terrible time when his dad died and Callie had gone and he'd taken that curve too fast, saw how easy it would be to end it all, be done. Only the thought of his mother made him yank the car back from the rail.

Since then painting kept him sane. It felt like his heart on the canvas, bad or good, but not to be denied.

Drying his hands on a paint-stained towel, he looked over the pieces he'd hung in the old Airstream he used as a studio. Most of his work fell short—too much paint, bad use of light, out of proportion, overpainted. Sometimes he wasn't good enough to paint bar scenes on velvet. The triumphs were his private joys.

He didn't have the focus to paint tonight. The planning and zoning meeting hadn't helped. As chair, he'd had to cancel for lack of a quorum. Banging the gavel, he'd noticed the triumphant smirk on Taylor Loft's face from his seat in the audience. He'd definitely had something to do with three commissioners who'd unexpectedly no-showed.

Loft was wearing them all down on the tax exemption. Go-along-to-get-along was too often the way in small towns, where you had to work, play, love and live with the people in power. Loft was the law in Abrazo and no one wanted him as an enemy.

But right was right and Deck expected people to stand up for it. Tax money was life blood to the small town. Why should Loft be exempt? Because his ancestor had founded the place? Named it Harriet, after his wife. He'd been cheated out of his holdings, according to Loft legend—and when the town incorporated they changed the name to Abrazo, Spanish for "hug."

Insult to injury to Harriet's progeny, in Taylor's mind, and he wore that chip on his shoulder with the same authority he wore his badge.

The man was trouble. A friend of Deck's, a county supervisor, had told him stories. Loft had been a security guard in Phoenix before he became sheriff. Working a convention for state officials, he'd covered up career-killing indiscretions for some pretty important people. As a result he had his hands in so many pies his fingers were permanently stained. "He's a malevolent little shit," Deck's friend had said.

Deck had to stop thinking about Loft. And Callie, for that matter. The burning in his gut had started up again.

Get over it.

Deck closed the studio and started for the trailer he called home, then stopped. Hell, he wouldn't be able to sleep. He needed a couple of beers and a soak in the springs.

Callie would be long gone, if she'd taken his advice, which was doubtful. She didn't give a damn what he thought. He'd better get all the use out of the springs he could before she turned it into a tiled hot tub. Dammit to hell.

He grabbed two Coronas, a towel and his bedroll and set off for the springs. The ranch house lights were mostly out. He zeroed in on Callie's window. Still lit. She was reading, no doubt. She'd been a big reader in high school. What did she sleep in? Something lacey and small, he'd bet.

These days women were too obsessed with their underwear. Those thongs had to be irritating. Naked was just fine with him.

Back then, Callie had worn bras that matched her panties. His favorites were white with hearts. She'd worn them the first time they'd made love in the springs and slept under the stars together. He could still picture her breasts spilling out of the half cup of that heart-dotted bra, innocent and brazen at once.

Deck took the turn through the rock formation. The springs steamed in the moonlight. He kept going to the private spring, where he laid out his bedroll and towel, cracked one of the Coronas, stripped to the skin and slid into the water.

The heat felt good. He lay back and let out a long, slow breath. Sipping cold beer, he let his mind go.

It snagged immediately on the sight of Callie loping toward

the barn on Wiley. This was the Callie he remembered as a kid, racing on Lucky, hair flying, a little scared but pushing on. He'd loved her determination, her energy. She'd been so lively, so full of fun. She just made him grin.

He missed her. Maybe she was still there under the big city act, the rush and self-importance. She said she'd missed riding. Probably missed the ranch, too. Would she stay?

Never. She needed more. That was why he'd let her go once she'd gotten through the worst of her sadness. She'd been bored. She wanted to be in town, hanging at the diner with the cheerleaders and football players.

He had better things to do than watch guys fling French fries down girls' blouses or race each other in their tricked-out trucks. He'd let ranch chores slide to be with her, blown his grades.

Callie had gotten what she needed from him, so he sent her back to her life. It hurt like hell, but he'd done the right thing. She'd seemed stung. He didn't get that. What was the point of dragging it out?

He pictured her in that goofy cowgirl outfit, the jeans so tight that Deck could hardly mount Brandy without causing himself injury. Holding her, brushing the dust from her ass, he felt the old hunger times ten. In fact, if she were here right now, he'd—

"Deck?"

He popped up, startled to find his fleeting fantasy standing there at the edge of the spring in a silky-looking black robe and flip-flops. She held towels and champagne in a bucket, a mason jar over the neck.

"I didn't think anyone would be here this late," she said, her gaze jerking around, telling him she was embarrassed.

"You took my advice," he said, surprised by that fact.

"I don't suppose you're wearing a suit…?"

He shook his head, grateful the water was opaque with minerals. "You?" He nodded at her robe, so thin he could make out her nipples. She was naked under there, all right.

She shook her head.

Great. Just that slight bit of cloth between him and her bare beauty. He had a hard-on so fierce he feared it might break the surface. "I'll leave." As soon as he lost his erection.

"No, no. You were here first."

"It's your springs."

"Don't be silly." She bit her lip, uncertain as she often was around him. "You shouldn't have to leave."

"We could…share," he said. "I'll stay on my side." He held up his hands. Like, what, he was going to jump her? His face felt hotter than the spring water, which hovered at one-oh-five.

"I…guess so." She laughed nervously.

"I've got another beer…." He nodded toward it.

"I have a whole bottle of champagne we can share." She bent to set down the bucket and her towels, the robe parting to show the curve of one breast, the top of a thigh.

She stood and started on the knot, then looked at him pointedly, circling a finger. *Turn around.*

"Oh. Yeah." It was just that he wasn't quite sure he hadn't dreamed her. She seemed ethereal, like she could drift away like the mist of steam off the springs.

He pivoted to brace himself on the rough stones and waited, catching the quiet swish of fabric, the grind of her bare feet on the sand, then the small splash when she let herself into the water, her soft moan as the heat hit her.

God. He recognized that moan. He'd made her do that many times. Fighting to look neutral, he turned back. He had a great poker face, but with Callie all bets were off.

She'd filled out a little, her breasts were rounder and she was a half-inch taller, but her shape was the same.

Touching her had been heaven.

"This feels so good," she said, leaning her head into the concave place in the rocks where they used to make love.

Don't think about that….

He cleared his throat. "So, champagne… You're celebrating."

"Trying to." A smile flitted across her face. "I've got a lot of work ahead of me."

"True," he said. It was nuts, but he'd keep his asshole blurts to himself. Instead he reached across the water for her bottle. "Shall I open it?"

She removed the mason jar and let him take it. "We can share the glass or you can drink from the bottle."

"The bottle's fine for me." Deck popped the cork, the sound sharp in the desert silence. He poured Callie a dose, then tapped the neck of the bottle against her glass.

"To old times," he said.

Her eyes flared and she shivered. No way was she cold in this water. Something else was going on and when she echoed his toast, her voice shook.

SIPPING THE CHAMPAGNE Deck had poured, Callie felt hotter inside than the steaming water that lapped at her shoulders. Deck's eyes locked on, gleaming in the moonlight. Startled, she backed into a hollow in the rocks, the perfect indentation…

Uh-oh. This was where they'd made love.

Did Deck remember? He was looking at her *that way*.

The last thing she needed with water wrapping her in warmth like the best of all hugs, was Deck naked, a mere arm's length away. She gulped more champagne, realizing too late that its fizzy deliciousness would unravel her inhibitions, making things worse.

Deck gave her a slow, big-as-the-sky smile. "Very nice…"

It wasn't until he lifted the bottle that she realized he'd meant the champagne, not her. Whew.

"I robbed the ranch's supply. I'll have to replace it. Ernie's carries champagne, right?"

"Even hicks enjoy the finer things. We don't all toss back a brew, then go shoot up highway signs for a good time."

"Come on. You know I don't think that."

He shrugged. "You left."

"And you stayed," she snapped back, defensive suddenly.

"To each his own." Was he jabbing at her, defending his choice, or being nice?

"As long as you're happy." Did that sound condescending?

"Exactly." Picking up the tension, he softened his next words. "Cal says your company's doing well. You set up parties for celebrities, right?" He lifted an eyebrow, like he couldn't believe she did that for a living.

"I do events, not just parties. There's more to it than cocktails and tenderloin satay." She held out her glass for more champagne. In Manhattan, top event planners were movers and shakers. Out here, though, she could see how it might sound, well, silly. "Human culture is built around points of celebration."

"Okay…." Another eyebrow shift.

"Events can make or break a new company, a product, hell, a relationship. In the right atmosphere, the right combination of people, food, setting and entertainment, deals can be cut, business ties forged, critical negotiations conducted. My mission is to bring people together for meaningful outcomes."

"I didn't realize parties could be so, uh—"

"Complex? Crucial?"

"Uh, sure."

Was he laughing at her? Probably. They both drank more.

"Maybe you could explain that some," Deck said, clearly trying to be polite.

"Okay," she said, deciding to pretend he was honestly curious. "First we consider the client's goals and determine the proper venue and approach. Sometimes direct mail, product placement, print and broadcast advertising will do. Other times, viral marketing works. Often, and this is where I come in, entertaining key clients, opinion leaders, media or city officials are a linchpin to the campaign."

She realized Deck's eyes had dipped to where the water

met the top of her breasts. Caught, he yanked his gaze upward
and cleared his throat. "Please go on," he said, gulping champagne, then refilling her glass.

"There's the budget," she said, fighting her response to his
roving eyes. "That's huge for client satisfaction and my revenue
stream. Clients want the world. You should try creating an elaborate, sumptuous reception for five hundred on a shoestring. It
takes artistry, attention to detail and fierce negotiation skills."

"I'm sure you're good at what you do, Callie." Deck leaned
closer. "You wouldn't take a job if it didn't challenge you."

"Thank you," she said, distracted by the sexual sparks
flying between them. Funny how the pale light of the moon
was all she needed to read him now. In broad daylight he'd
been a mystery to her.

"You're only as good as your last event," she said to distract
herself. "There's a lot of pressure, and word of screwups
travels fast."

Her mind wandered to Deck, naked beneath the water. Was
he aroused? She'd begun to feel the champagne. She had to
keep them talking. "How about you? What else do you do
besides the ranch? Not that that's not plenty."

Deck chuckled. "It's okay, Callie. You don't have to watch
every word. We got off on the wrong foot."

He reached across and touched her arm, his fingers warm
from the water. She couldn't help but sink lower and suck in
a breath. "Okay. That's good."

Deck withdrew his hand slowly. "I stay busy. Civic BS in
town—chamber of commerce, planning and zoning. I also
consult with horse breeders and buyers all over the West."

"And in your free time…?"

"I hang with friends. If I want music, I go into Tucson or
up to Phoenix. For that matter, New York's just a couple bags
of salted nuts away. I've been there."

"You were in the city? You didn't call."

"It was a long time ago. I was with someone." He shrugged.

"But I would have taken you to dinner. We're friends…"

"It was last-minute."

He was right. With their history, a double date over martinis and sushi would have been awkward.

"So is New York all you expected?" he asked.

"All that and more." She stopped herself. Why cheerlead? Naked in the springs, here with Deck, who'd always accepted anything she said, she told him the truth. "Is anything ever what you expect?"

"Maybe not."

"New York is indescribable. Intense. Vital. Important. The people are fascinating. There's so much to do—theater, museums, clubs, any kind of food you can imagine. It's the heartbeat, the pulse of the country. There's so much I love there."

"And…?"

She felt a twinge, like a new toothache, and took a big swallow of champagne before she answered. "It can wear you out. It's crowded. It's expensive. It's noisy and complicated."

"No place is perfect."

She smiled. "True. And I wouldn't live anywhere else." *For now.* That thought surprised her. "Part of it's my job. Especially after a twelve-hour day, when I have to schmooze the catering manager into one more round of appetizers, conjure a smile for the client from hell who's underpaying me, or cough up a joke before two business partners launch a fist fight with each other."

"Sounds like an ordeal."

"Does it? I guess it is. And, sometimes I feel…" She paused, not willing to say *lonely.* Too weak. In the city, you kept your cards close and your deodorant fresh. One drop of blood in the water and you were sashimi on an enamel plate.

Lately, since the breakup, she'd felt kind of alone. Even with Stefan, really, but she'd stayed too busy to notice.

"Overwhelmed," she finished. She'd love to ask Deck if he ever felt lonely, but they were too tentative with each other. "Your mom's doing okay?" she asked instead.

"She's happy. Harvey's a good guy and she likes Modesto."

"Do you miss the Lazy J?"

"Sometimes. Pop would never have sold. I'm sure he'd have hated that I was leasing the place. I had to hand off when I finally went for my degree."

"In what? Agribusiness?"

He laughed. "No. I got a BA in humanities. That and three-fifty will get you a venti at Starbucks. And, yes, I've been to Starbucks, Callie."

"I didn't say a word." At least they were joking. "Your dad wouldn't have wanted you to be strapped to the ranch forever. He'd want you to be happy."

"It wasn't a burden." He shrugged.

"You sacrificed so much for your mom, staying with her so long. Meanwhile, I left my dad all alone."

"You're out here a lot. You call all the time."

"Yeah, but I never know what's really going on. I think Dad puts on a happy face for me."

"That's probably true. You used to do that for him, too. You were a one-girl show. Housekeeper, therapist, entertainer."

"I just did what had to be done."

"Maybe Cal should have looked out for you more."

"Cheering him up cheered me, too." *Look happy and you'll be happy.* That was what she tried with everyone but Deck. With him, the mask fell away. It was falling away right now.

"It's hard for me to be here," she said. "It's like I get ambushed. I miss my mother so bad I feel sick. It's ridiculous. Eleven years have passed. What's my problem?"

"You left so soon after she died. Maybe that's why."

"I think losing our parents so young changed the course of our lives. I escaped to New York and you got trapped at the Lazy J."

"That's pretty dramatic. You were going to New York anyway. And I told you I liked working the ranch."

"Still…"

"Hey, hey. No regrets, remember? Live life with relish…" He paused for her to finish the old joke.

"And mustard?"

They laughed, looking into each other's eyes, sharing the warm memory. She felt close to him again.

"I think hard times make us stronger, Callie."

"I don't know about that. I was a mess." Every day had been a fight to stay at the surface, a desperate dogpaddle or she'd drop to the bottom like a stone. "If it hadn't been for you…" Deck had held her up. Deck and his warm arms and good heart.

"We were both in the same foxhole."

"Not exactly the same." The deeper pain rose like the hot steam around her. "You didn't cause your dad's death." She swallowed, struggling with emotion. She usually danced away from this idea.

"Your mother fell asleep driving. You weren't in the car."

"It was for my party. She drove all the way to Phoenix to get the stuff. If I'd settled for pizza at Dino's, she'd be alive today." She swallowed and blinked, embarrassed.

"Hey…" Deck moved to hug her, keeping the embrace high on their bodies. "I hate to see you in pain."

"I know." He had always been there for her. His skin against hers felt so right. She rested her cheek on his chest. It felt so good, as calming as back then.

Just like that, the moment changed. The comfort hug turned into something else, something more intense. Callie became aware of a hitch in Deck's breathing and her own. His arms around her were strong and sure, his fingers dug in.

She should push back. He should back off. Neither of them moved. She became aware of a tight ache between her legs.

They were inches apart. All either of them had to do was shift slightly forward and they'd be body to body, thigh to thigh, her breasts against his chest, her belly against his erection. It would feel so good. Like before, but new, too.

She *ached* to move closer.

"I remember how we were," Deck said, his voice rough.

They had to stop. This was dangerous.

"Me, too." She began to tremble. She wanted him so badly. She wanted to see how they would be together—without the grief and the frantic desperation. She'd been a girl, inexperienced in sex. Now she was a woman and knew exactly what to do and what she wanted. "I'd never felt like that before."

Or since, for that matter. Deck hadn't been her first, but sex with Taylor had been awkward and fast and all about him. Deck and she had moved together like two halves of a whole.

"We were young," Deck said, shifting infinitesimally closer. His chest grazed her breasts.

The ache between her legs felt like an injury. She wanted to lunge at him.

"Sex was new." Deck's eyes burned at her.

"Does sex ever get old?" Never with Deck. She couldn't imagine that happening. "It was more than that." She had to say it. She'd loved his seriousness, his self-confidence. He'd seemed free and brave and adult.

"Yeah," he said. "It was more." They were in trouble now, lost in the past, in their soft words, their naked nearness. "Lots more." With a decisive move, he pulled her against him, let her feel his hardness, took her backside in both his hands.

What are we doing? She couldn't say the words. She could only melt against him, weak with relief.

Deck's mouth found hers, his lips warm and giving, his tongue pressing gently, wanting in. She opened to him, welcomed his tongue, the slow slide of his lips on hers. The kiss was like water after a desperate thirst. She couldn't get enough. She wrapped her arms around him, dug in with her fingers, pushed her own tongue into his mouth, tasting him again, remembering, but discovering, too. They'd been kids.

How had this happened?

It was the champagne, the moonlight, the hot springs and

the memories. It was the way he smelled of cedar and sunshine. It was all that they'd meant to each other. And maybe more.

5

Deck was foggy on exactly how he'd ended up with Callie in his arms, her sweet tongue in hot pursuit of his own, but he wasn't one bit sorry.

He'd started it, he knew that. He'd meant to comfort her, but the past had come rushing back and they were so close and so naked in the water that he couldn't stop himself.

He gripped her backside with both hands. She moaned and trembled, wrapping her legs around his waist, locking on with her heels, as if for dear life.

He felt the hot drive to be inside her, making her come, coming himself, and fought to slow down, to manage this rush of need. He felt like a starving man dropped into a banquet.

Callie pulled back and looked at him, panting, her gaze flying across his face. "What are we doing?" She sounded scared.

"Acting crazy," he said, taking her mouth again.

She pulled away and looked at him, her eyes dazed. "Completely crazy." She blinked and shook her head, clearly fighting for control. "This would get complicated. We have to work together. Sex can make things weird. Plus…birth control…"

"True." What was wrong with him? He hadn't even paused to consider a condom. She was so beautiful, her eyes glittering, wanting him, her lips puffy from his assault. He wanted her so bad. He groaned. He couldn't help it.

"Don't do that," she said, as if begging for mercy. "I'm on the pill, though. And if you're healthy…?"

"I am. Completely. Very, very healthy."

She stared at him. "No. It's a bad idea." She shook her head, then looked at him, clearly wanting him to disagree.

"Very bad." Callie meant too much to him to act out of blind lust. Already, long-dormant feelings stirred within him. They could stop now, no harm done.

Then Callie darted in for a kiss, as if for a last taste of the forbidden. Her tongue pushed in, sampled him. She held his face in both hands while she explored him with her mouth. "But you taste so good." She moaned, rubbing against him. "You feel so good. I just—" She kissed him again, her whole body trembling, her hips rocking in response to a primal need she seemed powerless to oppose.

He had to touch her, so he braced her bottom with one hand and slid his other between her legs to stroke her where she was swollen with need.

"Oh, oh, oooh." She jolted as if electrified. "Deck, if you keep on…if you do more…" She pushed against his fingers, which slid the length of her, making her quiver violently. "You just…oh, you can't…oh…"

He lowered his mouth to take her nipple between his lips. His cock ached to be inside her. His fingers kept pace with her hip movements.

She pushed a palm against his chest. "Wait," she said, panting for air.

He released her nipple, stopped his fingers. "You want to stop?"

"We should. You know we should." She paused. "But I don't want to." She went for his mouth again. *That's my girl.*

"What about you?" she managed to say. "Do you want to stop?"

With her body against him, ripe with arousal, her breathing ragged, her eyes begging for more, he had no choice. "Not on your life," he said. He wanted to plunge into her and stroke them both into oblivion.

Somewhere in his half-gone brain he knew he was a fool, but at the moment he didn't care at all.

"Why are we doing this?" she said, her fingers around his shaft, moving up and down, killing him, making lust surge through him as unstoppable as the blood in his veins.

"For old times' sake," he offered, stroking her again.

"That's good. For old times." She could hardly talk. "Get… inside…me." She spread her legs, guided him to the place and he thrust upward, going deep, making her cry out.

"Oh. Yes, that is *it*." She threw back her head, then brought it forward on the last word.

"You feel so good," he said, pulling out, then pushing in. Her inner muscles squeezed him, urging him onward. He fought for a steady rhythm. He found her mouth and drank in her desperate breaths, drawing mews and sighs of pleasure from her. He cupped one breast, rolling the nipple between his fingers until she squealed in sweet agony.

His body was alive with the need for her. He would never get enough. The water steamed around them, splashing with their movements. Her ankles locked at his waist, she rocked faster, fighting for her climax. She used to panic like this, rub them both raw, as she raced for the finish line she feared she'd never reach.

"Slow a little," he whispered, gripping her hips, forcing her to stop. "Remember? Let it build."

She stilled and looked at him, dazed, struggling to make sense of his words.

He had to smile. "You'll get there," he said in her ear. "I know you." He shifted so he could push the base of his shaft against her clit.

"Oh, yeah." She shivered and a slow smile spread across her face. "I will. I definitely will."

She began to move, slower this time, squeezing his cock with her inner muscles, wiggling side to side, kissing him, sucking at his tongue, pushing her hips against his, making him suffer and fight not to explode too soon.

He groaned, then thrust hard, deep inside her, gratified by her gasp, by the flare of pleasure in her eyes.

They sped now, both of them, moving together, lifting higher, tighter, closer and closer. He tracked her reactions, her gasps, the rhythm of her hips, the way she held him with her body. He fought to stay with her, to not be too soon, to not interfere with the delicate trigger of her release. She began to breathe the way she did before she shot off.

"That's it," he said. "I can feel you."

"Oh…oh…oh…" she said, as if the roller coaster had just topped the rise and she was about to plunge into the joy of the speeding descent. "I'm *coming*," she cried out, going rigid, straining every muscle.

He came, too, nearly blacking out with the force of it, holding her body, keeping her head safe from the rock, losing himself in her sounds, her body, the way she clung to him, the rush and wonder of this most basic human act.

After their bodies stilled, they breathed into the night, holding each other, looking over each other's shoulders.

The world came back to Deck with a jolt.

He swore she'd been struck the same way. She went completely still, then leaned back to look at him. "Wow."

"Yeah," he said. "Are you okay?"

"Sure. I'm great." She hugged him, but it was a get-me-out-of-here embrace. She was embarrassed, he could tell. She backed toward the opposite side of the springs. "I should get back. It's so late." She gave a hesitant smile, then pushed herself up and out of the water.

He lifted a towel so she wouldn't be chilled in the cool air, but he stayed in the spring. "There's room." He nodded at his bedroll. What? Did he think they'd sleep under the stars?

"Thanks, but I need solid sleep tonight."

"Bedroll's thick. You won't feel the rocks."

"That's not what will keep me awake and you know it."

"Good point." Why was he dragging this out? "Shall I walk you back?"

"No, no. I'm a big girl. Just relax and enjoy." She tied on her robe, wrapped her hair in the other towel, grabbed the ice bucket, the nearly empty bottle of champagne, then the glass, which slipped from her nervous fingers.

He caught it midair. "Don't think this to death, Callie."

"I won't. Don't you, either. Don't think. Whatever." She flapped off in her flimsy rubber shoes. A few yards away, she turned back, shot him a smile, then soldiered on. Her stiff half run told him she was already sorry about what they'd done.

He should be sorry, too, but he wasn't. Having her in his arms felt right. He wanted more. Now *that* he was sorry about.

CALLIE WOKE smelling metal and dirt. It was her hair, which had picked up the mineral scent of the springs. It all came back to her in a rush. She'd had sex with Deck. The kind of sex where you couldn't wait for more.

For old times' sake? Come on. Who were they kidding? The only consolation was that Deck had had no more self-control than she'd had.

They would just have to act normal today. The whole incident had seemed like a dream anyway. Deck was a practical guy. He'd probably already tucked it away in his mind. Done and done.

The sex wouldn't quite leave her, though. The shower made it worse, hot water pouring down her body like Deck's wet hands.

To distract herself, she tried Dahlia's shampoo and conditioner. They smelled of herbs and citrus. The shampoo had a nice lather, the conditioner was creamy. Once she'd dried off, she tried the lotion, which went on smoothly with a lingering moisture that wasn't greasy. Dahlia's products were definitely worth considering for the spa. That was a relief.

She dressed quickly and set off for her busy day. The most

important thing was meeting with the first contractor this afternoon. After the second bid tomorrow, she hoped to sign with one or the other.

Intending to go over her plans with her father, she checked his room. He was already up and gone. Maybe doing the early trail ride with Dahlia. Callie skimmed downstairs, then slipped to the breakfast buffet to grab something. Several guests were putting away their plates, no doubt heading for the ride.

Cooky, the long-time cook, waved at her as she passed the kitchen. He made decent ranch fare and his baked goods were heaven. This morning the buffet held lard-fried eggs, flapjacks with fresh preserves, sausage patties, thick bacon, cornbread and caramel-cinnamon rolls as big as a child's head, one of Cooky's specialties.

For the resort, she would have to hire a fine chef and offer gourmet fare with Western options. That was the trend. She'd bet that Cooky, who was well past retirement age, wouldn't leave the kitchen until they pried the spatula from his cold, dead fingers. She sighed. That would be a tough conversation.

She caught Rosita on her way to dust and air the casitas and told her she'd catch up with her to do an inventory on needed improvements. Rosita would have year-round staff to manage, which meant a raise Callie hoped would entice her to stay.

In a hurry now, Callie wrapped a caramel-cinnamon roll in a napkin, grabbed a mug of coffee and set off to meet Rosita.

In the corral, she saw the riders were climbing onto their horses. There was Deck. Her heart fluttered at the sight of him. *Calm down,* she told herself. *It's just another morning on the ranch.* Still, she went over to speak to him.

He was squatting beside a small blond girl next to a horse. A man and a woman looked on from their own mounts. Her parents, she was certain. The little girl was obviously scared.

Deck patted the horse. "Daisy loves to give rides to little girls," he said.

"She does?" The girl looked up at the horse, which must look monstrous to her, then back to Deck.

"Here's how nice Daisy is. See that fly." He pointed at an insect on Daisy's flank. "Daisy's so gentle she lets that fly go for a ride, instead of flicking it off with her tail like all the other horses do."

The girl laughed.

"You just show her with your knees and the reins which way to go. Want to give her a try?"

The girl considered the horse again before turning back to Deck with a somber nod. He swung her into the saddle. Fear flickered across her face, but Deck placed her hands on the pommel and reassured her as he fitted her feet into the stirrups.

As Deck led Daisy in a slow circle, the little girl gradually relaxed until she was smiling. "This is fun," she called to her parents, who grinned with relief.

The ranch hand leading the ride started off and the guests fell into line behind him. Deck noticed Callie and came over. "Hey," he said, his eyes soft. "You get your sleep?"

"More or less." She flashed on being in his arms.

"Can I have a bite?" He nodded at the roll. "Cooky makes them with extra caramel when you're here."

"That's nice of him." She extended the roll and watched him bite into it. His tongue flicked out for a bit of frosting. The man turned eating into a sex act.

She handed over her coffee mug and he took a sip. Handing it back, his face got serious. "Listen, about last night…" He was going to point out that it was a one-time deal they should just forget about.

No way was she letting him say it first. "Forget last night. We were under the influence. Hot springs…champagne…old times. We didn't stand a chance."

"Right. Good." Clouds crossed his face again. Or maybe it was the shadow of his hat. She couldn't read him at all now.

"You were sweet with that little girl," she said, changing

the subject fast, before he could notice how upset she was. "Do you like working with the guests?"

"When I have time. The ranch keeps me busy. At least until now." He hesitated, looked at the ground, then back at her. "I'll stay until you get squared away, Callie. After that, I'll be gone."

"I see." Why did she feel slapped? There was a spark of something in his eye—disapproval, exasperation, irritation. Tension sprang between them again as if they'd never been in each other's warm, wet arms. "Up to you, Deck. You seen my dad?"

"They headed off to Tucson. Some Native American herb show. He said to tell you he'll be back this afternoon."

"Thanks." She wanted him here for the contractor visit.

"I'd better get back to it," Deck said. He turned away abruptly, shoving his hat harder onto his head.

She felt dismissed. What had she expected him to say? He was mad about her and had to have more? What was the point of that?

The morning went downhill from there.

First she saw that the casitas were in worse shape than she'd expected. The three adobe ones, historic though they were, would have to go. They smelled like mud and Rosita gave her an earful about how hard they were to clean.

Then the contractor called to cancel. He was too busy for another job. Worst of all, when she called to verify the second builder's visit, his secretary said he didn't have it on his calendar and was swamped until next summer, anyway.

Now what? Swallowing her frustration, she decided she'd track down another contractor and keep moving. A little glitch. It was only the first day, after all.

Her stomach was rumbling, so she headed into town for lunch and to pick up the mail. As she drove down Main, she noticed that Taylor's new strip of offices had a few vacancies. She hoped that wasn't a problem for him.

She parked in the older part of downtown, grabbed the

mail—the post office was at the back of a gift shop—then headed into Ruby's Diner. The smells—lemon meringue, hamburger grease, milkshakes and coffee—brought back happy memories of hanging with her friends. Until her mom died, life had seemed effortless to her. She'd had no idea how bad things could get. Fighting the twist in her chest, Callie moved forward. She always did.

"Well, if it isn't my girl." Taylor Loft stepped away from the counter and grinned his old grin. He looked good in the crisp uniform and he'd stayed fit. His eyes seemed a little different, kind of wounded, a little wary. That came from working with criminals, no doubt, or maybe a painful divorce—Julie had been the one to leave, she knew.

"Hello, Taylor," she said, accepting his hug. He held her just a few seconds too long. She hoped he had a girlfriend because she hadn't felt a twinge of interest in him on any return visit. If he got flirty…ish. The truth was she doubted she'd ever been truly attracted to him. They'd been friends, had friends in common, and he'd been wild about her. That had been enough at the time.

"You haven't changed a bit, has she, Ruby?" Taylor said.

"Hell, Taylor, she's here every few months. What's to change?" Callie liked Ruby's sadder-but-wiser kindness with a twist of sarcasm. She was a straight shooter and a good friend to all. "Sit anywhere, Callie. I'll be right with you."

"You care for company?" Taylor asked.

"Sure." She slid into a booth and he sat across from her. "Your office building looks good," she said to steer the conversation away from personal questions.

"Development's a good fit for me. I take after my great-great-granddad that way. Abrazo has to grow or die, I believe."

"What can I get you?" Ruby said, giving Callie an eye roll over Taylor's big talk. He was trying to impress her. In high school, he'd been humble about his popularity and football success and leaned on her for praise.

She ordered a salad and a diet Coke.

"You have time for a meal, Chief Loft, or is the call of crime too strong?" Ruby's sarcasm nearly dripped onto the table.

"I'll have the strip steak rare, no sides. And coffee. From a fresh pot, not the usual mud." He winked at Ruby.

"Got it," she said. "Don't let him shovel it too deep, Callie, or I'll never get the place mopped out."

When Ruby was gone, Taylor shook his head. "That woman can sure dish it out."

Callie liked that he'd let Ruby's insults slide off his back. He'd grown past his high school insecurity.

"God, it's good to see you," he said with a boyish grin. "You look great, like I said."

"Thanks. You, too."

"I work at it." He patted his belly. "Gotta make an effort when you're single." Hurt flashed in his face, then flew away.

"I was so sorry to hear about you and Julie."

"Don't be. Starter marriage. No biggie. When I got back from the army, we were both lonely. At least we didn't have kids, so no one got hurt." Except him, she could see plainly on his face. Her heart went out to him.

"You still with that guy your dad mentioned to me? Steven?"

"Stefan. Yeah," she said, cringing at the fib. They were still partners, if not lovers.

"So how's that going?" He sounded way too hopeful.

"Ups and downs. You know." Faking a boyfriend would be the best way to save Taylor's ego, she figured.

Their order arrived and they dug in.

"So, Cal says you've got plans for the ranch," Taylor said after a bit.

"I do. Yes." She told him a brief version of her plan.

"That's ambitious," he said. "Take it from me, construction gets more complicated than you expect. I learned the hard way. You get a loan?" He sounded kind, not nosy.

"I have investors, yes," she said.

"Think they'd be interested in opportunities around here?"

"They're mostly East Coast. Vacation properties."

"You never know." He paused. "So when do you start work?"

"Not sure at the moment, to tell you the truth. I need a builder. I lost the two contractors I had leads on."

"Yeah?" He put down his fork and grinned. "I just might have the solution to your problem. My guy. Garrett Templeton. He built my complex. He's out of Albuquerque. New around here."

"Do you think he would be available?"

"For a friend of mine? Of course."

"If I could have his number, that would be great."

"I'll do you one better." He fished a BlackBerry from his front pocket and began clicking buttons.

"You don't have to do this now."

"Now's when you need the help." He patted her hand. "I'm here for you, Callie. Besides, he needs local referrals."

"I really appreciate this."

In seconds, he had the guy on the phone and filled him in, winking at her while he gave directions to the Triple C. "He'll be out first thing in the morning." He slid the BlackBerry into his shirt pocket, then gave it a triumphant pat.

"He did a good job for you? On time? Reasonable bid?"

"Yeah, yeah. He's great."

"Thanks so much, Taylor. I really, really appreciate this."

"I can fast-track your permits, too. I know people."

"That would be great."

He tilted his head and his gaze went soft. "We had some good times, huh?"

"That was so long ago." Enough dredging up the past.

"What's changed?" Taylor shrugged. "Life's high school. People on top stay up. People on the bottom stay down. You and I were always on top. And now you're back."

"Just for the renovation. A few months."

"I should take you to dinner in Tucson one of these nights. We can catch up, talk about old times."

"Once I get a handle on the job, sure," she said. She could hardly say no after the help he'd been. She had Stefan for protection, at least. "I'm swamped right now."

"Even big-shot resort developers have to eat sometime. We can do wine, a nice meal, maybe find some music." He gave her the eager puppy look that used to charm her. Now it annoyed her.

Before she could respond, the entrance bell clanged and in walked Deck. *Save me* was her first thought. "Hey, Deck."

"Callie." His eyes softened, then he noticed Taylor. "Chief." He nodded, his jaw tight.

"How's it going, cowboy?" Taylor said. "Sorry about the meeting last night. Your commissioners played hooky. Must have been a game on."

"There was a game, all right," Deck said levelly.

"Taylor saved my butt. He hooked me up with a contractor after I lost my builders," Callie said to lighten the moment.

"Is that so?"

Taylor kept watching Callie.

"By the way, Chief, check with the high school principal," Deck said, his hostility like heat off a summer sidewalk. "She knows something about who vandalized the town Welcome sign. Some students with black ink on their hands and a lame story."

"I've heard a dozen theories. It's just kids being kids. The sign's fixed. Let it go."

"How's your pop doing?" Deck asked, but the question wasn't friendly. "He's out in Green Valley, right?"

"Good. Plays a lot of golf. Entertains the ladies."

"Tell him we miss him for me, would you?" Taylor's father had been police chief before he'd retired.

Deck's dig registered in Taylor's face.

"See you later," Deck spoke to Callie, then moved off.

Taylor stabbed at his steak, clearly fighting anger. He shot a look at her. "That guy... Always the superior asshole, throwing his weight around. He's got the mayor in his back pocket. They're locked in the past, the two of 'em. They'd run this town into the ground if they could."

"I guess people have different opinions and ways of—"

"You ever wonder why he's hanging around your ranch, brownnosing your dad?" he said, leaning forward.

"My dad needed help and he wanted the work."

Taylor snorted. "Don't kid yourself. He's after the ranch. He thinks Cal's in trouble and figures to steal it for a song."

"Why would you say that?"

"People talk, Callie. He was sniffing after a loan at the bank." He seemed to catch himself. "Sorry to be so hard with you, but not everyone is as good-hearted as you are."

"I imagine you see the dark side in your job," she said.

"Just don't trust him. That's all I'm saying."

At least Taylor's nasty attitude toward Deck had nothing to do with when she and Deck had been together. She hadn't deliberately hidden the relationship, but it felt too private, too linked to her grief, to breathe a word about it.

At school, she had forced herself to be the optimistic, bubbly girl everyone expected. The pity on people's faces had been torture, so she'd fought hard to act normal.

Only Deck had known her secret agony.

She looked over to where he was talking to two men at the counter. One patted his shoulder, as if to thank him. He took a few more steps before a woman stopped him to talk. At the next booth, a couple with a child spoke to him.

He'd mentioned being busy with civic stuff, which might be what Taylor meant about him throwing his weight around. Could Deck be after the ranch? He certainly acted proprietary about the place and he disdained her plan. But he was reserved, not secretive and direct, not sneaky. If he wanted the Triple C, he would have told her straight out. Wouldn't he?

As if he felt her gaze, he shot her a sharp look. *What are you doing with that guy?* He would no doubt warn her against

Taylor just as Taylor had warned her against him. Had to be some male-primate, chest-thumping routine. She sighed.

Meanwhile, Taylor was smiling tenderly at her. "Hiring Templeton gives me an excuse to come out and see you now and then."

"That will be…nice." Just great. As if she didn't have enough trouble with one rekindled flame. Now she had Taylor to handle. Judging from his hopeful, tender expression, she'd need kid gloves.

6

RETURNING TO THE RANCH, Callie saw her father and Dahlia getting out of one of the ranch pickups. Dahlia held a shopping bag, and when she saw Callie she beamed.

"You should see what I picked up," she said, holding out the sack. "I got some great herbs I can't wait to use." Near Callie she stilled, then leaned close to Callie's hair and sniffed. "That's my shampoo and conditioner!" She sniffed again. "My lotion, too!"

"Uh, yeah," Callie said, unsettled by the woman's bloodhound act. "I liked them a lot."

"Oh, I am so happy," Dahlia said. "Did you hear that, Calvin? She liked my products."

"That's no surprise," Callie's father said.

"We'll need to discuss pricing and quantities for an order," Callie said. "A small one at first."

"I am so, so excited. This is fabulous. Isn't it, Calvin?"

"It's fabulous."

His voice was so weak, Callie's gaze shot to his face. "Are you all right, Dad?"

"Just a little tired." He smiled.

"He needs some protein," Dahlia said, reaching into her voluminous satchel. She pulled out a wrapped bar, which she handed to him. "I need to make us lunch." She went into the ranch house.

Her father bit into the nut bar, then made a face. "Ick. What I want is one of Cooky's jalapeño bacon burgers, but we're watching my cholesterol." He winked and linked arms with Callie as they headed in.

Inside the family kitchen, Dahlia had pulled a compartmentalized plastic container from her satchel and was looking over the labeled sections. "I know exactly what tea we need," she said, tapping a square.

Peppermint. Go peppermint.

"No food for me," Callie said to Dahlia. "I just ate." She turned to her father. "While she's cooking, maybe you and I could talk over the plans?"

"Excellent idea. I wanted to talk to you, too. We'll be in my office, sweetheart," he said to Dahlia.

"Oh. Okay. Sure. And while we eat, you and I can talk about the spa products, Callie? Maybe you can nibble…?"

"Sure," she said. "That would be great." Might as well get it over with. Which was no way to feel about the woman her father loved. Dahlia took some getting used to.

They headed for her father's office at the back of the house. "Isn't she something?" her father said as they walked. "She carries her life around in that satchel. Of course, having to travel between our places, she doesn't have much choice."

"Are you thinking of changing that?" she asked. "I mean, the living arrangements?"

"I'd like Dahlia to move here, sure," he said, then frowned. "But she loves her house. We'll have to see."

"You wouldn't move to Tucson, would you? The ranch is your home." Surely Dahlia wouldn't force him to leave it.

"Sure it is. It's the family home." There was some hesitation in his voice—as if he wanted her approval or a confirmation. Before she could probe, they were inside the office, crowded with bookshelves and big furniture and framed photos of the ranch. The desk groaned with papers and folders and an older computer.

"How do you find anything, Dad?" she asked, welcoming

the leather and pipe-tobacco scent. Dahlia had gotten him to give up his pipe, she knew, and for which she was grateful.

"I know what I need when I need it and where to find it," he said, sitting on the worn leather sofa under a window. She sat beside him. This was where he'd taught her to play checkers and always let her win.

"So," he said, "best to get right to it. Deck tells me you want to sell off the herd and the acres by the river."

"Deck told you?"

"I have to say that I'm with Deck. That land is zoned for grazing, not housing. And let's not be hasty with the livestock."

Anger stabbed Callie. Deck had run to her father to criticize her plans? That was more than insulting—it was devious. "The cattle cost us more than we net right now, Dad. I'm trying to save the ranch. We have to cut losses. The best cash source is a higher occupancy rate. And, as I told Deck, I was *considering* selling those acres. It's only an option."

"I wish you'd give Deck a chance," he said gently. "He's right that I let the herd dwindle. He has some ideas on advertising and such that might work."

She fought to stay calm. "I've done the research and the math. Business as usual won't cut it. A few ads and some steers won't reverse the decline. You asked for my help, Dad. I thought you gave me full rein."

"I know. And I'm not second-guessing you. I just wish you'd take it slower. You were always in such a rush, even as a girl. Take a deep breath, study all the options, then make a move."

"I know what I'm doing. This is my business." She had a plan and a schedule and she couldn't afford delays.

"Deck knows the ranch and how things work out here. Between the two of you, you'll nail this, I know."

She stared at him, fighting not to snap. She'd dealt with clients like him—they wanted improvements, but not if they had to change their business model or approach.

Callie knew she could pull out all the charts and graphs

and profit/loss statements in the world, but it wouldn't change her father's mind. He needed time to adjust to the paradigm shift. She had to be patient. She wanted to do this right. Soon enough, she'd be back to New York and her life. She sighed.

"I won't sell anything right away. And I'll talk with Deck." Oh, yeah. The minute she could get out of here. "But I'm going ahead with the resort changeover. Are you okay with that?"

"Of course. I gave you full rein."

"I have a contractor coming out early in the morning. I'd like you to meet him with me."

"I can't, I'm afraid. There's a concert in Tucson, so I'll stay at Dahlia's overnight. Deck can be my stand-in."

"Your stand-in?" This was too much.

"With the two of you working together, what could go wrong?"

Plenty. Everything. Her simmering anger was sending up stinging splashes. "Where is Deck, by the way?"

"Out in the south pasture, I believe. He drove some fencing supplies out to the hands."

Her father seemed to pick up her tension. "I meant it when I said the place is yours to do what you want. I just don't want you to disappoint yourself. You always put your heart on the line."

"I know what I'm doing, Dad."

Dahlia tapped on the door, then peeked in. "Lunch is on!"

In the kitchen Dahlia poured sienna-colored tea into three mugs. A tray of falafel and a bowl of Greek salad rested on the table.

Callie would drink a little tea to be polite, then take off. The brew smelled bitter, not minty. She held her breath and sipped. The biting liquid shriveled her tongue, just as Deck had described. "This is different," she said, dumping in more honey.

"Isn't it amazing?" Dahlia beamed. "It's hibiscus, rose hips, ginseng and a sprinkle of my little secret."

"It's quite…intense."

"That's because it's fresh. You'll feel clear-headed and vibrant today, I promise."

"I need that, all right," she said. *Got anything for seething frustration?* She couldn't wait to confront Deck. What if he *was* trying to sabotage her so he could buy the ranch? Maybe he'd changed, after all. Or maybe she'd overestimated him from the beginning.

"My beauty aides offer the same healing properties for the skin," Dahlia continued. "They repair free radical damage and rejuvenate cells. It's the ingredients, of course. My base is jojoba oil. Then I add various natural elements—aloe vera, yucca root, mesquite honeycomb, desert sage…."

As Dahlia rattled on, Callie wanted to scream. Her heart was racing, her scalp felt tight and she'd begun to sweat. Probably all the held-back tension. "I'm sorry, but I really need to talk to Deck. How about we meet about your products tonight?"

"Oh, but we have a concert." Dahlia sounded stricken.

"Then tomorrow? If you get here early in the morning, you can meet the contractor, Dad. I'd like that."

"Deck will do right by the Triple C. I won't interfere. I won't have time. Dahlia keeps me too busy."

"*Too* busy?" Dahlia asked. "Do you feel like I push you?"

"Only when I need it." He reached for her hand.

"That's good." She relaxed. "Drink your tea, darling."

Very sweet, but it put Callie's teeth on edge. She barreled outdoors, only to find nothing to drive except the ATV used for spraying ditch banks, a tractor or a horse. She chose Wiley, hoping she wouldn't give the poor guy a stroke riding full-out.

Wiley managed an easy gallop, and the pleasure of riding him distracted her a little from her anger at Deck, though her heart was doing an odd race-thump she couldn't attribute to her irritation. What the hell was it?

Soon she could see the truck and the hands working on the fence. She stopped Wiley in the shade of a mesquite, looped the reins over a branch, then started toward the workers.

Deck headed her way, looking curious and concerned. "Is something the matter?" he asked when he was close.

"Yes, something's the matter." She ignored her heart's strange rhythm and focused on what she'd come for. "You undercut me with my father. You said I was wrong about the ranch."

"He asked me what I thought and I told him," he said calmly. "I said the same thing to you, Callie. What's the big deal?"

"Are you after the Triple C? Is that what this is about?"

He paused and something flickered in his eyes.

"So it's true. You do want the ranch."

"I considered making your pop an offer, yeah."

"And you looked into getting a loan."

"Where did you hear that?"

"Abrazo is a small town. Word gets around."

"It was Loft, wasn't it? If you believe more than a third of the BS he spews, you're a fool."

"He has an equally high opinion of you, Deck. As far as Taylor goes, I *appreciate* the help of a *friend*."

"You think that lazy, conniving asshole would do a thing for you without payback? He's not your friend, Callie. He wants in your pants."

Possibly true, but Deck had no basis to say that. "You're a fine one to talk about being conniving. When exactly were you going to tell me you wanted to buy the ranch?"

"Cal said you were coming out, so that was that. Why bring it up?"

"And it's just a *coincidence*, huh? That you were trying to talk him out of the changes I want to make?"

"Look, if the Triple C were mine, I'd tighten the operation and grow organic beef. I wouldn't pander to bored tourists. But Cal handed the place over to you. If that's what you're into, go for it." He shrugged. "I hope you realize it's a hell of a lot more work than planning a party."

"What?" His smug look sent the truth roaring through her. "I get it. You think if you discourage me I'll give up and you can buy the ranch from Dad." She was seeing red now, burning with betrayal. "I never would have thought that of you."

"You think I would plot against you?" he said, low and angry. "You know me better than that, Callie."

"I don't know what I know. I thought you were my friend."

"I *am* your friend. You want to build Club Med in the desert, go for it. Your father asked my opinion and I gave it. My conscience is clear."

He was telling the truth and she knew it. Had known it. Deck would never hurt her or her father. Why was she so outraged? So eager to fight with him?

"What's going on?" He stared at her. "You're pissed at me after last night. That's what this is about."

"That's not true," she said faintly, though she began to wonder. There had been a measure of relief to have a reason to be angry at Deck.

"I *am* your friend, Callie," he said again, fire burning in his eyes. "And as your friend I have to warn you about Loft. His dad was an honorable guy who worked hard for the town. I don't know what went wrong with Taylor. Maybe he expected the sea to part because his dad was chief, and when it didn't, he decided to cheat. I've seen his handiwork. Don't trust the guy. For your own good."

There was that smug tone, that I-know-best arrogance that burned her up, even when he was right. "What is it with you and Taylor? Are you jealous of him?"

"Of Loft?" He snorted. "Frankly, I don't know what you ever saw in that clown." He glared at her and she glared right back. He *was* jealous, even if he wouldn't admit it.

"I know what I'm doing, Deck," she said, ignoring the Taylor argument to return to the ranch. "My father seems to think you have all the answers. He insists I include you in the plan."

"Smart man," he said.

"Whatever. The contractor will be here early. I'd like you there for any questions I can't answer."

"I can do that." He paused. "Listen, at least check the builder out. Talk to other clients besides Loft." He raised his hands. "Sorry. Like you keep saying, you know what you're doing."

"And if I want your input, I'll ask for it." Now she seemed to be trying to out-asshole him.

"You're the boss." He ran a finger along the brim of his hat in a mock salute, just this side of sarcastic.

"And please refrain from going behind my back to talk to my father."

"Your father knows his own mind. Take a deep breath here. I'm on your side. I just happen to disagree with you."

"Then we understand each other."

She would check out Garrett Templeton because it was sensible, not because Deck told her to do it. He made her so damn defensive.

He had a point about her anger, though. The aftermath of sex at the springs still bothered her. She'd been irritated by his casual response, alarmed by how much it had meant to her.

Okay, so he was right about that. He was wrong about the resort and if he couldn't help her, then he'd better stay out of her way.

CALLIE LIKED Garrett Templeton right away. His bid was reasonable, he had money-saving ideas, and he seemed enthusiastic about the project. Deck showed up as requested, but said little and disappeared the minute Garrett left. The tension between them had been palpable.

After Garrett left, Callie put in calls to two of his previous clients, talked with Stefan and read her e-mail. Looking for travel writers she might pitch a story to, she learned that the National Travel Writers Association would be holding a conference in Phoenix in late April. Groups like that often booked nearby excursions for before and after the meeting.

Rancho de Descanso could be ready by then, even adding time to Garrett's optimistic estimates. On the Web site, she found the name and number of the conference chair. A half hour later, her infectious enthusiasm and rock-bottom bid earned her a tentative yes. What a coup. She would save thousands in advertising dollars, plus good reviews from travel writers meant credibility she couldn't buy.

Good, good, good. Callie was working her magic. Things were beginning to click. To top off the morning's good news, Finn Markham from Valhalla e-mailed that he'd be out in two weeks to see the ranch.

Buoyed by her success, she decided to hit Ernie's for some healthy snacks to keep her from succumbing too often to Cooky's deadly caramel-cinnamon rolls. She swung by the kitchen to see if she could pick up groceries for him. He seemed so happy to see her, she dreaded telling him he'd no longer be ranch chef.

Cooky's list in hand, she climbed into the ranch's oldest pickup to head for town. She was flying down the dirt road halfway to the highway when the truck abruptly quit on her.

She tried the starter twice. Nothing. Slamming the steering wheel with her palm, she swore a blue streak, then got out to check under the hood, which was a pointless exercise.

Unless the truck needed water or oil, she didn't have a clue what to do. It was two miles to the highway, where she could hitch a ride to town, except then she'd need a ride back with a load of groceries. Her only choice was to walk back to the ranch and snag another vehicle. She hoped that more than the ATV and Wiley remained.

Looking up the endless dirt road, she wanted to scream in frustration. The pace out here was maddening. No one seemed to mind delays or distractions or side trips. Even Garrett had sounded pretty laid back. She hoped that wouldn't mean he couldn't meet her deadline. She would be so glad to get back to New York, where things moved fast—a speed she preferred.

She trudged down the road, wishing she had something to

occupy her mind—a book, a magazine. She could think through some marketing ideas, but she brainstormed better at a keyboard.

She hated being stuck with her own thoughts.

As she walked, she couldn't help but notice how pleasant it was out here. The sun felt just warm enough. A light breeze lifted her hair and brought the smell of the river to her. Nice. The hills were a pretty blue in the distance. The sky was bright blue with cotton-ball clouds.

Enjoy the moment, she told herself. *Be here now.* That was a common theme in meditation, therapy and stress management, though she'd never had much luck with any of them.

She looked back to check how far she'd traveled. The truck sat on the road barely two football fields away. Damn, damn, damn. She'd lose the whole day this way. She turned back and began to race-walk. Might as well get a workout.

A few yards farther and she heard a vehicle approaching. This was good. This could save her. It was a Jeep. As it neared, she recognized Deck behind the wheel. This could be uncomfortable, but she held out her thumb anyway.

Deck grinned through the windshield.

She smiled back, the friction gone for the moment, and walked up to his window.

"I didn't think to warn you about that truck," he said. "The alternator's about shot. I'm heading into town for lunch. Can I give you a lift?"

"I'd slow you down. I have to grab groceries."

"I got time." Like everyone else out here, Deck didn't seem to mind a delay.

She climbed in, aware of how close they were. The silence soon became unbearable. They both spoke at once.

"Deck, I—"

"Listen—"

They laughed together, the sound almost musical.

"You start," he said, keeping his eyes straight ahead.

"I want to apologize to you. I know you wouldn't plot against me. I...I don't know— I was upset."

"You know me better than that."

"Years have passed. You might have changed."

"Are you kidding? I don't even change my Stetson. I'm the same guy you knew back then."

"Yeah," she said. "You are."

"And I still care about you, Callie." His words reassured her, warmed her. Then he wrecked it. "That's why I don't want to see you do something foolish."

"That's exactly the kind of patronizing remark that pisses me off."

He started laughing.

"You think it's funny pissing me off."

"I think it's funny that whenever I talk to you I turn into an arrogant jackass."

"For God's sake, quit it!" She laughed, relieved to feel the taut string between them sag and swing in the warm air. "And you were right. I guess after last night, I felt upset." Her face burned. "I swear I'm not really such a bristly bitch."

"So, how about a truce?" He held out his hand and she took it, liking the strength in his grip.

The silence was easy now, as if they'd opened a window in a stuffy room and were at last inhaling fresh, clean air.

"I guess I'd better confess, too," Deck said when they were nearly to town, his smile mischievous, his expression mock sheepish. "Maybe I am a little jealous of that jerk."

She laughed. "Tell me something I don't know." Then she got serious. "I know this job is bigger than event planning, Deck. I've done my homework, but I could be over my head."

"No chance in hell. When you set your mind to something, you're a sight to see."

"Thanks." She wanted to hug him with gratitude. His faith in her meant a lot.

"So, what did you think of Garrett Templeton?" she asked.

He paused, as if not certain how to answer.

"Be honest. I swear I won't bite your head off and feed it to my young."

He chuckled. "Okay. He promised a lot. But builders always do that. Add twenty percent to the time and costs he estimated."

"Of course. I'm going to talk to some clients. If the reports are good, I'm going with him. He can start right away."

"The job's pretty straightforward."

"Maybe he'll come in early and under budget."

"You know the chance of that." Then he seemed to catch himself. "Sorry. Let's let the glass be half-full for once."

"Thanks," she said, relieved at his attitude.

Deck parked at a meter between the diner and the market. "Lunch at Ruby's, then groceries?"

"Sure." She touched his arm as he was getting out. "I *am* counting on you, Deck. I value your advice."

"Whatever you need, Callie. I'm there."

For the first time, she felt as though the burden wasn't solely hers. She had Deck on her side. As long as she kept her needs strictly professional, they would be just fine.

7

THEY'D BARELY STEPPED into the diner when a man called Deck's name. He wore a police uniform and sat across from a young woman. They both grinned up at Deck.

"What have we here?" Deck said. "The brains of the Abrazo police force are off duty? The town's in trouble." He turned to Callie. "Callie Cummings, this is Officer Tad Renner and Ms. Suze Holcomb, secretary to the chief and general in-the-know person."

They greeted each other, then Deck spoke. "You liking your new digs, Suze?"

"Way too fancy." She shook her head.

"Suze…" Officer Renner warned.

"Don't shush me, Tad. Only the best for Chief Loft." She rolled her eyes.

Renner frowned at her, then spoke to Deck. "Thanks again for your help on that bust."

"You did the job. I'm just one nosy citizen. For that matter, the Smiths started it by complaining about cars all hours of the night down their road." He turned to Callie. "Some low-lifes plonked a trailer out west of town and started making meth."

"The Smiths were no help. They complain if coyotes howl," Suze said. "You saw the guy had a truck bed full of antifreeze. How did you even know that was an ingredient?"

"The chamber had a presentation about signs of a meth lab." He shrugged.

"And then Tad took over," Suze said to Callie. "Staked it out *on his own*."

"Suze…I was doing my job."

"You get no support, Tad, and you know it." She looked at Callie. "So Tad watched the place and arrested them." She beamed at Renner, who colored. They were obviously a couple.

"No big deal," he said. "I woke 'em up at 3:00 a.m. They were too groggy to argue with me."

"It was good work," Deck said. "And congratulations on your promotion." He patted Renner's shoulder. "Nice to see you both. I'll be over to check out the new john, Suze."

"Be careful. The gleam off the gold faucets could blind you."

"Suze," Tad warned, but his tone was affectionate.

When she and Deck had moved away, she murmured, "So those two are together, right?"

He put a finger to his lips. "Regulations say no fraternizing on the job. Tad's serious about the rules."

"Yeah, but in a small town? There aren't that many eligible single people."

"Rules are rules to Tad. He was trouble in high school but turned it around. He's loyal to Loft for giving him a job right out of the academy."

"See, that's one good thing Taylor did."

But Deck's attention was drawn by someone calling his name. She recognized Mayor Dickson in the booth. He was about to dig into one of the overloaded burgers Ruby was famous for.

"Hey, Mayor," Deck said.

"Deck." He nodded gravely. "And Callie. Good to see you back. Your dad says you're building a five-star resort out there. Our visitors' bureau thanks you. Not that we have one, but if we did it would sure be grateful."

"I'm happy to do my part," she said, hoping her success would benefit the town.

"Tax revenue must be damn good," Deck said. "With the police station getting that facelift."

"Taylor got a line on some funding." The mayor shrugged, then honed in on Deck. "You think any more about what I said?"

"It's not for me," Deck said.

"Sure it is. The mayor's job is mostly networking and buttonholing. Some grant-writing and listening to folks bitch, but you hear lots of that with the chamber and the commission."

"That's plenty for me."

"Why not get official credit for what you're already doing for free? Tell him he'd make a great mayor, Callie. I want to retire, sell the drugstore, enjoy my grandkids more."

She turned to Deck. "You'd be a great mayor, Deck," she said playfully, pleased to see she'd annoyed him. "You should do it."

"See you later, Mayor." Deck took Callie by the arm and pulled her toward an empty booth. "Thanks a lot for encouraging the man."

"What? I was just doing my civic duty." She batted her eyes innocently as she slid into the booth. "Abrazo needs great leaders."

"You're relentless, you know that?" Deck was about to join her when a woman grabbed him by a belt loop. "Hey, you, not so fast." Callie recognized Anita Hall, who'd been a rebel in high school, oblivious to any criticism of her wild ways.

"Hey, Callie," Anita said. They hadn't moved in the same circles, but they'd been on good terms. "How's New York?"

"Great. You took over the real estate office, right? Lester retired?" Anita had been an agent in Tucson. She'd returned to Abrazo after divorcing her husband, who'd been something of a rat, Callie had heard.

"Yep. I'm a broker now. Building the business." She turned to Deck, giving him a once-over that told Callie a lot. "I need you to check out this horse I'm boarding at the Circle U."

"Give me a call anytime."

"I'll do that," she said. "One of these days."

As soon as Deck sat, Callie said, "You slept with her!"

"Excuse me?" He went pink.

"Don't deny it. You're blushing."

"I don't kiss and tell."

"I remember," she said. Deck had stayed quiet about their time together, too, though they'd never talked about it. It was as if it hadn't been quite real for either of them.

She realized they were staring at each other. "So! Anita," she said to change focus. "She's pretty. Kept her figure."

"She's a good person. Escaped a bad marriage."

"Taylor did, too. Maybe *they* should hook up."

"Please."

"Now, now. He gave Tad the promotion he deserved, remember?"

"Even a snake knows a good hire when he sees one."

She slapped him with the menu.

"Relax. I said he was a snake, not a viper."

"God!" She was pleased with their new camaraderie. "And why don't you run for mayor? I've seen you here twice, and people practically throw you a ticker-tape parade when you walk in the door."

"I do what I do because I want to, not because it's a job." Deck grabbed the menu and pretended to study it. "The crab fritters are still great," he said, not looking at her.

"I know. I always have them when I—" She stopped, realizing what he meant. He looked straight at her over the menu.

"Oh," she said. "That. Yeah." She had had trouble eating back then and Deck had brought home a takeout order of Ruby's crab fritters and fed them to her, bite by bite, filling her stomach for the first time in days.

They locked gazes, their minds raking through the past, pictures flying, memories racing by.

"What'll you have?"

Still looking at each other they both said, "Crab fritters," then laughed softly.

The moment seemed too bittersweet, so Callie broke off the gaze and reached into her purse for her to-do list. "So, Deck, I want your opinion."

"You *want* my opinion?"

"Only if you can give it without going jackass on me."

"You ask a lot. I'll do my best."

"I want to keep the Old West feel to some degree. I can get a good price on some Conestoga wagons from a theater company, so people can sleep in them like the pioneers did."

He gave her a sideways look. "You're serious?"

"A ranch in Colorado says it's very popular with guests."

"We already do overnight pack trips. You'd have storage and maintenance. Canvas rots, remember?"

She pondered that. "Good point." She crossed out that item.

"You're taking notes?"

"Always."

"Then cross off Wild West shows, too. Your dad hired an acting troupe to do shootouts one season. The noise made the little kids cry."

She laughed and pretended to write. "No…shootouts. Good. Any classes will be self-sustaining. We have to watch costs."

"What kind of classes?"

"Bird-watching, weaving, maybe photography. We'll offer special-event packages. Valentine's Day lovers' getaway, Fourth of July fireworks. For Halloween, we'll call it Ghost Ranch and do a murder mystery."

"Oookay." His eyebrows were wiggling again.

"Don't you dare laugh." She pointed a finger at him. "I know what I'm doing on this. I'm boosting our wine cellar and we'll do sunset trail ride wine tastings."

He opened his mouth, then seemed to stop himself. "I get it. Sophisticated guests with sophisticated palates."

"You're catching on."

"By the way, Trinity Church is changing its community

hall. You could score padded folding chairs for next to nothing for songfests on the patio."

"Are you making fun of me?"

"Gently. That okay?"

"This once." She smiled.

"If you're looking for a decorator, talk to Caroline Bestway. New owner of the gift shop. She did the Dicksons' house. Bank manager's, too. Saved them tons. She makes the curtains herself."

"Really? She makes curtains?"

"Don't sneer. She had her own interior design business in Chicago before her husband got the ranching bug."

"I'll stop in to see her. Thanks. I've got to save where I can, since I can't salvage the adobes."

"Why not? They're historic."

"And they smell like dirt and crumble like crazy. Rosita says they're hell to clean."

"You need to keep Rosita happy, that's for sure."

"Luckily, she's willing to supervise more staff. I want to keep as many employees as possible." She remembered her biggest employee problem. "Do you have advice on how to break it to Cooky that I'm hiring a gourmet chef?"

"Why would you do that? Cooky's great."

"At what he does, sure. He can stay on as sous chef and baker, but I need a fancier menu than steaks and cowboy beans."

"Cooky thinks you love his food."

"I do. It's not that." She paused. "He'll be devastated, huh?"

Deck nodded. "So tell him what you want and let him try to make it."

"You see him handling braised elk osso bucco with Madeira mushrooms? Really?"

"A good cook is a good cook. He's been written up for his mesquite-grilled steaks and jalapeño blue-corn bread, you know."

"This has to be spectacular."

"You owe him an audition."

"You're right. I'll talk to him." She took a breath and smiled at him. "Thanks. You were helpful without being—"

"An asshole?"

She nodded. "I'm proud of you."

"I'm glad we're friends." Deck put his hand over hers.

"Me, too," she said, not happy about the more-than-friendly feelings that thrummed through her body at his touch.

She returned to the ranch in time to hear from both of Garrett's clients. They had good reports, so she offered Templeton Construction the job. Work would begin Monday.

Checking off those items on her list, she smiled. Things were moving. She was making progress. *When you set your mind to something, you're a sight to see.* Deck's words hung in her head. Deck hung in her head, too, for better or worse.

Glancing out her bedroom window, she saw the sun had begun to drop. Nothing beat the startling brilliance of a desert sunset. She headed out to the porch for the full effect.

She nodded at the couple on the bench swing drinking beer and shelling the roasted peanuts provided free to guests, then slipped into a creaky pine rocking chair at the far end of the porch.

She rocked slowly, noticing the curve of the seat smoothed by so many people over the years, letting the breeze stir her hair. She felt good here, she had to admit.

But then who wouldn't love winter in Arizona?

Except she'd never minded summer, either. The heat felt right, like a hot pad to sore muscles.

This was just a working vacation, really, which explained the pleasure. She'd be glad to get back to her life, be done with all the memories and hassles.

She breathed deeply, closed her eyes, relieved to notice the bees in her brain had ceased buzzing. She felt present. Content. She heard a murmur, a whinny, then footfalls.

She looked toward the corral, where Deck was swinging

onto Brandy. He galloped the horse around the corral, leaning over to talk to the animal, a hand on her withers.

Callie pictured that hand on her body and shivered. Before she knew it, she was at the fence, her chin on her forearms.

Rounding a turn, Deck saw her. "Callie." In the failing light, his teeth gleamed white in his huge smile.

She grinned back. "You're working overtime."

"There's no time clock on a ranch."

"True. Looks like you've got Brandy eating out of your hand."

"She loves to run, so I let her have her head." The horse tossed her mane, high stepping around the corral.

"She looks fun to ride."

"Want to give her a try?" He climbed off the horse and brought her close to the fence where Callie stood.

"I'm out of practice." She would love a spirited horse beneath her, a lovely sunset ahead, Deck at her side.

"You two will get along fine. You're both full of heart." He held out his hand and she let him help her over the fence.

"I remember those jeans," he said, checking her out.

"Just my old Wranglers."

"I happen to know the right back pocket has a tiny hole and the left is missing a rivet."

She craned to look. Deck put his finger first on the small hole, then on the pocket. His touch went straight through her.

"You don't miss much, do you?"

"Not about you, no."

She'd never missed much about him, either, back then. The way he cupped her face before he kissed her, how silky his hair felt, that tiny scar on his chin, the way he listened to her, head cocked, as if her words meant everything to him.

They stood too close together and Deck leaned down, close, closer, his breath rasping, ready to kiss her.

She tilted her face, closer still, ready to kiss him back.

Brandy bumped them apart with her nose.

"Smart horse," Deck said.

"I guess." Why tempt each other? That was childish. Their new rapport was too important to risk. They both knew better.

"You need help up?" he asked.

"Not with sensible jeans on," Callie said, taking the reins, running her hand down Brandy's neck. "Hey, girl. You okay with me on top? Can I climb up? Go for a ride. Hmmm…?"

Oh, yeah, Deck thought. *On top is great. Or on the bottom. Sideways. Ride me any way you like.* Every word out of Callie's mouth got him hot and hard. If she'd described scrubbing grout, he'd be ready to slam her against a wall. He'd almost kissed her, for God's sake. So stupid. Sex would knot the loose rope that held them together as easy partners at the moment.

She would have responded. He knew that. If he'd hauled her into his arms, she'd have gone as far as he wanted to go. She would be content with just sex, he was certain. For him, there was no "just" about sex with Callie. Not any more. Maybe not ever.

Callie swung herself gracefully onto the saddle. Brandy shimmied sideways and lowered her head, threatening to rear.

"Whoa, girl," Deck said, reaching for the hackamore.

"We're fine," Callie said, locking her knees onto the horse's body, giving a quick, hard tug to the rein, showing Brandy she wouldn't put up with any nonsense.

Brandy snorted, chewed the bit and tossed her head, then shook herself and settled, responding to Callie's handling. Callie was a natural and a great match for Brandy.

When he was certain she was ready, he opened the gate, then mounted Ranger and caught up with horse and rider.

"I forgot how fun this was," she said, her color high, her smile so big it lit her eyes, which gleamed in the dusk light.

Maybe she'll stay. The idea floated up from his belly like a bubble of hope.

"Too bad I got all caught up in being cool and stopped riding." She shook her head, puzzled at herself.

Lucky died and broke your heart. But he knew better than to say that. She would bristle. He grinned at his newfound wisdom.

"What's so funny?" she asked warily.

"Nothing, just, let's see…." He looked at his watch. "It's been four hours since I last made a jerk of myself."

She smiled, then hesitated. "You don't have to walk on egg-shells, Deck. We cleared the air. You can be honest."

Forget New York and come home. Stay here where you belong.

"Within reason," she added. "No telling me my butt looks big in these jeans or anything."

"Your butt looks great in those jeans. In the tight ones, too. Hell, in a burlap sack. You have a great ass."

"Now that's my kind of honesty." She laughed and he joined her, the sound rising in the dusk, making his heart float up to join that bubble of hope that she would stay.

They rode fast for a few minutes, side by side, glancing at each other. Callie looked thrilled. He nodded toward the shortcut to the creek, allowing her enough time to slow Brandy and guide her onto the winding trail.

Brandy led the way along the stony path and before long they'd reached the creek. The horses drank and he watched Callie survey the horizon, where the descending sun tossed color to the sky. She was so pretty against the sunset palette. Feminine and strong, tall in the saddle. The breeze lifted her hair from her shoulders and he was glad she hadn't worn a hat so he could see her entire face.

"This feels so nice," she said, lifting her face to the sky.

"It's been a mild winter." He was afraid he'd start carrying on about how pretty she looked.

"But I never minded the heat."

"That's because you're a true Arizona girl."

"My mom said the desert made all its inhabitants tough as nails—plants, animals, people."

"She was right, your mom."

She smiled, looking out at the horizon. "You don't get

sunsets like this in the East. Of course, when you see this every night, you probably take it for granted."

"I try not to. In fact, I've painted this scene more than once. Can't always do it justice."

"So you're still painting?" She turned to him as if startled by the idea. "You were so shy about your art back then. I only saw the canvases because we spent time in your trailer."

"I still use it as my studio. I hauled it over here."

"Really?"

He remembered holding her on the cot, the air smelling of linseed oil, paint streaking their bodies from where they'd brushed against the countertop.

"I can't believe you didn't mention this when you told me how you spend your time. Do you show your work anywhere?"

He laughed. "I paint for myself, Callie." Art didn't have to be on display to have value.

"I'd like to see your paintings." She turned in her saddle to look at him directly, leveling her gaze, unrelenting.

"One of these days, sure."

Brandy whinnied, then turned as if ready to run, wanting her head, which relieved Deck of further grilling. "She can't stand still any more than you can."

Callie fought Brandy until she settled into an uneasy stand. "I can't believe Dad bought this horse for someone like Dahlia."

"I think Cal bought her for himself."

"Why? He has his own horses."

"Maybe to feel younger."

"You mean Brandy's his red Corvette?"

"Possibly."

She pondered that. "Maybe he hopes Dahlia will get interested in the ranch." She paused, biting her lip.

"What?" he asked, knowing she had more to say.

"It's that I don't like how she treats my dad as if he's old and sick and she has to nurse him back to health."

It wasn't his place to mention the heart scare, but he wished to hell Cal would tell Callie what had happened. "Maybe that's how she shows her love," he said lamely.

"I wouldn't know," she said, then paused. "Have you been in love, Deck?"

Not since you. A fool-ass thing to even think. "Not really."

"Come on. With all the ladies in town falling all over you?" She was teasing, but there was something deeper, too.

"What about you? Were you in love with your partner?"

"I thought so. He was the kind of person I wanted—smart and funny and cool. We had everything in common. Work and friends. We cared about each other, but it wasn't love. We were more like social props for each other." She seemed troubled by that admission.

"He wasn't the right guy, is all. You deserve someone you mean the world to."

She turned to him. "You'll be a great husband, Deck. I hope you know that." Then she had to lighten it up. "Assuming you tamp down your arrogant-asshole side."

"I'll do my best."

"What are you looking for?" She tilted her head at him. "In a wife, I mean."

"I'm not exactly looking. And I don't have a list of traits, if that's what you mean." He shrugged. "I'll know her when I'm with her. She'll enjoy simple pleasures. Horseback rides at sunset. Quiet nights listening to music, reading. Now and then a night out, the occasional naked swim in the river."

Stupidly, he pictured Callie naked in bed, reading him a funny part of her book while he coaxed her into making love with his fingers until she dropped her book with a sigh....

"And 'romance,' of course." She made quote marks.

"Gotta have romance." Then he decided to stop joking. "We'll wish each other the best, no matter what."

"I hope you find her," she said, but her smile didn't reach her eyes, which looked lost and sad.

"What's wrong?"

"I wish I were as certain as you," she said. "About finding someone, about having those feelings." She shook her head, then laughed.

"You will. Of course you will." Maybe she was sick of guys like her ex. She'd sounded weary talking about the big-city lunacy of her life. Maybe she was ready to settle somewhere familiar and warm.

Like his arms.

"We should head back," she said. "It's getting dark." She turned Brandy and set off. Running again.

The way back took them toward the hot springs. As they approached the turnoff, she said, "Feel like a dip?" Her eyes shot to him, shining in the dusk, and she was holding her breath, waiting for his answer.

Hell, yeah. But he knew better. "I don't think that's wise," he said, sounding like a pompous ass.

She stiffened, embarrassed she'd suggested it, he could tell. "You ever get tired of being so damn sensible?" She managed a wry smile, then kicked Brandy into a run.

"Hang on," he called to her, riding fast and cutting her off, stopping so they were inches apart, facing each other. "Don't think for one second I didn't want you naked in my arms." He held her gaze, demanding she not look away. The breeze lifted a strand of her hair across her mouth. He smoothed it away. "I can't just have sex with you, Callie. I'm not built that way."

"Oh." She let that sink in.

He hoped to hell she didn't think he'd carried a torch of undying love all these years.

Yeah, right, pal. Like you haven't.

He couldn't let her feel humiliated. And if the truth kept her from suggesting they make love again, he'd endure the wound to his pride. More of that would only stir emotions best left alone. He did his own brand of running, too.

8

—————

AGAINST HER BETTER JUDGMENT, Callie went to the hot springs after supper. She'd earned a quiet moment in hot water under the desert sky after working out a spa products order with Dahlia and enduring another of her teas, this one tasting like alfalfa and seaweed.

Surely, he'll come. Lying in the water, she noticed her scalp felt tight and her nerves tingled. Yes, she was nervous about being with Deck again, but that didn't account for how her brain seemed to want to burst from her skull.

Was it Dahlia's tea? She'd had an odd reaction from the last cup when she raced out to confront Deck. Dahlia's teas were herbal. How could a few shriveled blossoms make her heart race or her brain throb? It had to be her emotions.

She looked up at the night sky and forced herself to relax. The night air cooled her face, the hot water warmed her body and the steam lifted around her like low, magical clouds. She was relaxed but listening hard for footsteps.

They could pretend to be surprised to see each other, but neither would be. They wouldn't talk. They would simply meld their bodies again. It would be amazing, healing, perfect.

Minutes passed. Ten, fifteen, twenty, a half hour. Callie began to feel foolish. After forty-five minutes, shriveled and soggy, she had to conclude Deck wasn't coming.

He was a man of his word. She'd known that. She just couldn't stop wanting him. Maybe it was the memories of being with him, the way he'd accepted her in all her moods, laughing, crying, silent or chatty. He could stand her pain. Taylor wanted the old Callie, always chipper, the life of any party.

Deck let her *be*. What a blessing that had been.

But that was a long time ago. Deck knew it. He'd sensibly concluded more sex would be a dead end and had taken the high road. He was so damned *mature*, so friggin' *wise*.

He was right. Hell, Deck's perfect woman was the anti-Callie.

Funnily enough, sitting on Brandy beside Deck at the creek, she'd actually pictured herself as Deck's woman—content in his arms, lying under the stars or before a roaring fire, sharing a martini at sunset and, yeah, a naked swim in the river.

But that had been a fleeting fantasy. No doubt it was because she was ready to make a move when she got back to New York but was trapped in limbo in the meantime.

She hated limbo. Make a decision and take action. Because if you stood still, thoughts came—regrets, sorrows, feelings.

The point was that she would never be a person whose big thrill would be going to Tucson for a movie or bingo night at the Trinity community hall.

Don't be mean, Callie. She understood the appeal of a small town, all right, but she didn't see Deck there somehow. Why had he limited himself to Abrazo and the ranch? He was so smart, so good with people, so interesting. He belonged out in the world.

In her world? Was that what she meant?

In the meantime, she realized a water-logged sex act wouldn't help her one bit. Relieved she'd dodged her own bullet, Callie dried off and trudged back to the ranch house, walking away from the letdown as if it had never happened at all.

ON MONDAY, the machinery, trucks and men arrived as promised. Over the next few days the roar of dozers, the grind of the cement mixer and the calls of workers were tangible proof that Callie's plan was in operation. She stayed close to the work as much as she could, and Deck helped her by keeping an eye on things when she was in town. He seemed to avoid her except when they had ranch business to discuss. He was pleasant but distant, acting exactly as if nothing had happened.

Stupidly, she felt hurt by how easily he'd set it aside. No lingering looks, no silent longing. Deck had never been demonstrative. Whatever he felt, he held back. Which made her an idiot to expect more.

Things were clicking nicely along until the day before Finn Markham was to arrive. After a successful meeting with Caroline Bestway, who would do the interior design on the makeover at a great price and a quick turnaround, Callie returned with samples to test against the walls and found the work site abandoned, stacks of lumber waiting to be used for framing.

Irritated, she walked to the site, surprised to notice Deck riding to her on Ranger. He climbed down and approached.

"Where's the crew?" she asked, pulling out her phone to call Garrett.

"I let them go early."

"Why the hell did you do that?" she demanded.

"I'll show you." He motioned for her to follow him to the stack of boards. "This is a poor grade of wood. See the knotholes, the inconsistency? Not framing quality."

"Did you check it all? Isn't some of it usable?"

"You want the building to collapse?"

"Of course not."

"Call Templeton. I left him a message already."

"That's what I was doing," she said, not appreciating his tone. She got Garrett's voice mail. "No answer."

"Keep calling."

"I will," she said through gritted teeth. "We'll lose days getting replacement lumber."

"Talk to Templeton. For that matter, he needs to manage the workers better. Most are inexperienced kids. The older Hispanic guys are pros, but they want to work hard and keep their heads down. They're not interested in supervising the kids or correcting their mistakes."

"What are you saying?"

"I'm saying this crew needs a boss. Get Templeton or a site manager here every day."

She dialed Garrett again and got voice mail. Damn. She clicked off her phone. "I don't need this."

"Delays are inevitable," Deck said.

"I thought you agreed to stop sounding smug."

"You asked me to keep an eye out for you." He shrugged.

Resisting a snotty comeback, Callie headed into the ranch house to keep working. While she tested the fabric samples, she half listened for Garrett's call.

Nothing. No call. Unable to sit still, Callie went back to Caroline's shop with her selections to finalize her order.

It was six when she walked out of Caroline's shop. Just as she reached her car, Taylor pulled to the curb, parked and got out. Damn, damn, damn. One of the hazards of small towns was how hard it was to avoid anyone. Taylor had been out to the ranch every couple of days, supposedly to see how it was going, but managed to tie her up for a while each time.

"So how's it going out there?" he asked her, leaning on his car as if expecting a leisurely chat. "Haven't seen you for days."

Exactly four, but who was counting? "Not so good at the moment," she said, too frustrated to hide it. "We've got low-grade lumber and I can't get Garrett on the phone."

"That's completely unacceptable," Taylor said, reaching for his Blackberry. "And surprising. Let me try him."

"You don't need to. It's after six. He'll call tomorrow."

"I have his private number, Callie. Not to worry." He moved to sit on the Harriet Taylor Loft memorial bench outside town hall and motioned her to join him.

Within seconds, Taylor handed her the phone to talk to Garrett. He was out of town on a family emergency, but promised replacement wood in two days or he'd deliver it himself. He also agreed to be on-site every day.

Callie handed Taylor back his phone. "You saved me again."

"That's what I'm here for." He beamed like a kid.

Warmed by Taylor's kindness, she said, "How about that dinner I promised you? A steak at Ruby's on me? To thank you?" It was the right thing to do and she was happy to do it.

Taylor hesitated and she remembered he'd wanted to go to Tucson, drink wine and reminisce. This was much better. A well-lit, unromantic place was perfect for Callie's purpose. Plus, Taylor wouldn't be driving her home, so there would be no quiet moments for an experimental kiss.

"Everybody's got to eat, right?" she coaxed.

"Sure. Okay." Clearly disappointed, Taylor managed a smile.

The diner was reasonably busy and Taylor guided her with a hand at her back to an open booth at the rear. She felt diners' eyes on them and caught several knowing smiles. Small towns. Gossip that she and Taylor were an item was about to fly, she realized, but there was nothing she could do now.

Once they were seated, the waitress arrived and they each ordered a beer. "Anything else?" she asked.

"How about the nachos?" Taylor asked her. "You used to love them with…what was it? Cherry cola, right?"

"You were the nachos fan, Taylor," she said, smiling. "Just the beer tonight."

"Same for me," he said, smiling across the table at her.

"So, how's policing these days?" she said to steer the conversation away from wistful memories. "I heard you busted a meth lab. Or rather one of your officers did."

"Where'd you hear that?"

"Deck and I ran into the guy who made the bust. Tad Renner?"

"Yeah. Tad's a good cop. He works hard. He's loyal."

"And you promoted him for his actions."

"He deserved it. Small towns don't have a lot of crime. Drunk and disorderlies, parking fines, a domestic here or there. Once in a while a burglary. It can make you think hard about what was so almighty special about being a cop in the first place."

The beers arrived and Taylor took a giant drink from his bottle, as if to wash away his bitter thoughts. They placed their orders—steak for Taylor, a burger for Callie—and she leaned forward. "Still, it's important work, Taylor. People appreciate what you do even if they don't say so."

"Sure. I guess." He seemed to brush that away. "So, I did want to thank you for writing those letters when I was in the army. I was pretty lonely, I won't deny it. I read them until they fell apart." He laughed at himself.

"I'm sorry I didn't keep it up," she said. She'd managed three letters, then feared he would read more into them than she intended.

"You got busy. You had school." She could tell he'd been hurt. He ran a finger through the condensation ring on the table, frowned, then looked up at her. He seemed to force away the bad mood. "Enough of that sad crap. You moved on. I moved on. Life moved on."

Their food arrived and Taylor ordered a second beer. Callie had barely started on hers. "Sure you don't want one more? Glass of wine maybe?"

"I'm fine, Taylor."

"I know it's ancient history, but don't you miss high school? It was so simple. You knew what to do. School, practice, go out with your girl, hang with your crew, have some laughs. No mortgages or meaning-of-life crap to hassle with."

"I had fun," she said. "Until senior year, of course."

"Right. Your mom got killed." He jerked his gaze to hers. He'd obviously forgotten. "I guess I wasn't too understanding back then. When I bought those tickets…I thought they'd get you back on track."

He'd spent a fortune on concert tickets the week her mother died. When she'd turned him down, he'd gotten a cold-dead look in his eye and punched the door near her head. She'd never seen him lose his temper before and she'd been a little scared. They'd broken up and Deck became her refuge.

"I was too sad to go anywhere," she said.

"I was a kid. I missed you. What can I say?"

She'd figured that out eventually. He'd apologized, heartbroken, and it was easy to slip into the old pattern, especially after Deck had sent her away.

"You were good to me, Callie. You kept me going. You made me want to do good, to give you everything. Remember that dress I bought you? You looked so hot in it."

"I remember." She pictured the hooker halter dress dangling forlornly in her closet. "Anyway, Taylor, is it tough to juggle police work with real estate?"

"Yeah, right. Enough of the old days. You won't want to go out with me if I don't cut that out, right?" He frowned. "I guess I'm more interested in development right now. It might be time for a change. When it's time to move on, you move on."

"That's my philosophy, too."

"You're a smart lady." He tapped his beer against hers. "And your guy in New York…that's serious?"

"Looks that way," she said, crossing her fingers under the table. What else could she do with Taylor looking moony at her?

"Things change, right?" He winked. "Whenever you get lonely, you call me. Dinner, drinks, whatever. No more old-times talk." He crossed his heart. "Hope to die?" He leaned closer, grinning.

"Stick a needle in my eye," she finished. They'd used that ghoulish childhood vow over ridiculous issues back then. Despite his promise, Taylor couldn't seem to help calling up old memories.

Callie glanced at the clock over the door to see how soon she could pay the check and leave. The door opened and Deck entered. This time he was the last person she wanted to see.

She looked away quickly, hoping he wouldn't notice them

in the far corner. He walked straight to the counter to talk to Ruby, thank God. She wasn't up for more of these two pissing in corners around her.

"WHAT'S COOKIN', handsome?" Ruby leaned across the bar while Deck tried not to stare at Taylor, who kept saluting Callie with his beer. What a creep. How the hell had she gotten stuck eating with that loser again?

"Better suck your eyes back in your head, Deck."

"What?" He jerked his gaze to Ruby.

"You still into her?"

"What are you talking about?"

"Come on. You never took your eyes off her at the funeral. And I was the one who packed up your take-out fritters."

"That was a long time ago," he said, startled that anyone had known about him and Callie's time together.

"Some things keep." She pushed a piece of raspberry-rhubarb pie—his favorite—across the counter at him.

"Loft got Callie a builder, so she feels obligated to be nice to him. The guy does nothing without a price. He won't leave her alone." As he watched, Callie laughed at something Loft had said. Deck dug into the pie.

"Taylor's harmless," Ruby said. "He's lonely, is all."

His gaze shot to her. "You seeing the guy?"

"God, no. I feel sorry for him. He puts on a tough act, but he takes things hard. Julie leaving tore him up. He wanted kids, but she told him she didn't think he'd be a good father."

"He tell you that?"

"Nope. Julie did. She wanted to hurt him for not being the man she wanted is what I think. Kind of vindictive of her."

"There are two sides to every divorce, I guess."

"It always ate at Taylor that he wasn't as good as his dad. That's why he brags so much. He's insecure."

"He pay you to say that?"

She laughed. "Eat your pie, cowboy."

He looked at Loft and Callie again. He couldn't help it.

"Don't worry, Deck. Callie's got his number. Look at her body language—arms crossed, bored smile. She keeps checking the clock. She's indulging him."

"So, Dr. Ruby, that's quite the psychoanalysis."

"You run a diner, you see a lot. People come in here to fight, flirt, fall in love, celebrate, make plans."

"You hear a lot, too, I bet. You hear anything about Loft misusing state funds to redo his office?"

"Who told you that?"

"Suze Holcomb hinted as much."

"Taylor bends the rules, sure, but usually to help somebody. He talked Craig Cosgood out of filing charges when Luther broke the mirror behind his bar."

"Maybe, but he picks and chooses the laws he wants to enforce. That's not good in a police chief."

"So run for mayor and fire his ass."

"I don't like politics." He pushed the half-eaten pie away, too upset to enjoy it.

"Politics is people, Deck. Finding out what they want and giving it to them."

"Or promising it and not delivering."

"You wouldn't be like that. What did you say to Randall at the bank to get me my loan, anyway?"

"I told him you shouldn't be punished because your ex-husband screwed up the finances. I also reminded him that he got his first job busing tables here. But what cinched it was when I pointed out if Ruby's closed, your Christmas tamales would be history. His wife's family cuts him a lot of slack because of those tamales."

"You see? That proves my point. You understand people. You know how to get things done without hurting anyone."

"I don't know." He shook his head. The mayor thing kept coming up. He would have time on his hands once he left the Triple C. He lived simply enough that he could survive on the money he made brokering horses until he figured out where to spend the Lazy J money. He could buy a spread, but it had to be the right property, the right price, and it had to feel right. That would take some time. What was he waiting for?

He'd told himself he'd stayed in Abrazo for his mom, but she was happy in Modesto, and here he sat, doing what he'd done all his life. Callie's arrival had made him restless.

"You want something else instead?" Ruby nodded at his barely touched pie.

"Not at the moment, no." Talking with Callie about the woman he wanted had stayed in his head. Maybe he was ready to settle down with the right person. Someone who made him smile just thinking of her. Someone who made him laugh and made him ache—in a good way. Someone who challenged him.

His gaze went to Callie. She caught his eye. He nodded toward Taylor, asking her if she wanted rescuing.

She gave a tight shake of her head. She had it under control. Okay. She was an adult. Smart and strong.

Still, if that asshole laid a hand on her, Deck wouldn't be held accountable for what would be left of the guy.

THE FOLLOWING FRIDAY Finn Markham arrived later than Callie expected. He climbed down from a rented black Escalade dressed in elaborate Western clothes. She fought a laugh, remembering how Deck had made fun of her red-leather ensemble. City slickers stood out like flies in vanilla ice cream.

"I'm here at last, love," he said, coming up the porch and kissing both her cheeks, before leaning back and smiling. "The Wild West's been good to you. You look so healthy and tan."

"Thank you. You look…Western."

Finn was midthirties and balding, but he dressed well and was charming enough to get away with flirting with any female over the age of sixteen. "Sorry I'm late. I stopped in your town to get directions—my GPS went AWOL—and made the mistake of talking to your sheriff, I guess? Or police. He was in a uniform. Loft was his name?"

"Taylor Loft. He's our police chief, yes."

"So he's talking me into a tour of the town, saying it's a gold mine for development, how he's got this building, and would I consider a partnership? The guy's got a pair of brass ones."

"I'm sorry," she said, cringing at Taylor's boldness. "He's very enthusiastic, I guess. Let's get you settled so we can talk." She led him to the casita she'd booked for him for the weekend. "I'll show you my plans, the budget, the ranch house and annex. Then I thought we'd take the sunset trail ride."

"Sounds good…" he said, but his attention had been drawn to four girls coming back from a hike to the river. College students from Paris, she knew. "Do you suppose those darling girls will be riding?"

"Possibly," she said. She hoped not. She wanted his undivided attention on the acres she thought Valhalla might buy.

They'd barely finished the overview tour before Finn began whining about his feet hurting in the boots. He was hungry, too, so Callie had Cooky fix an early meal and a waiter carried it out to Finn's patio.

While he ate, she showed him her plans and the budget, though he only let her get through a few screens on her PowerPoint before stopping her. "This cinnamon roll is incredible. What is it, toffee?"

"Caramel," she said on a sigh. "Shall I go on?"

"Just give me a printout to take back. Everything looks great. You're doing fantastic." An emotion flew across his face. "In fact, you're further along that we expected. Perhaps you might slow down a bit?"

"Why would we do that?" She tensed.

"I'm just saying there's no rush." He patted her hand, as if to reassure her. "So is it time for that ride?" He was watching the French girls head toward the corral.

"Looks like it," she said. So much for keeping Finn's attention.

Sure enough he spent most of the ride joking with the French girls. When she pointed out the river acres, he nodded. "Has potential for the right buyer. You should market it." That was that.

She'd planned to entertain him all weekend, but at breakfast the next morning, he informed her he'd booked an earlier flight. She was reasonably certain that was because the French girls had shut him down.

"Thanks for a lovely time," he said from the driver's seat of his Escalade. "I'll praise you to the skies!" He waved the folder she'd prepared, crammed with the printout, photos, plans and the budget. She was disappointed, but relieved that her investors had confidence in her work.

Watching Finn's SUV disappear down the road, she heard voices and turned to see Dahlia and her father descending the porch steps. Dahlia had on jeans and a vest, not her style at all, and she wore a nervous smile.

"What are you two up to?" Callie asked.

"I'm taking Dahlia on that horseback ride I've been promising her for so long," her father said. He looked pale.

"You feeling okay, Dad?" Callie asked.

"Got a bit of heartburn, is all," he said.

"No more sausages." Dahlia wagged a finger at him, her concern outweighing her fear for the moment.

"Who's riding Brandy?" Callie asked, hoping it wasn't Dahlia. Brandy was too spirited for the clearly terrified woman.

"Calvin is," Dahlia said, her lips trembling. She was acting brave for Callie's father's sake, which touched Callie. Maybe their relationship was two-way, after all.

"Want to come with us?" her father asked.

"Too much to do," she said, "but thanks."

She sat on the porch to place a call, watching her father help Dahlia onto Wiley, who would be perfect for the woman.

Her father moved so slowly. Did he have arthritis after all? *One day he'll die.* The thought froze her heart.

She watched them ride off, Dahlia sitting rigid with fear. The things you did for love. Maybe by the time she returned, Dahlia would be as in love with riding as her father was.

An hour later Callie was deep into working out a promotional timeline when her cell phone made her jump.

"You have to help us!" Dahlia's voice was high and scared. "Calvin fell. He says it hurts to breathe. I can't lift him."

"Where are you?" she said, fighting to stay calm.

"I don't know. By the creek somewhere. Near some trees. We've been riding forever."

"Did you notice the trail sign? Was it the Good Luck Trail?"

"I was too busy trying to stay on the horse to look at any signs. I knew this was a bad idea. I just knew it."

"Don't panic, Dahlia. I'll call 911, then head out to get you. Keep my father in the shade, his legs up. Do you know CPR?"

"He says he just got the wind knocked out of him. Hurry, please."

"Stay calm. Keep my father calm. I'll call you right back."

Her heart in her throat, fingers shaking, she got emergency services on the line. The county dispatcher promised an ambulance from Tucson. To save time, Callie would bring her father to the highway to meet them.

She called Dahlia's number and got her father on the phone. "Nothing is broken," he said, but his voice was tight and he seemed to fight for air. "I blacked out and fell. I'm out of breath, that's all." He was minimizing his condition, she was sure. What had happened? A stroke? A heart attack?

Please let it be minor. She assured him help was on the way, then called Deck for help.

"I'm ten minutes away on Ranger," he said before she finished explaining. "Borrow Garrett's truck. Throw in a blanket, water and ice. Grab the first-aid kit from the barn. Meet us at the trailhead. I'll ride in and carry him out."

Moving with crazed speed, Callie gathered what Deck had requested and drove to the spot. She parked and watched for them, praying they were in time, that the paramedics would be swift, that her father would be all right. They were only fifteen miles from Tucson, but heart damage happened quickly. Her own heart jack-hammered in her chest.

If something happened to her father...

The thought made her entire body twist in agony. It all came back to her, the horror of the call, the terrible words. *Your mother was in an accident.... They did everything they could, but her injuries were too severe....*

Just like that her mother was gone. No goodbye. There would be no more advice, no more hugs, no more sweet smell of the strawberry lotion her mother wore. And not another birthday party ever.

Gone. All gone.

This was no time to relive the past or sink into hysteria. Callie forced herself to take slow breaths, to steady her pulse, to stay calm. She caught movement in the distance and made out Deck barreling full tilt toward her. Her heart lifted.

He pulled up short, and she handed over the supplies. "It'll be all right," he said, low.

Not necessarily so. Things could go terribly wrong and they both knew it. Deck held her gaze for a moment, wishing her courage. "Don't assume the worst, Callie. This is not the same."

The exact words she needed to hear.

Deck turned Ranger toward the trail. The horse seemed to sense his urgency and moved swiftly.

Callie called Dahlia to tell her to watch for Deck. After that, all she could do was wait, straining her ears for the sound of voices, hooves on the trail. All she heard was the coo of a nearby mourning dove and the faint swish of cars on the highway. No siren yet.

Hurry up. Panic threatened.

It'll be all right. Deck's words blew through her like a cool breeze, settling her. He always slowed her down. What had he said about not rushing? You caught more details. Yeah. She studied a lizard skimming a mesquite trunk, then a pair of quail foraging in fallen leaves.

Before long, she heard noises—twigs snapping, the thump and click of horseshoes on hard soil and stones. Soon her father came into view, riding in front of Deck on Ranger. He looked pale as death and his face was tight with pain. Deck held Brandy's lead and Dahlia followed on Wiley.

When her father saw her, he put on a smile. "Don't worry about me, Callie," he said. "I'm…fine."

Deck helped her father into the truck while she got into the driver's seat. "Drive like hell," he said, sending her off with a pat on the side panel of the truck.

She did exactly that, shooting looks at her father as she raced for the highway. His face was pasty and damp with sweat and his breathing labored. He kept rubbing his arm. That was a sign of heart attack, wasn't it?

She wanted to crawl out of her skin with anxiety.

"This is a lot of fuss over a faint," her father said, unable to hide his grimace of pain.

Coordinating with the dispatcher, Callie met the ambulance halfway to Tucson. The three paramedics moved quickly and efficiently, asking her father questions about his pain level and the medicines he was taking, all while taking vital signs, shifting him onto a board with a collar—a precaution in case he'd been injured by the fall—putting in an IV and oxygen and giving him baby aspirin to chew.

Callie ran for her purse, then climbed into the passenger seat of the ambulance, which took off immediately, siren wailing. Callie chewed her lip and fought panic.

In a minute or two the paramedic in the back with her father stuck his head between the seats. "You doing all right up there?" He sounded so calm and cheerful she had to believe her father would be okay.

"I'm fine. How is my father?"

"We've got his pain down to a two out of ten and we'll work it down to zero before we get to the hospital."

"Did he have a heart attack?"

"He may have had one. Right now, he has an irregular heart rhythm and his pulse is erratic. He's doing fine and we'll be there soon."

A heart attack. God. The paramedic gave her a sympathetic pat on the arm, reading the terror on her face. "Hang in there," he said kindly. She nodded, blind with tears, unable to speak.

Her phone rang. "I'm on my way," Deck said. "Do not think what you're thinking. This is entirely different."

He'd read her mind, and she was so glad he'd once again be at her side.

9

AT THE HOSPITAL Callie's father was swept through the emergency entrance and down the hall to be treated, leaving her to talk to the admittance nurse, give insurance information and contact her father's physician. After that she was ushered into a family area where people sat and read or watched TV, all looking worn, worried or bored.

With nothing to do but wait for the doctor, she was pacing the hall when she looked up to see Deck striding toward her, Dahlia trailing behind.

Callie threw herself into his arms, letting him hold her, giving in to her feelings as she had after her mother's death. "I'm so scared," she said into his shoulder, her body trembling. She fought to keep from sobbing.

"I know, sweetheart. I know."

"If I lose Dad, I don't know what I'll do."

"We got him here fast. They know how to help him."

She buried her face in the cave of his chest and breathed in the cedar and sunshine smell of him, wanting to hide forever in his comforting arms. Realizing Dahlia must be watching, she composed herself and broke away.

Except Dahlia had gone. "Where'd she go?"

They turned to see her emerge from the hallway leading to the patient rooms, looking utterly bereft. "They won't tell me anything because I'm not family." She sank into a chair, tears streaming down her cheeks.

"They haven't told me anything yet, either, Dahlia. It's his heart, they think. That's all I know."

She looked up. "But I've treated him for that."

"What are you talking about?"

"He had a…problem…a few months ago."

"A problem? You mean an attack?" Callie was horrified.

"Just chest pains."

"Oh, no." Callie sagged, shocked. "He never said a word." She glanced at Deck. His face told her he wasn't surprised. "You knew about this? Why didn't you tell me? Why didn't he?"

"He didn't want to worry you. You were in the middle of a big project."

"So what? Nothing's more important than this. I needed to know. What if he'd…*died?*" She felt like someone had dumped ice water on her head.

"We've watched his diet," Dahlia said. "He's had my teas. This can't be right."

Dahlia and her teas. Callie fought the urge to say something harsh about how crazy that sounded.

"It's the ranch," Dahlia blurted angrily. "It's killing him, but he won't let go of it."

"Dad loves the ranch. Don't blame this on the ranch. Heart disease is in his family. His father died of it, though he was much older…." Her voice caught. What if the disease took her father younger?

"Let's wait until the doctors talk to us," Deck said, putting his arm around her. "He's getting the care he needs here. He's safe."

"Safe? He's not safe!" Dahlia wailed. "Hospitals breed disease. They administer poisons, cut into people for profit. What he needs is my tea." She fumbled in her satchel, pulling out the plastic container with all the tea compartments. She studied the sections, mumbling to herself, tears dropping onto the cover.

"We're all upset, Dahlia," Deck said in the voice he used to settle Brandy. "We'll get Cal home as soon as we can."

Dahlia gave up her search, set her tea box on her lap and wiped at her nose with a tissue. She looked miserable.

"How about we head downstairs for some coffee?" Deck said.

"I'm not thirsty," Callie said.

"Just in case," he said, reaching for her hand. He squeezed hard, as if trying to get through her panic, make her feel him, warm and strong beside her. "Let's take a moment."

He leveled his gaze at her and she took a deep breath. "All right."

"I'll wait here," Dahlia said, staring ahead.

"Can we bring you something?" Deck asked.

She shook her head.

Deck led Callie to the elevator and when the doors closed, he put both arms around her. "You'll get through this," he said, looking straight into her eyes. "You're not alone. I'm here for you. In whatever way you need me to be."

"Thank you, Deck," she said, letting him wrap her tightly in his arms. They stayed that way all the way down, as the door opened and closed, letting people on and off at different floors. As they held each other, whatever wisdom or caution or fear that had kept them apart melted away. Deck had offered himself to her and she was deeply grateful.

When the elevator doors opened, Deck had trouble letting Callie leave his arms. He'd meant what he'd said. He'd be what she needed—friend, sounding board, assistant…

Lover?

Yeah. That, too. No point trying to pretend he'd be smart or cautious now. Seeing her in the waiting room, small and scared, he'd remembered her pale face after her mother's death.

Her grief had seemed bottomless. She'd tried to hide it, pretending she had it all under control, but he'd seen she was dying inside, lost and alone, raw with pain.

His own misery was still so close to the surface that he'd

ached for her. Together they rode a sea of grief, the choppy waves choking them with salt and sand.

He'd be here for her now, too, no matter the cost to his peace of mind.

In the cafeteria she drank a few sips of soda before she insisted on heading upstairs again to wait for the doctor. He was holding both her hands, trying to still her trembling, when the doctor came out.

The introductions over, he sat across from Callie. "It looks like your father has atrial fibrillation," the doctor said, pausing to let the words sink in. "That means the upper chambers of his heart aren't beating correctly. His heartbeat is too fast, so—"

"Can it be treated?" Callie interrupted.

He nodded. "We have some effective medicines to control his heart's rhythm and thin his blood, reducing the risk of a clot or stroke."

"So he doesn't need surgery?"

"We have good luck with these meds. If they fail, there are electrical procedures that sometimes work."

"You mean with paddles?" Callie asked breathlessly.

"Along those lines. Also, radiofrequency ablation, which is where we send pulses of heat to kill off the misfiring heart cells. It's painless and works very well. But we have no reason to believe he won't respond to the drugs."

The doctor stood, preparing to leave. "So, if there are no more questions…?"

Callie lunged to her feet and threw her arms around the doctor, unbalancing him. "Thanks…so much." She sounded almost hysterical with relief. Deck's heart ached for her.

"It was a simple diagnosis," the startled doctor said. "I did nothing extraordinary. We'll keep him overnight, make sure we've got his rhythm regulated. If all goes well, he'll likely be released tomorrow afternoon."

"Can I see him now?"

"He's pretty sleepy, but you can take a minute."

Callie went in, but her father was too groggy to do much more than squeeze her hand and murmur that he was fine. Dahlia went in, too. She declined Deck's offer of a ride home, saying a friend would get her when she was ready to leave.

Callie was quiet on the drive to the ranch, though he caught her looking at him from time to time. They pulled up at the entrance to the house and he stopped to let her out.

She leaned in the window to say goodbye. "Will you be all right?" he asked.

She nodded wearily. "I need a shower, then I'll try to do some work."

He wanted to take her in his arms and just hold her, but he'd promised to do what she needed. He had to let her call the shots. "Mine's the trailer with the blue-striped awning," he said, pointing toward the mesquite trees. "If you want company."

"I think I'll be okay," she said. "Thanks, though."

An hour later a soft tap on his door caught him just out of the shower. He knew it was Callie before he opened the door. Her wet hair clung to her cheeks and she smelled of coconut shampoo and flowers.

"I changed my mind," she said, and flew into his arms, the force nearly detaching the towel he'd thrown around his hips. She kissed him, making it even more difficult to keep his towel in place.

"I can't get it out of my mind—what might have happened. It's making me crazy. I need something else to think about."

"Do you want a beer, some coffee, a movie?"

"No," she said softly. "I want you. Your body. Your arms. I want to be swept away that way."

"Are you sure?" he asked, his body tense, eager to do what she'd suggested. He had to be certain.

She nodded. "You make me feel better. Safe. You help me forget."

She was so pretty, fresh from the shower, no makeup at all. Just Callie.

She kissed him urgently, drawing his tongue into her mouth.

He kissed her back, matching her ferocity, then swept her into his arms and carried her to his bed. He lay over her, braced on his elbows, letting her feel how much he wanted her through the sweatpants she wore and his now-meager towel.

He'd meant what he said. He'd be what she needed, no matter how much it hurt when she left. Because she would leave.

That's what Callie did. She left.

He kissed her deeply for a long, slow time, feeling her body relax under him, feeling her let go of her panic and pain.

She wrapped her legs around his, pushed her hips up against him and held on tight. "Too many clothes," she said.

"Right." He pushed her long-sleeved shirt over her head and off, took down her pants and tossed away his towel until their naked bodies were in full contact. She felt so good, so right in his bed, against him, quivering and eager, soft and firm at once.

"I want you inside me," she murmured. "You're my medicine."

"Whatever you need," he said, but he realized if he entered her, things would go too fast. He wanted to give her a release that was all hers, with no distractions.

He wanted to taste her, something they hadn't done all those years ago. He took a nipple into his mouth and sucked gently, enjoying her moan.

Then he ran his tongue between her breasts, then down the center of her ribcage, adding his lips so he could kiss his way down her torso, shifting himself lower as he went.

"Deck…?" she asked uncertainly.

"Just be still," he murmured. He cupped her ass, ran his thumbs along the impossibly soft skin inside her thighs while she trembled in his grip.

"We've never…you've never done this befo—ohhhh." When he found her clit, she jumped, as if electrified. He licked the length of it, while she bucked and cried out. He liked the warm smell of her, the clean, sweet taste of her sex, how slick and swollen she was against his tongue.

This was heaven.

She locked her fingers in his hair, as if she had to hold him in place—as if he'd leave until he was finished—her breathing labored in the silences between soft cries and mews of enjoyment.

He sucked her swollen button, which went tighter. Her body rocked as she rose from the pillow, then squealed as she fell back. "I'm coming…" she breathed, but he already knew because he felt the throb against his tongue. He stayed with her for those long and lovely seconds that she writhed and shivered through her climax.

Once she stilled, she tried to talk. "I can't…I don't…how did you…? I can't…make words…"

"Don't bother," he said, kissing his way up to her mouth, grinning between kisses. "You already said it all."

"Oh," she sighed, watching him climb up her body, catching her breath. They kissed for a few moments, then she rolled him over onto his back and rose to her knees. Watching his face, she placed him at her opening and lowered herself, pushing him deep.

He groaned, finding himself in her soft, tight space. Her muscles tightened around his shaft, demanding more, which he wanted to give. He would never get enough of this woman.

THIS, THIS, *THIS* was what she needed, Callie thought as she slid up and down on Deck, still dizzy from her climax.

"You okay?" Deck asked her, seeming to sense her wooziness.

"I'm fabulous," she said. She'd been so relaxed when Deck used his mouth on her, completely free, absolutely open. She never felt that kind of abandon with a man, especially when he was doing *that* to her. But this was different.

This was Deck.

She rocked up and down, wanting to feel him deep. Deck held her gaze, taking in every nuance of her expression. He was no doubt timing himself to match her next climax. What a lover he was. It was like he was in her head. She was startled to realize she was already close.

She wanted never to stop, never to remember how scared she'd been. She focused on the moment, on the way the golden lamplight slid in pools along the dips and curves of his body, the way his muscles tightened, shivered across his chest and arms as he gripped her hips, then cupped her breasts as she leaned forward. He was so strong and he felt so good inside her.

Her release came closer with each stroke, each lift and drop of her hips. She fought to hold back, to prolong the luxury, but she…just…couldn't…stop….

"I'm coming," she gasped.

"I know," he said, and she felt him go off inside her. They bucked and gasped for glorious seconds until the waves subsided. She fell forward onto his chest, felt his heart pound against her own, his breathing rasp in her ear.

Finally she dropped to his side in the narrow bed.

Deck shifted her to spoon against her back. "You feel good." He wrapped his arms around her, his hands on her breasts. She looked down at his fingers, then opened a palm. He had a working man's calluses stained a rainbow of colors. He knew hard labor and delicate art. In some ways he was the whole package. Smart and funny, loyal and kind. He'd be so devoted to the woman he chose.

She had come to him because of their history, the bone-deep healing power of their sex. It wasn't forever. Or for very long. Was that unfair to Deck? He'd said he'd be whatever she needed, but she didn't want to hurt such a good and tender man.

"Stop thinking, Callie," Deck said in a husky voice. "Sleep now. Think tomorrow."

"I can't help it." She turned her body to see his face. "What are we doing?"

"We're sleeping. Close your eyes." He closed his, then opened one. Seeing her still staring at him, he opened the other. "We're spending time together. How's that?"

"And that's enough for you?"

"It's plenty."

"You mean that?"

"When have I ever said something I didn't mean?"

"Never," she breathed. "I love that I can count on you. Right now I need someone dependable and steady and—"

"Boring as hell. I get it. I'm the Wiley of your world."

"But I love Wiley."

"With his tired old body and white whiskers?"

"That's where the comparison ends. You're tireless and your body is gorgeous."

"Good to hear. Now go to sleep." He turned her around and settled her tighter against him. His erection pressed between her cheeks, his legs twined with hers.

Feeling wicked, she said, "But I'm not sleepy." She rubbed her backside against his penis. "And neither are you."

"Mmmm," he said into her hair, rocking against her.

She was on fire again as if she hadn't just had two orgasms. She moved onto her stomach, pulling him over her body.

He reached under her to hold her stomach, while he slid his cock slowly up and down her crack.

"Yessss," she breathed, pushing back, inviting him where she was hot and wet and slick for him.

He entered her like a deep breath, stroking deep, sliding his hands onto her thighs, then pressing her clit with greedy fingers. "You feel so good. Slippery and hot and wet."

They rocked slowly. Her muscles clenched and released over and over, feeling so good. She wanted more, so she lifted herself onto her hands and knees, pushing herself up, presenting to him like a female animal in heat.

He pulled out slowly, his entire length, like he was denying her. "Tell me what you want," he said.

"Go deep," she said. "I want to feel you all the way through me." The pressure of this angle, the intensity of the pressure made everything tight and vivid.

He did what she'd asked and she gasped. His fingers stroked her clit, while he moved in and out, tracing her, pushing her closer and closer to orgasm. She loved the slap of her butt against his groin. They were liquid and juicy and moving like one body. She felt helpless, pinned there by his hands, by the relentless strokes, by him taking her, making her his.

"Come for me, baby. Come," he coaxed.

The words were like the trigger to an explosion and she went off. Her knees went liquid and gave way and she dropped flat to the mattress.

Deck stayed wrapped around her and inside her while she climaxed. When she finished, she felt him come within her, groaning, overcome.

Afterward, he fell back, holding her against his chest. She turned toward him so they lay face-to-face. "That was incredible."

He nodded, breathing hard.

"Can we do this while I'm here? Be together this way?"

"Is that what you want?"

"It can't be just me."

What could he safely say? Deck thought for a long moment before he spoke. "It's what I want," he said finally, lying to Callie for the first time.

He wanted more. Way more. Deck wrapped his arms around Callie and felt her heart flutter against his chest. Could he handle this?

He'd have to. He'd lock his fingers into her mane while she tore through his life, jumped all his fences and trampled his grass. Maybe he'd burn out, be done with her before she took off again. She wanted the clatter and crowds and distraction of New York. She could no more sit still, so sunset could gather around her shoulders with its soft peace, than she could leap the Rio Feliz.

Except, she'd said she sometimes felt overwhelmed, hadn't she? She clearly loved being back on the ranch. Pain had made her previous trips hard. Now that was passing. She'd never taken the time to experience the pleasures of life out here.

If he showed her all that was here, maybe she'd change her mind. Daily routines and free-time activities weren't that different no matter where you lived. With someone you cared about at your side, the ordinary could seem extraordinary.

It might be crazy, but he was going to give it a try. He smiled into Callie's hair and felt her fall asleep on his chest.

10

In the morning Callie awoke to the smell of coffee and a note on Deck's pillow:

C: I'm off to work. No rest for the sexually whipped. The coffee is Starbucks. Even in the boonies we get the good stuff. Call me if you want company picking up your father.

She smiled, feeling good in Deck's bed, her body tired from all the sex. She liked the cozy familiarity of leaving each other notes and offering company for errands. She hoped Deck really was okay with this. The scare over her father had pushed her into his arms, but she felt better than she'd felt in a long time.

This was for now, for a little while. That was why it could be so magical. There was a time limit, a clear end in sight. Even too much dessert got old.

Reaching to the floor for her purse, she fished out her phone and called the hospital, where the nurse told her that her father would be released later in the day. She would go to see him and stay to take him home.

She sat up in Deck's bed, rubbing her back from where she'd been wedged against the trailer wall and looked around the room that was so small it barely held the bed and a small bureau. The open closet contained a few clothes, a couple pairs of boots, running shoes and dress loafers. One of everything, nothing extra.

She padded down the short hall into what passed for a living area and kitchen. Everything was neat and tidy and spare.

The walls held two paintings. Realizing they must be Deck's work, she stopped dead to study them. One was a horse running through a pasture. The animal seemed to pop from the canvas. The other showed a pair of coyotes at the river at dawn. They looked so alive she expected to see movement. Deck used thick layers of paint that managed to be delicate, too, making the fur seem feathery, the eyes wise. They were so good they made her shiver.

She *had* to see the rest of his work—and soon.

Walking on, she saw that the small table held photos of his parents, his mom with her new husband, and Ranger. The shelf over the kitchen sink held an aloe vera plant, some round creek stones and a long brown feather—Deck's treasures, no doubt.

The man lived like a monk. Maybe he had few needs and wants. Or maybe he didn't allow himself to desire more. He claimed he was happy here. Maybe he was. They saw life so differently. Deck stayed put and she kept moving. She heard his voice from that long-ago night. *Stay with me.*

She'd had the melting desire to give up, to sink into the warm comfort of Deck's arms, to just stay. But she'd known better then and she knew better now. She would never stay and Deck would never leave. They would enjoy each other while they were together and not look for more.

Two hours later, Callie drove to the hospital and found her father dressed and sitting on the edge of his hospital bed eating soup. Dahlia stood over him, supervising.

"Dad," she said, going to hug him. "How are you feeling?"

"Fine as frog hairs, Callie. And that's pretty damn fine." Was he pretending for her benefit?

"You look tired."

"Who can sleep in a hospital with them waking you up to ask how you are every two hours? I *am* fine. My stress test came out decent. I have to watch my cholesterol, but that's not new.

I'll take some medicine and my heart will be back to normal."
He flashed a look at Dahlia, as if to warn her not to argue.

"Eat your soup," Dahlia said. "It will help heal you."

Callie caught a whiff of fish and B vitamins, but her dad
sipped without making a face.

Catching her watching, he said, "That's all there is to it,
Callie. That and a bruise the size of Texas on my behind
from the fall."

"Okay," she said. "I believe you."

"We're just waiting for the wheelchair so we can leave.
They have to take you out in one. Some kind of liability issue."

She wished she could have a private moment with her
father, but she could hardly chase Dahlia out. "Why didn't you
tell me about the first time you had heart trouble?"

"You would have worried. It was minor. They didn't even
know what it was."

"What if something had gone wrong?" Her throat tightened. "I need the truth, Dad, no sugar coating. I'm an adult."

Her father studied her. "You have nothing to worry about.
I'll follow the doctor's orders. And Dahlia's." He reached up
to pat the woman's hand on his shoulder. "She's going to wait
on me hand and foot. I'm staying at her place for a few days."

"Really?" Callie wasn't sure she liked the idea.

"Don't worry. I won't let him out of my sight," Dahlia said.

That didn't make Callie feel better. "I came to take you to
the ranch, Dad. It's no trouble."

"I couldn't be in better hands. You focus on the ranch. I'll
be well taken care of."

"But, Dad…"

"Come out and see us when you can," he said, his tone
ending the discussion.

"I will, Dad. For sure. Tonight."

The wheelchair arrived, and Callie walked beside her father
as he was pushed to the exit, where Dahlia pulled up in her
Prius to take him away. Callie felt strange, waving goodbye.

She should be relieved he'd be in loving hands, but she felt…uneasy.

She was still standing there when her phone rang. "You need me, Callie?" Deck's voice warmed her.

"I need you to tell me if I'm crazy." She explained what had happened and about her odd feelings about Dahlia.

Deck listened closely, and when she finished, he said, "It sounds like your father is safe and that he'll be cared for. If he'd come home, what would you do? Stand over him? Hound him? I doubt he'd appreciate that."

"That's true." She had to laugh at Deck's insight.

"You can call every few hours, and we'll go see him tonight. How's that?"

"That sounds good," she said. Deck had put her concern in perspective, dragging her from the edge of that whirlpool of worry she'd been sliding into.

"Maybe we can bring him some of Cooky's corn bread."

"Too much lard. Dahlia would never approve."

"Good point. Brace yourself for bad tea."

She laughed a real laugh. "Thanks. I'll see you later."

She drove home. It was Sunday so no work was being done on the annex. She would catch up on e-mail, touch base with Stefan and formalize her offer to the travel writers' group.

She'd barely gotten into her room when she heard a knock and opened to Deck, who whipped into the room, grabbed her and kissed her. "I had to touch you," he said. "Just to make sure I didn't dream you."

"I'm real," she said. "And so are you." She pressed her palm against the bulge at his zipper. "Very real." She was happy to drop into the mindless pleasure of their bodies together for a while.

Deck lifted her off her feet and carried her to the bed, where they fell together. Clothes flew, legs tangled, mouths grasped and gasped and moaned. They were so rough, so urgent, so quick, that Callie's skin felt chafed.

After they'd finished, Deck fell back beside her, holding on to her. They caught their breath for a few minutes, then Deck rose onto his elbows and looked around. "You realize this is the first time I've been in your room? Pretty girlie, Cummings."

"I know. I'd love to update it, but I'm afraid it would upset Dad."

"Why? You don't live here anymore. You and your dad seem to spend a lot of time protecting each other."

"You think so?"

"Don't you? You're both sturdier than you think."

"Maybe." It was something to think about. She squinted at her clock.

Deck, who was closer, held it out to her, then studied it. "What's with the fish?" he asked.

"Pisces, my astrological sign. My best friend in eighth grade gave it to me for my birthday. We were into astrology at the time. Supposedly, I'm changeable and indecisive. I prefer to think of it as flexible and forward thinking."

"It's all in the spin, I guess. When is your birthday?"

She swallowed, not really wanting to talk about it. "March twentieth."

"That's soon. We should give you a party."

"No, thanks. I don't usually celebrate it."

"No?"

"I just don't like to make a big deal."

"Ah." He seemed to realize something. "Because of your mom?"

Her gaze shot to his. She nodded. "It's stupid, but at first it felt like if I ignored the day, I could pretend she wasn't gone." Despite how tight her throat felt, she was glad to say it out loud. "Skipping it became a habit. Does that sound crazy?"

"Not at all. It makes sense. At least back then it did."

"But I should be over it by now?"

He shrugged. "Birthdays can be simple. A cake, some candles, a gift or two. People who love you all around. You can make a birthday what you want it to be."

"What? You're my shrink now?"

"Sorry. Just a thought. Roll it around in your mind."

"I will." She let her mind go back to her birthday, the terrible one. She moved with mental care, on tiptoe, and found that she felt…okay. Sad, but not tortured. "Hmm," she said. "I still feel sad, but it's not…agony."

"It wasn't your fault, remember?" he added gently.

"You're right. It wasn't. I wasn't driving, like you said."

She laughed, surprised at the change. "I hadn't ever said it out loud until I told you. I assumed it would always hurt like hell, so I avoided the thought. Maybe it helps to open the window a little."

"Kind of like what you said about my pop and selling the ranch. I'd felt guilty for leasing it out, but you were right. He would have wanted me to be happy. He wanted me to go to college. I knew that, but guilt was a knee-jerk reaction."

"Exactly. We're pretty damn good shrinks after all," she said, laughing. Talking with Deck, dipping her toe into the icy lake of memories, she'd become accommodated to it. The cold water became refreshing instead of painful. It was like aversion therapy for phobias.

"Nice to have a second calling," he said, lying back, holding her against his chest.

She smiled, feeling happy. Then she remembered something. "Speaking of knee-jerk reactions, Deck, what you said about your painting is wrong. You're good. I saw those pieces in your trailer and I want to see the rest."

"They're not that good."

"I want to see."

"God. You're not going to let this go, are you?"

"Nope."

"One of these days, then." He rolled back, then shoved his hands beneath the pillow. "What's this?" he said, pulling out her vibrator, which she'd stuffed there for easy access.

"Give me that!" She tried to grab it, but Deck held it out

of reach. It was an elaborate but diabolically effective model, though in Deck's hands it looked ridiculous.

"So, this is what you use for *romance*.... So many buttons." He pushed the one that made the middle section turn small beads round and round. Deck's eyebrows shot up in amused surprise. Lights flashed white, pink and blue. "It's like a carnival. Except we need sound. Boom-chicka-bowow."

"A girlfriend bought it for me after my breakup."

"A *girlfriend,* huh?" He clearly didn't believe her. He pushed more buttons. Now it pulsed and the beads rotated back and forth. "How can a man compete with this? We have nowhere near the staying power of…how many batteries?" He opened the battery door. "Four double As. That's a lot of jiggle power."

She grabbed it from him. "Don't make fun. It works."

"Show me," he said, the joking gone from his voice. He took the vibrator and, watching her face, placed it where her thighs met so that the rabbit ears trembled against her vulva. "This how it works?"

She couldn't help but pivot her hips. "Yeah… You…uh… got it."

"Is this how you do it?"

"Kind of," she said, beginning to gasp. Having the device in someone else's power made it intense. She didn't know what he would do next, and wondering and waiting upped the excitement.

"How's this?" He nudged her thighs apart and placed the clear plastic tip at her opening.

"That's good, too," she said. *"Veeerrry gooooood."*

He watched her. "Faster? Is that better?"

"It's…great…good. It's…all…good." She was getting more and more aroused, her body tightening and tightening.

"I want to play," he said. "Turn over."

She did and he slid the vibrator beneath her, angled so the beads turned against her clit. He spread her legs from above and entered her from behind.

"Oh. Wow. Ohh…" She was instantly brought to intense arousal. He stroked her inside while the vibrator buzzed the rest of her. It was almost too much. Her mind shut down completely. Her hips swiveled, she made inarticulate noises, her clit tightened to the breaking point and she burst like fireworks in release. She was vaguely aware that Deck had surged inside her, bucking as he came. The moment went on and on, the vibrator humming, Deck tight within her, waves and waves of pleasure poured through her. Deck traveled with her the entire time.

After long, lovely seconds, finally catching her breath, she managed to roll away and switched off the vibrator. "Omigod," she said. "I can't believe that."

"You didn't have to work for that one, huh?"

"What do you mean?" She fought for breath.

"You usually work to come, like you're not sure you'll get there if you don't push hard."

"Huh," she said. "I never thought about it, but maybe you're right. I do put in effort. I usually need to." She studied him. "Except with you."

"I know you." He smiled softly.

"You do. You know what I like."

"And I want to know more. Show me how you like to be touched." He kissed her mouth, then her neck.

"You already know."

"But I want to get better." He placed her own palm on one breast. "Show me how you like your nipples to be touched."

His words sent a rush of desire through her. She'd never been so lost in sex, greedy and needy at once. She ran her finger slowly around a nipple.

Deck imitated her on the other breast. She squirmed. This was the sexiest sex she'd ever had.

DECK DIDN'T THINK he'd ever get enough of the woman beside him. She was so beautiful, her face fresh, flushed with desire. No pretense, no decoration, just Callie to the core.

Watching her trace one nipple, while he did the same to the other while she shivered and writhed made him so hard he wasn't sure how long he could keep from slamming into her body.

He had to know more about what pleased her. He licked his finger before applying it again to the tip of her breast. "How's this? Do you like this?"

"Mmm, yes," she said. "Maybe more pressure."

"Show me," he said.

She looked at him, her eyes burning, then used more pressure with her own fingers.

"Ah, I see. Like this." He imitated her move.

"Both of us touching me makes my brain buzz."

"Mmm. Brain buzz. Sounds like we're getting there. What do you like next?" She looked too dazed to respond, so he slid his other hand down to where she was swollen for him. "How do you like being touched here?"

"Like that. Slow and soft." She bucked up against him, biting her lip. "Just like that."

"Anything else?"

"Sometimes, I like…" She reached down and slid a finger inside herself.

"Can I play?" He put his finger beside hers.

She made a noise deep in her throat and moved more quickly, responding to the pressure they were both applying. He was completely on fire. He wanted to get inside her, bring her off, go off himself, all of it at once. He stayed still, though, and watched her as her hips pivoted and her eyes rolled back and her tongue darted out to lick her lips.

When she was ready to come, he removed both their fingers and pressed his cock inside to ride with her, convulsing with her as she lunged into release, going there himself.

Afterward, Callie flopped back onto the pillow. "That was incredible. I never in my life—" She seemed startled and happy and he kept smiling.

Stay here. Don't go. The words played in his head. Too

soon. She was as skittish as Brandy. He had to be patient. Patience was his gift. "How about a trip to the hot springs?" he murmured into her hair.

"I can't even move," she groaned.

"I don't want you to get bored."

"Bored?" She pulled back to look at him incredulously. "I can't even think straight."

"Good. So after we visit your dad at Dahlia's, there's a band I like playing at a bar in Tucson. We could take in a set."

"That would be nice," she said, looking a little puzzled but pleased. His plan to show her the joys of staying around seemed to be off to a good start.

THE VISIT TO DAHLIA'S went well. Callie felt reassured that her father was all right there. Later, the band was great. Deck kept asking her if she was enjoying herself, no doubt to be sure she wasn't worrying about her father.

The next evening, she decided it was time to see his art, so she knocked at his door with a plate with brie, crackers, grapes and one of the wines she'd been sampling for the Rancho de Descanso cellar.

"How about a private showing, Mr. O'Neill," she said playfully. "I brought refreshments."

"You sure?" he said, leaning forward to kiss her.

"Mmm. More on that later. Show me." She stepped back away from the door, waiting for him to lead her to his studio.

"Let's get it over with," he said, taking her to the rounded silver mobile home she recognized from years ago. Inside she got that familiar smell of paint and…turpentine, maybe? She set the tray on the sink counter, which was splotched with dried paint in a dozen colors, then turned to look around.

A few canvases hung on the walls, and a couple dozen more were stacked backward against the baseboards. At the far end was an army cot. She nodded at it. "Is that the same?"

"The very one."

She pictured them as they'd been then—frantic, their bodies glued together, striving for release, for peace, the air around them smelling of paint and canvas and turpentine, but somehow intimate all the same.

"Have at it," he said, waving her toward the stacks of paintings. "None of it's that good." He stood in the doorway, as if anxious to leave, a muscle ticking in his jaw.

The hung paintings were close-ups. One was a cactus study, little squares of detail from a century plant, a second was a triptych of parts of a horse at full gallop—chest and withers, hindquarters, muzzle. The third was three pieces of tack, so close the braided rope looked surreal, light as air, the brass ring glowing as if on fire. "These are wonderful."

He did not react, so she turned around several of the leaning canvases. They were more of the close-in works of desert plants—mesquite, saguaro, creosote—and more parts of horses. There was a series of clouds. Spring wildflowers. Landscapes of the ranch, some in full light, some at sunset. The river, also at dusk. He'd mentioned painting this scene more than once. He'd captured it with extreme and vivid realism.

Each painting showed Deck's distinctive style—detailed and realistic, vibrant with colors, the paint thick but delicate. Each piece was a surprise, showing ordinary objects in a new way. She'd never noticed how the spikes on a century plant looked like eagle talons, how blood vessels squiggled beneath the hide on a horse's head.

She didn't need an art degree to see that Deck was a clear talent.

"You get the idea," he said, holding the door, the tray in hand, as if he expected her to leave.

"Hang on, Deck. These are brilliant." She picked up a small painting of an agave plant. The light made it look luminous, almost edible. "I can't believe you've never had a show."

"Don't flatter me, Callie." He seemed almost angry.

"I'm not, Deck. I don't do that. You know me."

He stared at her.

"I'm telling you, this is good. It's fresh. You have an eye for detail and light and color. You could sell in New York."

"Like I said, I paint for me." There was a stubborn resistance in his voice. "I have a lot to learn."

"You're marketable now. I have a client who owns a gallery. She shows avant garde stuff, so I doubt you'd fit, but she'll know where you belong. It's all word of mouth in New York, so—"

"No," he said, then softened his voice. "I don't need to sell a painting to feel good. Let's get out of here before this cheese takes on the taste of linseed oil."

"But you should get recognition. Hell, make some money."

"I don't need that or want it. Maybe one day."

"What are you afraid of?"

He looked at her, fighting an angry response, she could tell. When he spoke, he spoke in a deliberately quiet voice. "Manhattan might be the center of the universe to you, but it isn't to me. When I want a show, there's a co-op gallery in Tucson I'd approach. But, as I said, I don't want that now."

He was warning her to let it go, but she couldn't stand seeing his talent wasted. "Aren't you even curious? I could take digitals of a few pieces and e-mail them to my client."

He looked at her for a long silent moment.

"Don't say no, say maybe?" she tried.

"Let's go." That was as close to giving in as Deck would get.

11

THE NEXT TWO MONTHS flew for Callie. Except for a few hitches due to the inexperienced crew and Garrett's family problems, construction continued steadily.

Caroline Bestway had come through with the new furniture and fabrics. Already the casitas, lobby and dining room had been updated. The spa—an extension off the expanded recreation room—turned out great, the tennis court had been poured and work on the pool would begin in a week.

The hot springs upgrade even met Deck's approval. She'd put in a handrail, but left the rest alone. The massage ramada and meditation garden turned out well. Deck grudgingly admitted they added something to the spot. She would wait to scoop out another soaking pool until she saw how high the demand became. She'd kept the far pool private for family use.

Managing the construction, planning for the launch, arranging marketing and advertising and hiring additional employees kept her so busy her head spun.

She'd kept all the hands and housekeeping staff, offering them good raises, and hired a new assistant manager, Jessica Swift, whom she hoped might become the manager when Callie returned to New York. The woman was calm, efficient and smart and had five years' experience as an assistant manager at a Vegas resort.

The big push now was for the launch party. A dozen travel writers had signed up for the postconference stay that weekend. She wanted the renovation as close to complete as possible and the system smoothed to an effortless glide by then.

With the deadline ticking relentlessly closer, Callie had to-do lists for her to-do lists, but she felt good about what she'd accomplished. If it all went as planned, Rancho de Descanso would be making a profit within a year.

She was under budget on Phase One of the makeover, thanks to economies here and there and cost-cutting construction moves. She hoped Garrett wasn't sacrificing quality, but the savings pleased her. She'd reported her success to Valhalla, but hadn't heard a response. She expected high praise when Finn brought two partners to the launch weekend.

When she wasn't busy with the ranch, Callie was on the phone with Stefan. She'd casually asked him how he felt about buying her out and he'd seemed relieved by the idea. Her e-mails with the managing partners of Ogden, Rush & Tillman had been positive, meaning she was poised to make her next career move when she returned.

She looked forward to that, anxious to be done with this exhausting project, ready to move on. Well, except for her father. And Deck. Deck was always on her mind.

Her father still worried her. After a week at Dahlia's, he'd returned, claiming to be a new man, but whenever she talked to him, she felt him gear up to sound energetic. Was he hiding pain or new symptoms? She wished he'd be honest with her.

She sensed a tug-of-war between her father and Dahlia over where to stay. Dahlia did not like the ranch, a fact that became clearer every time Callie encountered her on the property.

On the other hand, she seemed to have taken good care of Callie's father and she'd filled the spa products order in record time exactly as Callie had requested.

One annoyance was Taylor, who spun out every few days in his patrol car to check on the project. He was solicitous and he'd pushed through the permits for her on a fast track, so she shouldn't complain. The longing looks she caught on his face made her uncomfortable.

Nights with Deck were heaven. The sex was amazing—intense, healing, intimate—and that made her nervous. They were tangling their lives as well as their limbs, and the separation would be painful.

Deck seemed to have launched a campaign to show her how action-packed and cosmopolitan life could be out here in the desert. They stayed clear of Abrazo, wordlessly agreeing to avoid tongues wagging about their relationship, but spent many evenings in Tucson. They went to an art show at the co-op gallery he'd mentioned, saw a photography exhibition, attended a lecture at the University of Arizona, went to a poetry slam at a coffeehouse off campus, ate at all the hot restaurants, went to movies and even a Broadway production that was passing through.

His efforts touched her, but she worried that he thought she might stay. They had an agreement. Surely Deck would stick to it. She couldn't make herself bring up the topic. Things were going so well, she didn't want to risk it.

She was having too much fun. The sex, the nights out, working together, getting his thoughts on whatever came up. With him around, the ranch was a pleasant and interesting place.

She was a little troubled by how out of touch she felt with her old life. That became vividly clear the night three friends called from a girls' night out at a noisy bar. They were drunk and missed her, so they filled her in on the latest gossip, talking so fast, tossing out in-jokes she didn't get. They seemed as far away as the Triple C had seemed when she'd visited in the past. She missed them, but she felt distant from the talk of who was sleeping with whom, what agency had fired what account rep, what parties were hot and why.

It made sense, really. She was so immersed in the resort work and so much depended on her success, that ordinary life *had* to seem frivolous by comparison. She'd be back in the swing as soon as she returned. It might have been smart to book a few days in New York to hit some parties, schmooze the VPs at the agency she wanted to join, raise her visibility a bit.

She was just too busy at the ranch.

And strangely content.

Early Friday evening, a month before the Rancho de Descanso grand opening, she and Deck sat at the kitchen while Cooky unveiled his latest epicurean creation: a delicately spiced rabbit stew that exploded like fireworks of flavor on your tongue. Callie had taken Deck's advice and asked Cooky to step up his game. Cowboy gourmet turned out to be Cooky's niche. He'd added a down-home flair to countless upscale menu items, cooking his tough old heart out.

Deck leaned forward and dabbed at her cheek with a napkin. "We'd better get going if we're going to get decent seats," he said. The Red Elvises, a funky Russian group that did old rock-and-roll tunes, were appearing, one show only, at a Tucson club.

"Could we skip it?" she asked, hoping not to disappoint him. "I'm kind of beat."

"You want to stay home?" He looked delighted, but tried to hide it. "These guys don't tour much. Could be your last chance to hear 'Blue Suede Shoes' with Russian accents."

"I'll have to chance it."

"I got a DVD from Netflix we could watch at my place."

"Sounds great." She preferred Deck's place when Dahlia and her father were down the hall at the ranch house.

Deck grinned like she'd offered him the key to the city.

They didn't make it through half the movie before they were making love on Deck's sofa. Falling onto him afterward, she bumped a book off an overhanging shelf. She reached to the floor and picked it up. It was a sketchpad with a curling, charcoal-stained cover. "Can I look?" she asked. Deck shrugged, so she flipped it open.

There was a nude woman stretched out on a bed. "Is this…?"

"You? Yeah. I didn't quite catch this curve…." He ran his finger down the side of her body, while studying the drawing with a critic's eye.

"Or here, where your hair curls at your neck." He touched the place with a feather-soft stroke. "And this spot at the base of your throat." He brushed, then kissed the spot with a tenderness that melted her.

"I get so lost with you," she said. She felt torn—Callie at the ranch and Callie in New York were different enough to be two separate people.

"You're right here, Callie. I've got you." He kissed her, then noticed her face. "What is it?"

"I don't know. I guess I miss New York. I've been away so long." Or maybe she didn't miss it enough. "I feel out of it."

"You'll get it back." Distance came into his eyes. "If that's what you really want." He paused. "Is it?" The question hung in the air, impossible to ignore.

"My life's in New York, Deck."

"Things change," he said, looking away, trying to hide the emotion she heard plainly in his voice.

"This from a man who hasn't changed in eleven years."

"That's just my hat, Callie." She was relieved he'd joked in return. They'd tiptoed out onto the ledge, scared themselves and dropped back to the safety of their lovely limbo.

To change the subject, she flipped through the sketch pad. "You are so talented, Deck. I mean it."

"Hang on a sec," he said. He flipped back to the drawing, took a piece of charcoal from the box on the bottom shelf of his table and began working on the parchment, glancing at her body, then sketching, rubbing, then drawing more.

His focus was unnerving. His gaze was intimate, but dispassionate at the same time. She felt more naked than naked.

When he was finished, he turned it for her to see.

"You made me look sexy and…sensual, I guess. Relaxed."

"You are sensual and sexy. Relaxed, not so much, but I'll get you there one of these days."

"I'm just fine," she said, grabbing a charcoal to dash a moustache on his upper lip, then a goatee on his chin.

He raised up to see his reflection in the small window above them. "I look like I should be holding a goblet of saucy Cabernet and nibbling rumaki at some gallery opening."

"Not a bad idea."

He leaned down to kiss her, sliding his body against hers, slow and easy, getting into it again.

But she wasn't ready to sink into physical oblivion just yet. His talent fascinated her. "What goes on in your head when you're drawing or painting?"

"It's hard to explain. When it's going well, a place in my brain fires up and my hand shapes what my mind sees. More and more, what I have in my head actually appears in what I paint. Some days it's hard to put down the brush."

"Your paintings are so haunting. I noticed your pieces are either very close up or very far away—a solitary figure at sunset, a single cactus on a hill, a muscle on a horse's neck, light on a cactus spine."

"I hadn't thought of it that way, but that sounds right. Either way, it's like I'm unraveling the string of the thing, peeling back the light and color to get at the core of it, the essence…."

She loved the low intimacy of his voice, the fire in his eyes. Tingles and chills raced up and down her arms and spine as he talked on about how he worked. She felt he was letting her see his soul and she was in awe of him.

She loved when he described the world through his eyes. She wanted to see it that way. To hold still. To watch, to listen, to absorb. Which was not like her at all.

She wanted to share his work with the world, too. Which gave her a sudden idea. "What if I hang your paintings in the ranch house? Treat it like a gallery? In the great room and down the long hall? For the opening for sure. We'll post prices."

"You know what I think about that." He shook his head.

"You'd be helping me. I'll have artwork without breaking my budget. Come on. Help me out here."

"You're working me, aren't you?"

"Not yet, no," she said, running her finger down his chest, then wrapping her hand around his penis, which responded instantly. "*Now* I'm working you."

"Mmm," he said, kissing her hair.

"So, do we have a deal?" she said in her sexiest voice, playing with him, but serious, too.

"How can I say no when you have me in your grip." He moved her back onto the bed and rolled over her, masterful and sexy, and soon they were streaked in charcoal and slithery with sweat, their own private art project in rhythmic motion.

Afterward, lying in Deck's arms she realized how much she would miss this. For the first time in her life, she saw that moving on would hurt more than staying.

DECK LED CALLIE to the picnic bench outside his trailer and sat her down, hoping she'd like what he was about to do. The resort open house was next week, and Callie had worked nonstop. In the rush, she hadn't realized what today was, which made this a perfect surprise. He hoped to hell he'd judged right.

The night air smelled of spring, and a light breeze lifted her hair from her shoulders. She'd been letting it hang loose, naturally curled, not tamed and sophisticated as it had been when she first came. She wore only light makeup these days. He thought that was a good sign. She'd grown calmer. Her eyes were clearer, her skin a healthy tan, her shoulders more relaxed.

"What are you up to?" she asked him.

"Close your eyes," he said, "and I'll go get it."

"What is it?" she asked. "Tell me."

"Stop arguing and just close your eyes, would you?"

"Okay, okay. They're closed."

He started toward his trailer, then turned back. "No peeking."

She laughed, a sound he loved.

A minute later he carried out the birthday cake Cooky had made, so full of frosting flowers, doves, ribbons and lace that Deck had had a hell of a time finding room for twenty-nine candles.

He placed the cake, along with his newspaper-wrapped gift, on the table in front of Callie and sat beside her. The candles sent up a soft circle of warmth that made Callie's face glow.

"Now open your eyes," he said.

She did, giving him a quick smile before looking down at the table. She gasped.

"It's your day, Callie. I hope you're okay with a small celebration. I thank the stars you were born."

"Deck…" She swallowed hard. "I don't know what to say." She studied the cake and seemed to be gathering her thoughts. "I just…" She made a sound that was half laugh and half cry, then widened her eyes. "It doesn't hurt. It's my birthday and it feels good." She threw her arms around his neck.

"Good," he said, when she'd released him. "You mom would want you to enjoy your day. She was big on celebrations."

"She was," she said, nodding.

"I considered inviting Cal and Dahlia, but since there was a chance you'd throw the damn cake at me, I kept it just us."

"Very wise," she said, running her fingers through his hair, studying him, her eyes shiny and wet, her smile so big he wanted to laugh. "You're a wise man, Declan O'Neill."

"Open your gift," he said, embarrassed by his own emotions. "Sorry it's newspaper wrapping. Couldn't find a ribbon."

She tore the paper away. He'd framed his charcoal sketch of her in a simple red-enamel frame. "It's lovely."

"Not as lovely as the original, but good enough to frame." He was damn glad he'd made her happy. He leaned close to kiss her, then nodded at the flickering flames. "Make a wish."

She did and so did he. Watching her, he let the thought fly. *Stay with me.*

She blew out the candles and they carried the cake inside, though neither seemed interested in a piece. Callie clung to him as they stood in the tiny kitchen of his trailer. Her muscles, usually tensed as if to take off, seemed more relaxed, more settled. Maybe now, with him, she'd stay awhile.

This moment had weight, here in his place, gold with lamplight. Callie's eyes stayed with his instead of skipping away as usual. She seemed to be memorizing him. That was how he studied an object he intended to paint.

After a long moment she seemed to come to herself. "What are we doing standing here? We need the bed." She was definitely changing the subject, but he didn't mind. This was a big step for a woman as skittish as Callie.

He carried her down the narrow hall and they tumbled to his bed, Callie's laugh husky and deep. They undressed each other and he found his way inside her. He focused closely on Callie, the way she moved, her eyes, the hitch in her breathing, the small sounds of pleasure she made, happy that she no longer tried to wrestle her climax to the ground.

She knew he'd get her there just fine.

When it was over, he watched her sleep. She was so beautiful. And funny and smart and driven. She amazed him.

The work she'd done on the ranch hadn't been easy, but she'd managed it with grace and energy. She made employees feel like part of a team, crucial to the success of the new ranch. Everyone had geared up for the grand opening. The ranch hands were polishing up the tack and saddles like they expected the president. Cooky had tried out so many new dishes Deck had thrown on five pounds in the last month.

Deck had done what he could to help between his regular chores. He'd located the additional trail horses she needed, scoped out the livestock sales for when the time came, and checked on the construction, where his Spanish came in handy when Templeton went AWOL.

He thought he'd been good for Callie, too. She sure as hell

had been good for him. Now that he had her in his arms every night, something had clicked into place. Like his life was right at last.

He hadn't known what was missing. Of course, he'd been busy. He had work, people counting on him. He'd done what needed to be done. He'd been content. More or less.

He ran a finger down the line of her body he'd tried to capture in his sketch. She smacked her lips and cuddled against him. He was so damned happy.

What about when the ranch was finished? There was another couple of weeks' work on the addition. Callie would shake down the operation for a few weeks more. The new casitas and landscaping the surrounding acres weren't finished. She wouldn't have to be on-site to manage that. She'd hired a good assistant Deck knew she hoped could take over when she left. He'd said he'd stay on as field manager for a while.

Unless she stayed. She could manage the resort. Surely she had a personal investment in what she'd built. She *said* she missed New York, but she didn't act like she did. She acted…happy. She was coming around to it in her mind, he believed. That's what the long looks were about, the silences. She was working it out in her mind, trying it on for size.

He could push the issue, but Callie had to figure it out for herself. She already knew he wanted her here. He told her with every gesture, every kiss, every night out.

She would come around. Maybe she already had.

THE DAY OF THE OPENING Callie was in constant motion. So much hung in the balance. She couldn't miss a detail. She had help, of course, but she was the only person who knew all the pieces to the puzzle. When she wasn't advising employees, confirming the jazz trio she'd booked, making sure the guest rooms were in perfect shape, she was directing delivery people with potted plants, area rugs, flowers, food and wine.

The annex wasn't quite finished, so they'd had to fake a few things. At noon, she saw the furniture truck pull in with the beds, tables, chairs and sofas that would give the place the appearance of being ready. They'd have to haul the stuff away after the weekend, so the workers could put in windows and other finishing work.

She waved the truck toward the spot and dashed inside to make sure the annex was cleared and prepped for setup. The place reeked of the newly applied varnish. Four open cans with brushes sat in the hallway. Damn. The crew did not work neat.

They'd worked hard, though. Everyone had. And been ingenious while they were at it. When the electrical circuits for the annex kept blowing, Callie brought out kerosene lanterns, enlisting everyone to hammer up small wooden ledges in every guest room and down the hall, so that the rustic flair looked deliberate. She'd pulled out strings of twinkle lights from the ranch's holiday decorations and with a few strategically placed extension cords managed to create an elegant, festive effect.

She told the delivery crew what went where, then hastily moved the varnish cans into an alcove, blocking them from view with a decorative vase of pampas grass, getting her hands sticky in the process. She hoped to steal a moment to clean up.

She called Rosa to get the housekeeping staff to throw spreads on the temporary beds and add decorative touches.

Luckily, the refurbished ranch house rooms and the five casitas would be enough to house the travel writers and the Valhalla people. Finn had nearly canceled the trip, only coming through at the last minute. That worried her. Had they lost interest in the project? She expected him to bring the Phase Two check so they could start the new casitas and finish the landscaping. Already, Garrett had extended her credit for supplies and for clearing the lots.

With the annex more or less ready, Callie headed to the kitchen, where Cooky wanted her to taste the final versions of his appetizers, as well as his wine pairings. The man had become a manic foodie. But that was all to the good. He loved the new grill and wood-fire stove they'd installed.

After that, she would meet with the staff, including the nervous new employees, for a final pep talk and rundown. Caroline and Anita were sharing hosting duties, freeing Callie to tour the writers and do interviews.

She'd prepared media kits with photos and a dozen story ideas. If all went well, she'd have seeded travel magazines and newspaper travel sections with stories that would appear off and on throughout the year, leading to the steady increase in reservations she needed.

The travel writer weekend was the linchpin in her marketing campaign, which included direct mail, targeted print ads and a sponsorship on the Travel Network. She was close to being featured on an episode of a popular travel show, too.

In short, the renovation was Callie's best work. If she could pull off the launch it would be green lights all the way. Once the casitas were started and she had the kinks out of the operation, Callie could safely return to New York, checking in by phone and visiting every few months. If her plan worked, Rancho de Descanso would turn a profit before year's end.

What about Deck?

Her mind stalled whenever she thought about leaving him, so she pushed the idea away for now. Maybe they were finished with each other. These things tended to burn out, right? Couldn't they find a natural stopping place?

She looked at her watch. Hell, the travel writers were due soon. She'd sent a van to pick them up from their conference hotel. She was about to risk a quick shower when she noticed Taylor had pulled up and was heading toward her.

She forced a smile. He meant well. "Hi, Taylor."

He reached to shake her hand, but she held them up. "Sorry. I'm sticky with varnish."

"Things under control for tonight?" he said, scanning the

yard, where workers were placing the pots of flowers and plants she'd rented to make up for the unfinished landscaping. "Anything I can do?"

"We've got it handled so far. My guests should arrive any minute, though, so I have to keep going." *Hint, hint.* "I want to thank you for helping with those last-minute permits."

"Happy to do it. You know that, Callie. Anything for you."

She reached into her pocket for one of her complimentary stay cards. "If you and a date want a getaway, we'd be delighted to have you."

He gave her a sad smile. "I'm not after a freebie overnight, Callie."

"I just want to thank you somehow." She felt embarrassed.

"You have. Many times." Longing crossed his face, but he pushed it away, managing a tight smile. "That's what friends are for." He clearly wished for more.

Uncomfortable in the moment, she glanced past him to where Deck was walking a horse around the corral.

Taylor followed her gaze, then turned back. "I hear you're seeing the cowboy." His words were low, his voice dead.

How had he found out? She and Deck were careful. There were no secrets in a small town, she guessed.

"Your boyfriend know?"

"I don't want to talk about this, Taylor. I'm in the middle of trying to—"

"Because I guess I'm old-fashioned that way." Now he sounded angry. "I respected you. I believed you. If you said you had a boyfriend you were *serious* about, I wouldn't violate that. I guess not everyone has that kind of integrity."

"Taylor, I…I don't know what to tell you."

He shook his head, finished with the topic. "Doesn't matter." He held up his hands. He'd wrapped his hurt up tight. "Garrett says you've asked for credit. You overshot your budget?"

"It's just a cash flow issue," she said, wishing Garrett hadn't been so generous with information.

"It happens. You get overextended, you let me know."

"I appreciate that," she said. Was he offering her a loan? Did he want to buy in to the project? She did not have time to explore his intentions. She needed to escape.

"I'm looking out for you, like always," he said wearily.

"You've been a great help, I know." She felt bad that he knew about Deck and that she'd lied to him about Stefan. He thought she was a cheater and a liar. Why hadn't she told him the truth? He'd seemed so vulnerable, so easily hurt.

He tipped his hat at her, then headed to his car. Opening the door he turned to look at her for a long moment, which made her feel strange. Finally, as if he'd made some decision, he bent into his car and drove away fast.

The van of travel writers arrived then, ending her chance at a shower. Callie met with them over a fresh batch of Cooky's cinnamon rolls and coffee. She handed out packets, showed them their schedule, which included a sunset wine-tasting horseback ride, an overnight pack trip for the more adventurous, complimentary spa treatments and massages.

After the meeting, the writers were escorted to their rooms in the ranch house or one of the casitas. Her father came over to speak to her. "Anything I can do?"

"Nope. Just enjoy yourself," she said.

"I hope tonight is everything you want it to be." He pulled her into a hug, then held both of her arms. "You've worked so hard, how could it not be?"

"I won't rest until we're back in the black."

"Whatever makes you happy. That's all that counts." She thought that was an odd way to put it, but had no time to talk.

At two, Finn and two Valhalla partners arrived in an Escalade, bleary-eyed and rumpled. Claiming jet lag, they declined a meeting, but Finn promised they would take one of her tours before the reception. She hoped he had a check with him.

Shaking off her disappointment, she caught sight of Deck in the corral and went to him. He sent two travel riders off on a trail ride with one of the newly hired hands, then turned to where she stood at the fence.

"Hey, there, cowboy," she said. "You look amazing." He wore the fancy leather chaps and his dressier hat, as she'd asked.

"I feel like I'm in a rodeo parade, but you're the one putting on a show, I guess."

"I'd like to get you out of those chaps and into something warm and wet," she murmured. "Me."

"Mmm. Better not keep that up or I'll haul you over that fence and have my way with you in the barn."

"I double-dog dare you."

"If you meant that for a second, I'd do it."

She felt the usual hot shiver when he looked at her.

"After this is over, I say we sleep under the stars." His eyes burned at her, promising way more than sleep.

"I can't wait," she said.

Tonight they'd celebrate her triumph in each other's arms.

12

THE RECEPTION WAS in full and boisterous swing when Callie finally took a breather on a stool at the outdoor bar. She looked around. The place was packed, but the flow was comfortable enough that no one would feel claustrophobic or annoyed. Appetizers circulated, along with plenty of margaritas, and the music from the jazz group created the perfect background for lively talk.

She prided herself on producing events with the care of a movie director, and this reception had all the signature Callie Cummings elements—great ambiance, plentiful food and drink, careful hosting so everyone felt attended to. Everywhere she looked, people laughed, smiled and happily chatted, completely engrossed in each other.

The writers had asked tons of questions on their tour. The Arizona media presence had been big, too. Her throat was dry from talking, her legs ached from all the running around and her head still spun after the constant tweaks and behind-the-scenes adjustments an event like this required. She was out of practice, she realized, but she could get back to speed in a quick hurry. Event management was like riding a bicycle.

She noticed her father and Dahlia heading her way. She'd seen her father hanging with ranch cronies most of the evening.

"You're a miracle, Callie," her father said, hugging her. "This reminds me of one of your mother's parties. This is what we needed—your hand on the reins."

"I'm glad, Dad," she said. "I wanted to make you happy." This event meant more to her than all the parties, receptions and galas she'd produced in New York, that was certain, and his pride in her made every frustration worthwhile. "It's a good sign for the future." They'd achieved the first benchmark on her timetable. So far, so good.

"This has been just lovely," Dahlia said. "So many people took my samples." She'd circulated a basket with her products.

"I just wish Colleen were here to see you shine," her father said, his voice shaky. "She would be so proud of you."

"Do you think so?" Callie was startled by the sting of tears.

"Of course. But I'm proud enough for both of us."

"Thanks, Dad," she said, hugging him, hiding her wet eyes.

Her father and Dahlia headed up to bed, arms at each other's waists, and Callie watched them go, her heart full.

Only one bit of bad news hung in her head. Finn Markham hadn't brought a check. He'd obviously been trying to avoid her, and she had to chase him down and ask him directly.

"We're just a tad off on our funding cycle," he'd said, changing the subject to how many cute women were at the party.

She'd explained about the credit Templeton Construction had advanced her toward Phase Two of the build. Finn glanced at his partners, then shot her a showy smile. "Not to worry. Downstrokes turn into upswings quick in our biz. Let it ride a bit. It'll all come out just fine."

Now she'd have to work out something with Garrett, maybe delay the casitas for a few months, seek a loan. Her stomach churned, but she would not allow bad news to ruin her triumph.

She focused on the party. Guests sat on the curved stone bench around the new fire pit sipping wine, talking quietly, laughter bubbling up frequently. The firelight turned their faces golden, the wood smoke gave off that lovely campfire smell and the piano-and-bass piece the band played floated on the night air, smooth and sexy. Even the stars seemed to decorate the party, twinkling extra bright.

"You look happy." Deck's voice behind her flooded her with new warmth.

"I *am* happy. Take a look." She gestured out at the crowd. "This is why I love my job. Moments like these."

He nodded. "You're good at this. You're like your mother. She never knew a stranger."

"That's true."

"In a way, you've followed in her footsteps. She was a party planner, too, right?"

"She was. Yeah." Her mother held frequent parties at the ranch and chaired the committee that put on the town's Cinco de Mayo fiesta, Easter egg hunt and Fourth of July picnic.

"I hadn't put that together." Her own career was an unconscious attempt to do as her mother had always done. She could picture her in the middle of a party, eyes shining with joy as her guests ate her food, drank her special cocktails and played the unique games she devised.

Best of all, the memory didn't hurt. She missed her mother, but she was grateful for the years she had enjoyed with her.

"Thank you," she said to Deck.

"My pleasure. I can't wait to get you alone." He brushed her hair back, put his arm behind her back in gentle support. Deck was there. Always there. However she needed him to be. "Meet me after you've put your guests to bed."

So she did. When the fire was embers, the guests retired, her staff wearily taking out the last of the trash, Callie made her way to the far mesquite grove where Deck waited for her, already in the large sleeping bag. The air was mild, the breeze light and the stars bright in the velvet sky.

"I brought you a pillow, princess," he said, patting the white mound beside him. She'd complained of a neck cramp after their last night under the stars.

She removed her clothes and joined him, warmed by his naked body wrapped around her, pleased by the pillow. They faced each other, braced on elbows, legs twined.

"You did good, Callie," he said. "The party was a hit. I don't know how you manage it. That kind of thing wears me out."

"It makes me feel alive," she said.

"I can see that."

"And you! I saw Sold dots on three of your pieces."

"We'll see if they're still there when the booze wears off. When can I take my stuff down?"

"Why would you want to? You might sell more."

"I didn't want them up in the first place. You twisted my...well you know what part you twisted, Callie."

"But look how well it turned out. They look so good on the walls. Besides, I can't afford to replace them quite yet."

"Callie..." He sighed, but he seemed to decide to let the issue pass. "Leave them up for a while more, I guess." He leaned in to kiss her, urgently, as if to forget everything else.

She felt the same way. She didn't want to think of how she would miss him when this was over. They kissed and moved against each other, sliding into position, then joining their bodies, staying right here under the mesquite tree in this sleeping bag, where they belonged.

"When you're inside me, I never want you to go," she said, lifting her hips, inviting him deeper.

Deeper he went. She had to say more, to tell him what this had meant to her. "You've made this place feel like home again, Deck. I've loved being here with you."

Loved. Past tense, as in, *I'll soon be gone.*

Despite his promise not to let doubts assail him, Callie's words hit like a punch in the gut.

"Deck?" she said, sensing his withdrawal.

"I'm here," he said, forcing himself to keep on. He thrust deeper, loving the way she gasped, how her eyes flared hot.

All the same, he was backing away. He wanted her too much and she wasn't his. She had another life she preferred.

She moved more quickly now, giving the soft sounds that told him she was nearing release. He helped her along, holding her hips, intent on her reactions, breathing her in, pressing his fingers into her soft skin and the firm muscles beneath.

You're mine, he told her with every stroke. *And I'm yours.* She shivered and stilled, then cried out.

He broke open inside her, calling her name, too, embarrassed by how desperate he sounded. He wrapped his arms around her, absorbing her heat and giving her his, holding on. Was this how love felt? Like his insides had been run through a blender? Where was the joy? He felt trapped, tense, braced for it to go to hell.

Callie's heart fluttered against his chest like a bird cupped loosely in a palm.

Stay. Why couldn't he say it? *For once in your life, go with your heart, Deck.* He took a breath, ready to risk it, except Callie rose onto her elbows and smiled down at him. "I'd love you to see my place in New York."

"Sure," he said, an ache passing through him like a hot knife through butter. "Maybe I'll visit," he managed to say.

She blinked, as if startled by his reply. "There's so much I can show you." She bit her lip, then fell away from him to stare up at the sky.

He felt her absence like a cold wind. A taste of how he'd feel without her. He'd been a fool.

Maybe he'll visit? Callie felt stung. They'd grown so close over these months, she thought. She figured he didn't want it to end any more than she did.

But she'd been wrong. That was obvious. Once again he was ending it early, being sensible, practical, mature.

The distance between them suddenly felt as huge as the miles on a map between Abrazo and Manhattan.

She fought to sort it out, to be mature for once. What did

she think he was going to do? Come with her to Manhattan? Live in her apartment? Rent a studio so he could paint like the thousands of aspiring artists in the city?

"We've had fun, haven't we?" she said finally, her heart in agony. They cared about each other, but maybe that sprang from their past. Maybe they'd healed themselves so they could move on in their separate lives.

"Sure," he said flatly. "Lots of fun."

Did she love him? Probably, but how far could she go with her crippled heart? *Be sensible. This is better.*

For long, painful minutes they stared upward and took tense breaths. Callie couldn't stand it. She rolled back to look down at him. "Hey. Why so gloomy? I'm not leaving tomorrow. We've still got time."

He tried to smile. "Sure." He kissed her, but his lips were barely there. It was a ghost of a kiss.

She fell back onto the sleeping bag and they resumed staring up at the vast desert sky. They were together, but so alone. Callie's heart twisted in her chest.

Go, go, get out of here. Her mantra started up in her head. As soon as the resort's operation was set, the upswing assured, she'd get the hell back where she belonged. Whatever was left of her heart was already in agony.

IN DECK'S DREAM, Callie surprised him by agreeing to go on a horse pack trip. If it went well, she'd said she would stay. He was so happy until the campfire started to smoke. Billowing clouds of smoke had them both coughing and rubbing stinging eyes. Dammit, this would ruin everything.

He fought to move, to put out the fire. He had to save Callie, save her good feelings, keep her happy.

Danger. Wake up. Now. He jerked up, breathing hard. Awake. He'd been sleeping under the trees near the ranch house, Callie beside him. There was no pack trip and no campfire.

So why did he still smell smoke?

Flickering light drew his gaze to the annex, not a hundred yards away, where flames licked at the empty window frames. Smoke rose, ominous in the moonlight, a dangerous gray against the black night.

He touched Callie's shoulder. "Wake up, Callie."

She opened her eyes and blinked, dazed. "What happened?"

"There's a fire. Everyone's safe if the wind stays calm, but we should empty the ranch house just in case."

She nodded, leaning out of the bag, grabbing her clothes, shaking her head to wake up.

Deck dialed 911, dressing while he talked to the dispatcher. Rural Metro had a fast response time, he knew, but the fire looked well established, no doubt feeding on the newly varnished walls.

They jogged to the ranch house together. Inside, sleepy-looking people were already tromping down the stairs, led by Cal, Dahlia holding his arm. How the hell did they know?

"Fire trucks are on the way," Deck told Cal.

"I was making tea when I saw the fire," Dahlia said, her eyes huge.

"Here." Cal handed Deck a key. "This is the master. Check all the rooms. Make sure everyone's out."

Deck nodded and Cal led Dahlia out the door.

Callie was reassuring the guests as they headed outside. "You're in no danger. The fire is in the next building. We'll be back inside in a jiff." She managed to sound calm, though Deck heard the fear beneath her words.

After he'd checked the guest rooms, Deck searched the ground floor to be sure everyone was outside. In the Cummingses' kitchen, he found a teapot on the floor in a puddle of water, the stove burner glowing red. He turned it off, then checked the window. Sure enough, the fire was clearly visible from here. What the hell was Dahlia doing making tea at three in the morning?

When he emerged from the ranch house, he heard the low

whine of a siren. The guests, in pajamas or robes or wrapped in blankets, murmured and pointed at the fire, now roaring yellow against the dark sky.

The casitas, far enough away not to be disturbed by the noise, were dark. Except…he noticed three men outside the farthest one, silently watching. Callie's investors, he thought. What had awakened them?

The siren got louder as it hit the ranch road. But the vehicle wasn't loud enough for a fire truck and soon he saw that it was Taylor Loft, jerking to a stop at a reckless angle, kicking up dust, as if he had to rush to save the day. What an ass. It wasn't like the guy to even show for a fire. He wanted to look like a hero for Callie, no doubt.

Sure enough, he headed straight for her.

A second police car pulled up. Tad Renner got out, spoke to Loft, then began setting out unnecessary traffic cones and marking off the annex with yellow tape. Deck went to help him. Taylor, the officious prick, ordered the guests to move back, though no one was anywhere near the fire.

Within minutes two engines, a fire truck and an ambulance arrived and set to work on the fire. EMTs made sure no guests had injuries or had inhaled smoke.

Callie finished talking with the lead fire fighter and turned toward Deck. She looked devastated.

"You okay?" he asked her.

"The annex will be gone. They can't save it."

"You have insurance. Templeton, too."

"We had trouble with the breakers. Could it be electrical?"

"That's possible. I'm sure the varnish sped the burn."

"Varnish!" She gasped. "Oh, God. The workers left cans in the hall, so I tucked them in an alcove. Could that have caused it? Varnish fumes? I hid them with pampas grass. Dry grass! Talk about tinder."

"The temperature has to be high to cause combustion. You need ignition, a spark or something…"

"We had kerosene lanterns all over the place. Maybe we left one burning. The ledges were hammered in a hurry. If one gave way…" She pressed the heels of her hands against her temples. "Is this my fault? Was I negligent?" Her voice shook.

"It was an accident," he said. "And no one was hurt."

"That's true." She looked toward the guests. "What will the travel writers say about this? I have to go smooth this over. Lord knows how long it will be before they let us back in."

She started away, but he caught her arm. "Give yourself a minute, Callie. You've had a shock."

"I don't have a minute. I have guests." She set off with determined strides toward the crowd.

Soon she was gesturing and laughing, completely at ease, covering for a disaster that had devastated her. Which was exactly what she'd done at her mother's funeral—handed out food and drinks, offering solace to her mother's friends and her dad.

They should have been comforting her, Deck had thought at the time. Was he the only one who saw the misery behind her smile, the deadness in her eyes? He'd noticed her hair shivering against her collarbone. She was trembling, but no one else saw or cared. He'd gone to her and touched her arm.

"What is it?" she'd asked distractedly.

"Come outside with me."

"I have guests."

"Just for a second." He took her by the elbow and led her outside. "Now breathe for a bit, okay? You look like you're about to faint."

She stood still. Soon, tears began to spill down her cheeks. She brushed them violently away. "I have to go. I need to cheer people up."

"What about you? Who cheers you up, Callie?"

She blinked and seemed to fight a sob.

He pulled her into his arms. "It'll be okay. It will. Eventually." People's words from his father's funeral swirled in his head. He snatched the ones that had helped and offered them to her: "This is hell… It's unfair… You'll think you can't go on and then you'll wish you didn't have to. Take it day by day. Find what makes you feel better and keep doing that. Hang on for time to pass."

Callie looked at him, eyes wide, drinking in his words, nodding, slowly accepting. Gradually, tension drained from her face and body. He'd helped her and he'd been glad.

He would help her now. When she returned, he asked her what she needed. Her answer made him shake his head. She wanted him to help her haul booze out of the ranch house. She wanted to turn the disaster into a party.

When they'd brought it out to the casitas, Deck noticed her investors didn't join in. They stayed on their deck in the far casita calmly smoking cigars, talking quietly. Their investment had just burned to the ground. Shouldn't they be worried, full of questions? Maybe they knew more about insurance than he did.

"JUST A LITTLE added excitement," Callie said, passing out plastic glasses of beer, wine and tequila shots. She'd unlocked the unused casitas and turned on all the lights. "Wish I'd remembered the marshmallows and weenies. We could have a real roast out here." The joke was almost more than she could bear.

"Just a bit of a setback," she said to a clump of writers smoking on the porch. "We'll have the annex back in a jiff."

"You think so?" said a hard-eyed writer with a syndicated travel column vital to Rancho de Descanso's visibility.

"I know so." She had no idea how long it would take, but she had to salvage what coverage she could. "We still have accommodations for thirty. With our new amenities, Rancho de Descanso remains an ideal destination. Wait until you hit the hot springs tomorrow. And the massages! Our therapists melt every muscle into liquid…."

She kept talking, assuaging fears, assuring everyone that

by the time their stories saw print, the fire would be a distant memory. Meanwhile, she fought despair. Would insurance pay? How soon? With Valhalla holding back funding, what would she do for cash? As if things weren't bad enough, she looked up to find Taylor striding her way.

She met him as far away from her guests as possible, not wanting his uniform to upset them. "What's up?" she asked.

"I need to interview your people about what they saw or heard related to the fire. Should I set up in the far casita?"

"I just got them calmed down. No one saw anything, Taylor. Can we skip that? Please?"

"It's protocol for an investigation."

"What investigation?" Her heart thudded in her chest.

"A structural fire is considered suspicious until determined otherwise," he said. "Tucson will send out an investigator and you can expect the state fire marshal."

"You mean arson?" She was horrified. "They assume arson?"

"They'll look at who had motive and opportunity, consider who might benefit from the fire."

"Who could possibly benefit?"

"You'd be surprised, Callie." He paused. "I'm sorry to say this, but you and your father will be prime suspects."

"Why would we burn down the annex? We built it to make money on."

"Insurance. That's the obvious answer. To anyone who doesn't know you, of course." He paused, letting his words sink in. "The insurance company will send out investigators, too. They'd love to find a reason not to cover the claim. When John Granger's Feed & Seed went up in smoke, it took forever to settle. Brace yourself. This will drag on, I guarantee."

"This is terrible." Her throat closed so tight she could hardly breathe, and she felt dizzy enough to fall.

Taylor put his arm around her. "Are you all right?" For a second, Callie caught an odd light in his eyes, a twist to his mouth. Was it suspicion? Guilty glee? He looked *calculating*.

She blinked and stepped away. When she looked back, his expression was concerned, which was what she expected. She must have misread him in her panic.

"You won't be the only suspects," he added. "Your investors wouldn't be the first to use arson to get out of debt. Do you know where Mr. Markham was all night?"

"In his casita, I'm sure." In bed with that cute camerawoman from the Tucson TV station, if she guessed right.

"So…where should I set up for the interviews?" he asked.

She looked over at the guests. They'd been good sports so far, but keeping them around for endless questions would ruin everything. "Everyone was asleep. We woke them up to get them out. Please don't harass them."

Taylor studied her, then seemed to come to a decision. "I know this has been rough on you, Callie. Give me contact info on everyone and I'll take the heat for not doing the interviews on the scene."

"Thank you," she said, faint with relief.

"Don't let this get to you, Callie," he said. "It will all work out. You'll see." She caught calculation again. Odd.

"Everything all right?" Deck approached, standing beside her, leaning in as if to protect her from Taylor.

"I'll keep you updated," Taylor said to Callie, ignoring Deck. "Have a good night now." He walked off.

"What was he after you for?" Deck demanded.

"He says me and my father will be suspects for arson."

"That's nuts. That's Loft acting like a big shot."

"He said it's presumed arson until proven otherwise."

"I don't know about that."

"The Feed & Seed fire took forever to settle, did you know that?"

"There was a spat between the owners over the deed. Loft's just trying to scare you."

"He succeeded. The whole place was a fire hazard. I had Christmas lights plugged in, extension cords everywhere. And those varnish cans with the dry grass right *there*. Hell, it would look like arson to me, too."

"It was an accident. Don't assume the worst."

"You're right. I don't have time to panic." She was host to this awful bonfire party and she had to keep smiling.

She had the rest of the weekend to show the writers a good time, make them forget the fire. She made a mental note to have the spa manager make up gift baskets of Dahlia's products. She'd include free-weekend gift cards, too, giving away revenue she doubted they could afford.

When the fire crew gave her the all-clear, the guests shuffled back to their rooms and she headed toward the porch to go up to bed. "Do you want company?" Deck asked.

She felt a stab of sadness that he felt he had to ask. "Please," she said, not wanting to be alone at the moment.

Upstairs, in bed she felt exhausted but still wired, her mind swirling with concerns. Deck tried to hold her, but she was so tense it must have been like hugging a pillar. "Would it help to talk about it?" he asked.

"I don't know what will help. My mind is spinning. What if the insurance doesn't come through? Valhalla delayed the Phase Two check and Garrett advanced me credit."

"We don't know anything yet. You'll call the insurance people in the morning. You need information right now."

"Without the annex, there are only so many more bookings we can handle. And we need more bookings to turn the corner."

"You'll make it work. It'll just take more time."

"But I don't have more time! I have to go!" The words burst out of her. "I need this to be over."

Deck didn't speak, but she could tell she'd wounded him.

"I'm sorry, Deck. I've enjoyed you and I've enjoyed being here, it's just that—"

"You want to be done and gone. Yeah. I get that."

"There's an opportunity in New York for me and it won't wait forever. I'm selling out to my partner and joining a big firm…." Her words trailed off. She hadn't helped anything. They lay there, blanketed in tense silence once again.

When she heard Deck's breathing slow and knew he'd dropped off, she slid from under his arm and went to the window. She could see the charred remains of the new wing, black and jagged in the moonlight, the yellow tape flickering in the breeze.

Freaked out, she opened the window for some air, but the smell of smoke taunted her with its sour pall.

What now? What would she do?

A horse whinnied from the barn. As a kid, riding at night had been her secret thrill. Maybe that would help her now. Silently dressing, she slipped out of the room and down the stairs to find out.

DECK WOKE WITH A START to find Callie gone. He'd drifted off, but she hadn't. He wasn't surprised. He noticed the window was open and went to look out in time to see a rider fly by on a horse. Callie on Brandy. She looked so beautiful, leaning over, riding hard. She belonged here. It was so obvious to him. Here she was herself, simply Callie. Her own woman.

His woman.

Yeah, right. She couldn't wait to escape. He watched her slow, then ride to the charred remains of the new wing. She got off the horse and looked over the wreck. She seemed small and so sad he had to go to her.

He skimmed the stairs and loped out of the ranch house, reaching it in seconds. "Did the ride help?" he asked softly.

She spun to him, startled. She managed a tight smile. "I'm more tired now, I guess. Maybe that will help."

"Is there anything I can do…or say?"

She shook her head. "Thanks, Deck, but no. I just have to get through this." She was shutting him out. He could tell she wanted him to hold her, wanted his comfort, but decided she didn't dare accept it. Maybe she was right.

"I'll take Brandy back for you," he said dully, feeling the chill of winter though the air was warm with spring. "You head on up. You'll sleep better on your own."

"Thanks, Deck," she said. "For understanding."

He led the horse away, not understanding at all.

13

THE NEXT MORNING Callie woke, scratchy eyed, exhausted and missing Deck. She struggled to get up, shower and put on her happy face for the guests at breakfast. She felt heavy and sad and scared.

She was on the porch watching the morning ride leave when a fire department SUV pulled up. Presenting her with a search warrant, the two investigators drove close to the annex, then headed in to examine the wreckage. They wore gloves and carried cans she assumed would hold whatever evidence they found.

Evidence of arson? She hoped to hell not.

Taylor had gotten her thinking about who might have a motive for arson. Valhalla was on a down cycle. She knew that. They might well want their money back. Finn had shrugged off her apology, telling her it would all work out. Was that suspicious? Or merely kind? Hell, anyone could be a suspect. A fire bug. A disgruntled construction worker. Garrett could be in a money mess. Dahlia hated the ranch. Would she sabotage it to get Callie's father to sell? She had been the one who first saw the fire.

For that matter, Deck wanted to buy the ranch. He could have started the fire to get Callie to sell to him.

That kind of speculation was crazy. The fire was an accident due to the flammable materials in the annex. That was the obvious truth of it.

She called Garrett, who promised to contact his insurance

company right away. He swore they would work this all out. The Triple C's insurance agent promised the claim would be processed as swiftly as possible, but she suspected them both of trying to soften the bad news.

Callie got through the day as best she could, supervising the rest of the hosted activities, pleased to hear the guests rave about the food, the massages, the springs, the trail rides.

If not for the fire, the event would had gone off perfectly. She couldn't help thinking she could have prevented if she'd been more careful, slowed down, anticipated problems.

Deck was helpful, but quiet. They both knew they couldn't sleep together again. The feelings were too raw. Dragging it out would be like hanging around the terminal when a friend's flight was delayed. Awkward and anticlimactic, a slow agony.

The next day she was working over the books in the office when Jessica, her assistant manager, let her know Taylor was here to see her.

He wore street clothes and looked sympathetic, so she assumed this was not an official visit. He sat in the chair beside her father's desk. "How you holding up?" he asked kindly.

"I'm okay so far. The insurance adjuster is due tomorrow. The fire investigators will interview us soon."

"So I heard." He hesitated, then scooted to the edge of his chair, elbows on his knees. "I'm here as a friend, Callie."

"What is it?" she asked, ice water racing through her.

"I'm hearing they think it's arson. Multiple ignition spots. The fire burned fast and hot."

"Oh, my God. I don't believe it. Who do they suspect?"

"I hate to say this, Callie, but where were you when the fire started?"

"I was asleep," she said, shocked by his words.

"And you have a witness?" Something sparked in his gaze.

"I do. Yes." Deck had been with her and she could tell Taylor surmised as much.

"I assumed so," he said coldly. "I suggest you hire a lawyer before you answer any questions. You don't want to incriminate yourself. Same for your father."

"Why would we need an attorney? We did nothing wrong."

"Truth is in the eye of the prosecutor, Callie. What you need is a plausible explanation for your behavior and someone on your side who knows your rights."

"We have nothing to hide."

"Be smart. Be realistic." He held her gaze.

"I'll think about it," she said finally.

"That's good. And I have an idea that will help you." He offered a fleeting smile. "I am prepared to make an offer on the back acres of your ranch. The land where the river is."

"Really?" This came out of the blue.

He reached into his back pocket and pulled out a preprinted property sales form. "This is a generous offer and it should give you the cash you need to rebuild." He pushed it across the desk. The boldly inked figure was high for raw land.

She looked up at him. "Why would you do this?"

"I've got a buyer for my complex, so I've got cash to invest. These acres would make great country club estates."

"But you'd have to get zoning allowances and deal with water rights."

"I'm prepared to handle all that." He looked at her steadily. "I also have sentimental reasons. My great-great-grandfather used to own your ranch and thousands of acres around it. In his honor, I want it back. If I can solve your problem, too, it's win-win."

"I see. That's kind of you." Why was she waiting for the other shoe to drop? Taylor had been nothing but helpful since she'd returned to town. But the hairs on the back of her neck were prickling. He had that odd look in his eyes she'd seen last night for a second. Calculating. Cold.

"There's something else you should consider," he said. "This mitigates your motive for arson."

"How do you mean?"

His smile was smug and wily, as if he couldn't wait to let her in on some trick. "As far as anyone need know, we've been in discussion about this sale for weeks. That erases finance as a motive. Also—" He cleared his throat, looked down, then directly at her "—I'm prepared to forget you had varnish on your hands before the party."

"So? I moved the varnish cans. That doesn't mean I tossed a match anywhere."

"I suggest you deny any knowledge of how, when or where those cans were moved. For your own safety."

"Why should I lie?"

"Don't give them any more rope to hang you with."

Callie was shocked. Taylor was offering to perjure himself on her behalf and urging her to do the same. The old Taylor would never cheat anyone. He even looked different now. Cynical, sneaky, bitter. She shuddered inside. "I'll think about it."

"Think fast. This is a good-faith offer and I expect a good-faith answer. I'm considering other deals. I won't wait long."

"I'll let you know," she said, standing, holding out the form to him.

Taylor took it, but he shook his head. "This is no time to take risks, Callie. Do the right thing for everyone."

She walked him to the door. Closing it, she turned to rest against the wood to think. Setting aside Taylor's creepy suggestion that she lie, his offer would go a long way toward rebuilding, no matter what happened with the insurance.

And you can leave sooner.

No. She didn't dare think that. She had to do the right thing for the ranch. She would talk to Anita about the value of the land, whether the offer was decent, whether they'd make more money waiting. She would talk to her father and to Deck.

One thing she knew for certain. She would lie to no one, no matter what Taylor said.

DECK HEADED for the ranch house, since he was due to be questioned about the fire, along with Cal, Callie and Dahlia. He was irritated to spot Loft on the porch hassling Callie.

He walked faster.

"You get a lawyer like I told you?" Loft was saying when Deck bounded up the stairs.

"I don't need a lawyer," Callie said flatly.

"Hey," Deck said. "What's going on?"

"Deck," Callie said, sounding relieved. "The detectives aren't here yet. Dad and Dahlia are waiting inside."

Deck glared at Taylor. "What are you doing here?"

"Agency cooperation is the way we work these days, cowboy."

"Go on inside, Callie," Deck said. "I'll watch for them."

She hesitated, as if to object, then went in.

"Leave her alone," he said to Loft.

"Callie is an old friend. What's between us is none of your business," Loft said, so snakelike he practically hissed. "Why don't you go back to the bunkhouse, chew some snoose? We'll fetch you when you're up."

Deck took a step closer. "You cause Callie any more grief or fear or, hell, give her one bad dream, I'll come after you and they'll need a thousand yards of fishing line to sew you up."

"You're threatening an officer of the law?"

"I'm promising a jerk he'll get what he deserves. I don't care how much tin you wear on your chest."

"Watch your step, O'Neill. I have friends."

"No. What you have are *victims*. This town deserves better than you." There was too much play in Taylor Loft's line and it was about time somebody reeled him in. Taylor was hassling Callie for some nasty reason of his own, and Deck was going to find out what it was and do something about it.

BOTH TAYLOR AND DECK were red in the face and breathing hard when they brought the investigators into the office.

They'd argued over her? Probably. She shouldn't have left them alone, especially now that Taylor knew she'd been sleeping with Deck. Maybe she was lucky neither of them had thrown a punch. She had no time for their pissing match right now.

The investigators were Detectives Carl Mann and Michael Wares. Mann, who seemed to be in charge, was tall, with a formal manner and clipped speech. His fleeting smiles seemed forced.

Callie gestured toward the sofa, but Mann positioned a straight chair at the center of the table facing the sofa and sat in it before removing a tape player, notepad and pen from an attaché case. The case he placed precisely at his feet. He read from the pad, then looked up at her. "I'll see Calvin Cummings first. Everyone else can wait with Detective Wares. Please do not discuss the incident. Chief Loft, you're free to go. We'll contact you if we need anything from your department."

That was that. The three of them left the office. She was glad when Taylor kept going, shooting her a last meaningful glance. *Take my offer.*

Callie was the last to be interviewed. Her father, Dahlia and Deck came out of the office each in turn, her father looking puzzled, Dahlia scared and Deck irritated as hell. Callie's heart pounded. *Was* truth in the eye of the prosecutor?

Before she went in, Deck squeezed her hand, leaned in and murmured, "I'll wait outside, so we can talk."

She nodded and went in. Her father's office, usually cozy and warm, seemed cold and dangerous to her now.

Barely greeting her, Detective Mann clicked on the recorder, announced who was present, the time and the purpose of the interview, then proceeded to scare the bejesus out of her. The first questions were easy: Where was she when the fire began? What did she see? What did she do? Did she return to the burn site after the fire was out for any reason?

She answered completely, even telling him she'd ridden her horse to the site later that night just to look.

Had she stepped inside? Had she'd moved any items for any reason? She told him no, but he stared at her coldly.

He spent a lot of time talking about the varnish cans. She was completely honest, even telling him about the pampas grass and the shaky lamp ledges.

He moved on to questions about the ranch's finances, about Templeton Construction and Valhalla Investments. Did she know that Valhalla had pending legal judgments?

No, she didn't. A lawsuit was a hell of a lot worse than a down cycle, for sure, but she refused to believe Finn or his partners would commit arson.

By the time the interview was over, Callie was damp with sweat and trembling with tension. The fears Taylor had planted in her mind were running wild. People were falsely accused of crimes all the time. Maybe she should have hired a lawyer.

She walked the two detectives out, managing to be calmly polite. Detective Mann promised to be in touch. She watched the men drive off, then noticed Deck heading her way from the barn.

She sank into a chair at a white wicker table to wait. Maybe he could make her feel better.

"How'd it go?" he asked gently, sitting beside her.

"They obviously suspect arson. They asked all these questions about finances and insurance and the varnish cans. I don't know if they suspect me or Dad or Valhalla Investments or even Garrett Templeton, for that matter."

"They have to cover all the bases, Callie. They have protocols to follow, even when no crime has been committed. They're just being thorough."

"Maybe Taylor's right. Maybe we should have hired an attorney. Truth doesn't always win, you know."

Deck made a disgusted sound. "What is Taylor after, Callie? There's a reason he's trying to scare you."

"He's trying to help me," she said, but faintly, since she'd begun to have her own doubts.

"Yeah?" Deck demanded.

"He offered a lot of money for the land by the river."

"Really?" He considered that. "The offer was high?"

She nodded. "I think so. I have to talk to Anita."

"What's he up to?"

"He thinks it would make a good development project. His family used to own the land, so it's in honor of his family."

Deck sneered.

"Cut it out. You hate the man, I get that. I have to be practical. If he buys those acres, I can hold on to the ranch until the insurance comes through. *If* it comes through. That might be the smartest move I could make."

"See how the investigation plays out first. Find out about the insurance. Don't do anything hasty."

"He wants an answer right away."

"What's the rush?"

She shrugged. "He's looking at other properties, too."

"He's pressuring you. The offer's high for a reason. Get the facts first. Don't act out of desperation."

"But I am desperate, Deck. I haven't run the numbers, but without some cash fast, we'll be too far down to recover."

"I'll loan you the money," he said, low and serious.

"Deck. You don't mean that."

"I do mean it. I wanted to buy the place, remember? Consider me an investor. Pay me back down the line."

She shook her head. "I can't take your money. You should buy your own ranch, not rescue ours."

Deck blew out a breath. "Let me get this straight. You'd give away a valuable piece of the ranch to that asshole, but you won't take a loan from an honest guy who cares about you?"

"That's not what I'm saying."

"Let me help you, Callie. It's what I want. You can pay me interest if you want."

She let the possibility trickle through her. If Deck loaned her the money, she'd have time to evaluate the worth of those acres. Something *was* odd about Taylor's offer. She didn't like how he'd wrapped it around the lies about the fire.

"I don't know when I can pay you back. You'd be tying up your money for an indefinite time."

"Interest rates stink now, anyway. I consider it a long-term investment." He smiled at her in that way he had.

Her heart tightened and she blurted, "This can't change anything between us. I'm still leaving."

"Excuse me?" His face colored, and anger flashed in his eyes. "You think I offered you the money so you'll stay?"

"That's not what I meant. I'm just—"

"Leaving. Yeah. You said that. I get it." He looked away. His jaw muscle twitched and he remained that way for long seconds. He seemed to be pushing back harsh feelings.

When he spoke again his words were soft. "You've built something here, Callie. Why not see it through?"

"I *am* seeing it through."

"You seem happy here. Why not stay?" The words came out tightly, as if he'd held them in his throat for a long time.

"Deck…" How could he ask that? This was like his last-minute drunken demand she not leave for college. "My life is in New York. My work. My future."

"You could have a good life here," Deck said, his voice urgent. "You said yourself New York wears you out. You feel better here. I can see it in your face. You're more relaxed, more yourself."

"What are you talking about, Deck? I'm not some quiet country girl content to ride a porch swing every night. That's your fantasy." Anger speared her.

"You're running away again," he said.

"Again? I left for college. I wasn't running. And, for that matter, you broke up with me. If you wanted me, why did you push me away? Then wait until I was leaving to get plastered and tell me you wanted me?"

"I shouldn't have done that," he said stiffly.

"At least it was honest. You shared your real feelings. I guess I should be glad for that. Maybe I'm running, but you're hiding. You hunker down at the ranch like it's a cave."

"That's not true."

"Sure it is. Why can't you come to New York? You could rent a studio, you could paint." It sounded far-fetched, but it was an important point.

"What I want is right here," Deck said.

"And what I want is out there."

"Really? You want crowds, grime, traffic, expense, social chaos, an insane pace."

"You say that like it's a bad thing." The joke was her only defense against the emotions boiling in her and it fell flat.

It had cost Deck to say what he'd said, to admit what he wanted. They stared at each other, breathing hard, both of them upset.

"You can't even admit the truth."

"Don't you dare act superior," she snapped. She wasn't sure why she was so furious. Because he was being smug? Because he'd asked too much? Because it was over?

Because she ached and ached?

"We both had a tough lesson, Deck," she said, barreling into the fight with both feet. "We saw how fragile life can be. The people you love can be gone like that." She snapped her fingers. "But you don't lay back and lick your wounds. You get up and move on. You put yourself out there. You try."

"You mean chase your tail, like you do?" he snapped. "Stay so busy you can't think or feel, or figure out what you want, what makes you happy? Like with your boyfriend. You said you didn't even feel it when it was over."

"You're right. I didn't." The words stung. They were her own and they dug deep. "I don't know what love is, okay? I can't do it. I'm empty, okay?" Her voice went high and her heart banged her ribs. "Why would you want a person like that?"

His eyes flared with emotion. Was he going to say what she wanted him to? *Because I love you. Because I want to be with you for better or worse, richer or poorer, ranch or high-rise.* That was her foolish hope.

"Good question," he said, pulling back, his blue eyes distant now. "We live completely different lives. It's stupid to fight it."

"Right. Exactly. You're finally making sense." Deck's face wavered before her eyes and two tears dropped to the table. She swiped them away, pretending they hadn't fallen.

Deck ran his thumbs across her wet cheeks, not letting her get away with pretending. "We tried," he said softly, his anger gone. "At least that."

She nodded, trying to smile, though more water dripped from her eyes.

Deck wiped it away, too. "My offer stands, Callie. The money's yours whether you leave tomorrow or never speak to me again."

"I don't know…I mean…that would help a lot." It was true.

"There's one condition, though. Don't sign anything with Taylor Loft until I find out what he's up to. Promise me that."

"I promise." She looked into his eyes, their clear blue gone gloomy as a monsoon-stained sky.

They'd had a chance, a moment, to work this out. It was like they'd stood at the edge of a canyon and instead of helping each to safety, they'd jumped off, each alone, giving up altogether.

14

TREMBLING AND MISERABLE, her mind spinning from her quarrel with Deck, Callie wanted nothing more than to curl up into a ball on her bed and cry it out. Why did this hurt so much? She'd fallen in love with Deck. Or at least what passed for love with her crippled heart.

Was Deck in love with her? She didn't know. For all his friendly warmth, there was a wall behind which he hid.

Neither had said the words, of course. They were two poker players trying to bluff each other into folding first.

What kind of love was that?

Callie was a complete mess, but there was no time to feel sorry for herself. She had to talk with her father about Deck's offer—and Taylor's—and figure out what to do. She had to apologize for letting him down with the ranch. She'd tried before, but the words jammed in her throat.

Fighting back her pain and sorrow, she forced a smile on her face and headed for his room. Just as she reached it, the door flew open to reveal a terrified Dahlia holding a bloody towel. "Thank God, Callie. He fell and hit his head."

Callie rushed in to find her father on the floor, holding a bloody washcloth to his forehead.

"I got dizzy...hit the bureau," he said, but he was clutching his chest, too. "It looks worse than it is. I'll be—oh." He bent forward, overcome by pain, gasping for breath.

"Call 911!" she shouted at Dahlia, running for another

cloth. When she looked at the injury, the cut seemed too shallow for so much blood. What was wrong?

Her father groaned, opened his eyes, then vomited onto the floor. "I'm sorry, Callie. I don't want you to see this." He was in so much pain he couldn't hide it from her. "I can't…catch…my…breath."

"We'll get you to the hospital, Dad."

"This can't be happening," Dahlia said, sounding more outraged than scared. "I made him better."

What the hell was she talking about? "Is your car out front?" Callie asked, not willing to argue with the woman.

Dahlia nodded.

"Then let's go." They formed a carry hold with their arms and got her father downstairs, outside and into the back seat of Dahlia's car.

Callie climbed in beside him. "Drive fast," she snapped, pressing the blood-soaked cloth against her father's forehead. Was it a heart attack? Had the medicine failed? Why so much blood?

Dahlia drove as Callie had told her to. They didn't speak to each other and, after what seemed like forever but was only twenty minutes, they jerked to a stop at the emergency entrance. The moment was painfully familiar. Only a few weeks ago, Callie had made a similar trip. This time she was even more scared.

Again her father was rushed away. This time, however, instead of Deck, she had Dahlia at her side, pale as a ghost and wringing her hands.

Callie didn't deserve Deck's comfort anymore. Leaning on his strength had been cheating in a way. Taking care of yourself was best.

Once the papers had been filled out, Callie led Dahlia to the now-familiar waiting room. Neither of them spoke. Callie was too scared to even pace this time.

After an hour, the nurse told her she could see her father. The doctor would soon be in to talk with him.

"Can I come?" Dahlia asked, looking so scared Callie had to invite her along.

They pushed quietly into the room. Her father looked puny in the bed, hooked to an IV, getting oxygen, with all the tubes and monitors, grayed by the fluorescent light. The gauze bandage on his forehead was stained with a surprising amount of blood.

"Dad?" she asked softly.

"Callie…Dahlia. It's so good to see you." His words were slow, his smile loopy. Pain meds, no doubt. "What a lot of fuss for a blood-sugar drop and an upset stomach." He tried to pat Callie's hand, then Dahlia's, half missing both of them.

"Is that what the doctor said?" Callie asked.

Her father didn't respond.

"You have to tell me what's going on, Dad."

Dahlia patted his shoulder. "We'll get you out of here and get you treated, Calvin," she said firmly.

Callie bristled at her bossiness. "What are you talking about? He *is* being treated. Right here. In the hospital."

Before Dahlia could respond, a tall man in a lab coat breezed in, studying a clipboard. He looked up and smiled. "Ah, well. You're all here. I'm Dr. Reynolds."

They introduced themselves. Barely acknowledging them, the doctor dropped onto a rolling stool and scooted close to the bed. "You feeling any pain, Mr. Cummings?"

"None whatsoever," her father said, his eyelids drooping. He looked like he would nod off any minute.

"Good…good," Reynolds murmured, skimming the clipboard with a frown. "Seems like we have a puzzle here, Mr. Cummings, looking at your lab results."

"We do?" Callie asked.

"Have you been taking the medicines as prescribed?"

"Huh?" Her father seemed foggy and slow to grasp what was being asked of him. "Have I been—"

"He hasn't taken any pills," Dahlia interrupted. "I've been treating him with herbs."

"Really?" The doctor turned to Dahlia, rolling a few inches in her direction. "Exactly what have you administered?"

"Herbs to help his heart and prevent clots, of course. Sweet woodruff and foxglove, some white willow."

"Plant-derived medicines can be as potent as prescription drugs, sometimes more so," he chided. "Herbs are not to be toyed with." His patronizing tone annoyed Callie.

"I follow guidelines," Dahlia said nervously.

"Strength varies, preparation techniques, too. Herbs can interact with pharmaceuticals and each other." Now he was lecturing. "Amateurs can do more damage than they realize."

"I'm always very careful—"

"Adulterations are common," he said, talking over her. "There's no regulation of the industry to speak of."

"But I grew the woodruff and foxglove myself."

Foxglove. With a jolt, Callie remembered that was the purple-and-white flower in the pots Dahlia had put by the door. Sweet woodruff were the low leaves with white blossoms. Dahlia was growing the killing herbs on her father's own porch.

"You were poisoning him," she blurted. She'd thought the teas were just nasty-tasting placebos, not killer plants. She remembered feeling odd after she'd had some of Dahlia's teas.

"I was healing him," Dahlia said, tears running down her cheeks. "I'm so sorry, Calvin. I was careful. I was. Truly."

"Now, now," the doctor said, "let's see what we can find out." He rolled to a computer terminal and clicked keys. "I'm pulling up a phyto-pharmacology guide. Luckily I took a seminar about this very thing not long ago. Name the herbs again?"

"Foxglove for his irregular heartbeat and sweet woodruff and white willow to prevent clots." Dahlia's voice shook. "The white willow came from a very reputable supplier."

The doctor clicked a few keys, then read out loud. "Foxglove…the dried leaves are a source of digitalis…used to correct arrhythmias." He clicked again. "Sweet woodruff contains courmarin, a blood thinner. Hmmm." More clicking. "Same with white willow—the original source of aspirin."

"I'm so sorry." Dahlia broke into sobs.

"Don't cry, Dahlia," her father said, sounding dozy.

The doctor held up his hand. "Hold on. It's not that simple." He flipped a page on the clipboard. "You'd have to pour gallons of tea down his throat to get this result." He turned to Callie's father. "What's the story, Mr. Cummings?"

"Huh? Wha—" Her father's eyes flew open.

"You're getting too much medicine, sir."

"I took the pills, too," her father said in a low voice.

The doctor gave a pleased laugh. "That explains it then."

"You what?" Dahlia asked.

"I filled the prescriptions. I wanted to do all I could."

"You didn't trust me to heal you." Dahlia sagged.

"I didn't think your teas did anything. I was scared. I wanted to be safe, but I didn't want to upset you."

"Safe? You could have died, Dad," Callie said.

The doctor had the grace to stay silent, but she could see by his expression that she was correct. Her father could have killed himself doing what he'd done.

The three of them looked at each other. Callie didn't know who she was more upset with—her father for risking his life, Dahlia for messing with dangerous drugs or herself for not being more vigilant.

"I was trying to help you, and all the time you were laughing at me," Dahlia said. "Humoring me."

"I wasn't laughing, Dahlia."

"I never would hurt you." Dahlia shook her head. "If anything had happened to you because of me—" She put her hand to her mouth, eyes wide with horror, then rushed from the room.

"Go get her, Callie. Talk to her," her father said. "She's such a sensitive person."

"We're all upset, Dad. Let's let everyone calm down."

Callie wasn't sure what she would say to the woman if she caught up with her.

"It was my fault. I took the pills without telling her. Don't blame her."

"For now just get well," she said.

The doctor explained they would give her father medicine to reverse the effects of the excess drugs and give her father's system time to clear itself.

If all went well, her father could return home the next day. She tried to tell herself she was lucky it hadn't been more serious, but the thought of losing her father took her right back to the terror she'd felt when her mother died. This time Deck wasn't here to talk her out of her panic.

When the doctor was gone, Callie gripped her father's hand. "I could have lost you, Dad." Tears blurred her vision.

"I was stupid. I thought the teas were harmless."

"I should have checked on them, paid more attention."

"That's not your job, Callie. I should have told Dahlia the truth."

"But she pressured you about everything—your diet, the ranch, dragging you to Tucson. No wonder you lied to her."

"That's no excuse. Dahlia was looking out for me."

She almost killed you. Callie couldn't say it, not with her father so upset. Meanwhile she'd let her father down in a terrible way. "I'm so sorry about the ranch, Dad. I blew it, I know, but I'll make it right, I swear."

"You didn't start the fire, Callie. That was an accident. Just like this mess with me was an accident."

"I should have been more cautious," she said. "I was in too much of a hurry. I ignored fire hazards to make things look good." She shook her head, digging her nails into her palms in frustration. "We'll bounce back, I promise."

"I'm sure we will. Do what makes you happy, Callie."

She had to talk to him about the offers. Her father seemed

alert now, but still… "I wanted to talk about some options, but maybe we'll talk once your head clears."

"What is it, Callie? Tell me. I'm awake."

"Taylor Loft offered to buy the river acres. The price is good." She told him the price, explained Deck's loan offer and how if they doubled bookings they could squeak by. As she talked, she felt her energy drain away.

"You sound exhausted, Callie."

"I'll be fine," she said, forcing a smile, taking a deep breath so she could pretend optimism. "Just give me a good night's sleep and I'll be ready for battle." She bit her lip.

"What do you want to do?" Her father's tone was firm, no-nonsense. "Really and truly." He grabbed her gaze with his.

"What do you mean? I want to save the ranch for you."

"What about for you? Do you want it for you? Tell me the truth now. No sugarcoating, like you said."

She swallowed hard, surprised at the naked concern in his face. "I came here to help you, Dad. I love the ranch, sure, but your whole life is here, your memories of Mom."

"My memories of your mother are here." He tapped the side of his head. "They're always with me. I wanted the ranch for you, Callie."

"For me?" She stared at him.

"Everyone needs a home. I thought that once you got out here, you would decide to stay."

"But, Dad, my life's in New York." She remembered when she'd first arrived, he'd joked that she might stay. But he'd been serious about it. With a jolt, she realized Deck was right. She and her father hid important things from each other.

"Are you saying you don't care about keeping the ranch? That you'd sell?" The implications of that trickled through her.

"The ranch gave me a lot. After Colleen died, it kept me busy so I didn't dwell on how much I missed her. But I realized when I met Dahlia that I've been a hermit. If your mother were alive, she'd have kicked my butt for sure."

"You mean it's not Dahlia dragging you away, saying the ranch is killing you?" Her voice went high and sharp. "If I'd known that…" Her face burned and her chest felt tight.

"What, Callie?" he asked gently. "If you'd known…?"

She was too upset to fake it. "I never would have come. I would have told you to sell it and be happy. I would have stayed in New York. Avoided all this work and worry and agony and arson charges and—" She stopped herself. She had enough sense not to say *heartbreak*. "You should have told me, Dad."

"I'm sorry, Callie." Her father was clearly hurt by her words. "I didn't realize you felt so strongly."

Her stomach bottomed out. She hated upsetting her father. "It's a shock to learn this now, that's all. And the fire has thrown me off." She tried to make up for her words. "Of course I want the project to succeed. No worries."

"Do you want to take the loan and hang on or would you rather sell out altogether? It's up to you, Callie. Whatever you want."

"I don't know what I want," she blurted. Without warning, she burst into tears. She knew her crying would alarm him, but she couldn't help herself. "I'm sorry, Dad. I want to be optimistic for you. You're ill and I don't want to make you feel worse, but I'm a complete mess right now." She wiped her cheeks, swallowed hard, fought for control.

"Don't cry, sweetheart. It's okay. Did you hear the one about the two tomatoes on a hike…?" His voice shook.

"One was too slow, so the other one turned around and slapped him and said, '*Ketchup.*'" The old punch line came out wobbly, but she managed a smile.

"That's my girl," her dad said. "We'll both be all right."

That had always been their way. Joke away the sadness, pretend everything was fine. It felt hollow and wrong now.

"Sometimes I feel bad, Dad. That's how life is. You don't have to fix it for me. All I need is your love and support."

"You have it. One hundred percent. A father will always worry about his daughter. If I can save you pain, I'll do it."

"I know." She felt the same about him.

"What do you want to do with the ranch?" her father asked again. "It's your decision."

Sell, get out, get away, go home.

But that was her automatic response. She'd invested too much into the makeover to walk away now. She took a deep breath. "I want to accept Deck's loan and see what happens with the fire. I want to make the resort work. I do. If we sell, it won't be until we can get the most money for it."

That meant more time here, but it was the right thing to do. She would see it through. She would not run. Not until she was finished. For her father and for her.

THE BEST THING about investigating Taylor Loft was it kept Deck from moping over Callie. For the first time, he saw the advantage of her system: keep moving, keep doing, never let your mind rest and you'll never feel hurt or sad or heartsick.

Callie had inspired him after all.

And snapped his heart like a dried twig.

That wasn't fair. They were just too different. She loved the insanity of the city. He preferred simpler pleasures—desert nights when the stars went on forever, the relief of shade on a July noon, the rolling thunder of a summer storm, the hard work of a good roundup. No field trip to Tucson for a stage play would convince Callie she could be happy here.

He'd been a fool to think so.

Now he sat in Best Bet Realty getting an earful from Anita about Taylor Loft. Her anger was a gift, since she was telling him more than she ought to.

"So, last week, he comes in and wants me to market his office complex for free," Anita said. "Free. Can you believe the balls on that guy? I'm trying to get established and he wants freebies."

"Did he give you a reason?" Deck asked.

"Kind of. He claims he'll be making a killer sale that means he'll have tons of listings for me down the line."

"Interesting." The killer sale could be Callie's acres. "Did he say anything more about what he'd be selling?"

"Not really. But he waves one of these brochures under my nose." She pointed at a pamphlet about the ballot measure on the state trust lands. "'If you're looking to donate to a cause, this is the one,' he says. It's a good proposal, sure, but why does he care?"

"Must be something in it for him." The ballot measure drafted by a coalition of ranchers, developers and environmentalists would improve how state trust lands were traded and sold, helping cities with infill and giving more money to public schools. Deck had circulated a petition himself to get it on the ballot.

"I'm so sick of his I-have-powerful-friends bullshit," Anita said. "The man's an insufferable egotist."

"Don't hold back, Anita." He chuckled. "You think of anything else that might help me, holler, would you?"

"Absolutely," she said. "This guy needs a takedown."

"I'm doing my best." Deck gave a grim smile.

Two hours later, a check of county plat maps proved what Deck suspected. The Triple C backed up to state trust lands. Deck's county supervisor friend said Loft had been partying with prominent developers in Tucson and Phoenix.

Loft must know something he shouldn't about the value of the Triple C acres. If there was big money to be made through a sale or trade, it damn well better go to Callie and her father.

Deck would need tangible evidence of any wrongdoing on Taylor's part. He had an idea Suze Holcomb might know a bit about Loft's dirty dealings. Taylor's car was parked in front of town hall, so Deck eased into Ruby's to wait until Taylor left—early, as was his habit—so Suze would be alone for a chat.

Deck found a stool at the counter. Immediately the pain of Callie hit, as it always did when he had a quiet moment, making his gut ache, his brain burn and his heart jerk in his chest.

"What can I get you?" Ruby asked him.

Callie. Just Callie. "Coffee," he said.

"What's up? You look like you lost your best friend and want revenge on the guy who did it."

"I've got things on my mind."

"Sorry to hear about the fire out at the Triple C. I hear there's an investigation. How's everyone doing with that?"

"As well as could be expected. Loft's scaring the crap out of Callie, pretending he's got the inside scoop on the investigation."

Ruby laughed. "Trust me, Taylor is not on the inside of anything. The investigators came in for burgers and I overheard them grousing about having to trip over 'that local bozo' all the time. One said if he kept it up they'd file interference charges. They're sure as hell not confiding in the man."

"That's good to hear." He was relieved to have his theory confirmed. "You hear anything else that Loft is up to? Anything about a big real estate deal?"

"I mostly tune him out, Deck. Sorry."

The door clanged and Deck looked over to see Tad Renner enter in street clothes. When he caught sight of Deck, he froze, then nodded an uneasy greeting. He took a far booth. The kid wanted to run from him. Had to be a sign of guilt. He'd looked exactly like that when Deck caught him sneaking rides on horses from the Lazy J back when Tad was in high school. Deck hoped to hell he hadn't cooperated with Loft in some crime.

Deck sipped his coffee. He'd ease over and find out. Watching Tad from the corner of his eye, he saw the waitress bring him a beer, which he slugged back. Not even 5:00 p.m. and the kid was drinking? Something was up. He waited until Tad's burger arrived, then wandered over and sat across from him.

The kid looked startled. "Deck."

"Late lunch," Deck said. "You mind?" He nabbed a fry.

"I was busy earlier."

"Too busy to eat on your day off? That's a shame."

Tad shrugged, then looked down at his food.

"Go ahead and eat," Deck said. "I was just wondering if you'd heard anything about the fire investigation. The Cummingses are pretty flipped out, as you can imagine."

Color came into Tad's cheeks. "It's an active investigation. I can't discuss it." He cleared his throat. "Not that I know anything. It's not our case." He looked morose.

His instincts firing like pistons, Deck felt a surge of adrenaline. *Take it easy. Go slow.* "Sure wish I had something to tell them," he said slowly. "Calvin's got heart troubles and Callie's worked so hard she's beside herself with worry."

Tad lifted his gaze, stopped chewing. He swallowed dryly. "I wish I could help, but like I said, we're not involved."

"I understand. Except, I heard Taylor pissed off the investigators asking questions. You know why he's so curious?"

"How would I?" Tad's eyes flitted away, then back, avoiding Deck's gaze. "The chief's cooperating. Trying to be of use."

"I don't think it's that." Deck had to be very careful here. Tad was loyal to Loft. He wouldn't even allow Suze to criticize the gold faucets in the station john. But he'd also taken an oath to uphold the law, and that should override his misgivings about ratting out his boss.

"Between you and me, I think Taylor's up to something."

Tad swallowed hard. "Yeah?"

"Yeah. He's been trying to scare Callie, telling her she's the main suspect for arson on the fire."

"How would he know…?" Tad blanched and grabbed his beer to suck down the half inch that remained in the bottle.

"Exactly. Why would he want to frighten that poor woman?"

Tad stared at him, not moving.

"That bothered me. So I asked a few questions and it turns

out he offered to buy some of the Triple C. To help Callie out, he claims. They were together in high school, you know."

Tad blinked several times. "Maybe he's helping her as a friend." He blinked some more, clearly trying to justify whatever Loft had done in his own mind. He began to tear the label from his beer bottle.

Deck took a deep breath. "That could be. Sometimes we bend rules to help the people we care about. But the chief swore to uphold the laws. If he's breaking them…"

Tad's thumbnail stopped tearing. He looked up slowly.

"You're a good cop, Tad. You have good instincts. You work hard. I know you think the chief did you a favor hiring you, but he was just being smart to snap you up before someone else did."

Tad shook his head. "I don't know about that."

"Trust me, I do. Something's not right and I get the idea you agree. I'm hoping you'll help me find it out and fix it."

Tad's lips tightened and his jaw muscle rippled.

Easy, Deck warned himself.

Tad went back to shredding the label, more violently now.

"He's not above the law, Tad. You know it. I know it. He knows it." Deck hoped to hell he was on the right track. "Deep down he wants to be stopped. Deep down, where he's a good cop."

Tad didn't speak, but he seemed to hold his breath.

"All you have to do here, Tad, is your job. What you swore to do. To uphold the law."

More silence.

"If you don't speak up, can you live with the guilt?"

"I might be wrong," Tad fired at Deck through gritted teeth. "I could wreck his career. He had to be trying to help."

"Tell me what happened. We'll talk it through and figure out what to do about it." Deck waited, holding his breath. Everything depended on what Tad said next.

15

TAD HUNG HIS HEAD for a long silent moment. Finally he lifted it, looking miserable. "It's my damn bladder."

"Excuse me?" Deck said.

"I had to take a leak. That night. The night of the fire. The chief told me I could go home, but I needed to relieve myself so I circled around and pulled over into a stand of trees. While I was at it, I happened to look up and see the chief put something— looked like paint cans—into his trunk. I thought it was odd, but didn't worry about it. Then the next day, I realized I'd left my tool kit out at the ranch. I went to borrow the chief's. He was over at the diner, so I opened the trunk with the spare key. Our vehicles are department property. I'd been in the trunk before, so it wasn't a big deal." He shrugged, then swallowed hard.

"There were the cans. Completely black with soot, so I knew he'd taken them from the fire. I figured he'd collected evidence…." He shrugged.

"But you didn't believe that. Not really."

"It wasn't procedure. It was…odd."

"What did you do?"

"I checked later in the day and the cans were gone. I thought maybe he'd turned them over to the investigators."

"Did you ask?"

"That might have raised questions. There had to be an explanation. I figured it would work out." But he hadn't asked Loft, so he must suspect him. "He could have been protecting the Cummingses," Tad said hopefully.

"He tampered with evidence, good intentions or not. He broke the law. And, for the record, I don't believe his intentions were good, Tad."

Numbly Tad nodded. "This job is all I ever wanted."

"You're not going to lose your job. Not for doing the right thing. Loft is in more trouble than this, I'm sure, and I'm going prove it. I will need your help."

Tad looked away, his face going blank as he figured out what he would say. Finally he looked back at Deck. "I'll do my job," he said gravely.

"That's all I ask. I'm going over to talk to Suze, to find out what she knows, as soon as Loft leaves the station."

"I doubt she knows anything," he said, looking worried. "She doesn't like the chief. I don't want her losing her job because she spoke out of turn, gave opinions, not facts."

"Come with me, then. We'll talk to her together."

"What choice do I have?" Tad seemed resigned to his fate, but not happy about it.

This was good. Deck was closing in on the guy. Whether Loft set the fire and tried to cover his tracks or was trying to set Callie up as a suspect, he was up to no good. Deck figured Loft was trying to push Callie into selling to him.

"Whatever you need," Suze said once Deck explained what he was after.

"Not so fast," Tad said, holding her hand. "Only say what you know for a fact, Suze. Don't speculate. Don't guess."

"I know what to say, Tad," she said. "I don't like a lot of things going on around here and neither do you. Look at the tires on your car. Bald as hell. And your crummy Kevlar vest couldn't stop a BB gun."

"Suze."

"I think Chief Loft paid for the fix-up in here by faking a Homeland Security grant. He faxed the application and he left it in the machine. I read some of it. It was supposed to pay for new equipment and upgrades that we have yet to see."

"Can you get your hands on the application?" Deck asked.

"Probably. He never puts anything back. I can check tomorrow as soon as he opens his office door. His in-basket is piled high. And why does he lock his office, anyway? What's so secret? All the time, he's in there on the phone with the door closed. I know he does his real estate business on the city clock."

"I don't suppose you overheard any of these calls?"

"Not really. But I've taken plenty of messages." She reached over for her message pad. "There are NCR copies of all of them."

Deck flipped through the pages, noticing several state officials, including someone from the Bureau of Land Management. "This is interesting," he said. "Can I keep a few of these pages?"

"Take the whole book. I'll start a new one."

Deck asked more questions, probing what Suze might have seen that would help them. Finally she remembered noticing a map on Loft's desk he'd tried to cover with papers when she entered. The corner was sticking out, stamped in big red letters, *Proprietary. Not for Release.*

She would look for the map, too.

"You have enough from Suze?" Tad asked Deck, putting a protective arm around her shoulder.

"For now, yes, but I'm going to need help from you both tomorrow. Suze, you'll look for the application and the map. Tad, I need you to check the chief's trunk for any evidence of the cans. If he didn't clean up, there should be soot."

"I'll photograph what I find and take samples."

"As soon as you two find what there is to find, I'm going to confront him, bluff enough to get him to confess. I'll make sure he can't tell I've talked to you two. I'll record the conversation. It won't be admissible, but it might lead him to confess and it will be something to get the sheriff interested."

"I'll listen through the intercom," Suze said.

"I don't want you in any danger," Tad said.

"I can't imagine Loft would do anything violent," Deck said. "You'll be nearby, Tad, just in case. I'm betting he'll break right off, but if he doesn't he'll try to cover his tracks. Your job is to follow him, see where he goes, who he talks to, what he does. Whatever evidence we have, we'll take to the sheriff."

"Why not go there now?" Tad said. "Let them investigate."

"We don't have much more than hunches yet. Even if they believed us, they'd need warrants and that takes time. Time Loft could use to destroy evidence. As a citizen I can do and say far more than the sheriff can."

Tad nodded. "You sure you want to do this, Suze?"

"He's hurting people, Tad. The Cummingses. You. The department. The whole town. We have to stop him."

Tad turned to Deck. "Whatever you need, we'll do."

"I'll make sure you don't lose your jobs," Deck said. "We'll nail this guy, I promise."

Heading home, he decided to wait to tell Callie about Loft until after they'd enacted his plan. With any luck, tomorrow Loft would fold like a bad hand and he could relieve Callie of some of her worries. That and the loan seemed to be all he could do to help her at the moment.

THE NEXT DAY Deck was restless as he went about his ranch duties, listening for the phone. Finally, at noon, Suze called to tell him she'd found the map and the phony grant among Loft's papers. So far, so good. As soon as Tad had examined Loft's trunk, Deck would go after the guy.

Two hours later, Tad called. Sure enough, there'd been an ash outline of the cans in Loft's trunk. Even better, Tad had found the cans themselves. In his arrogance, Loft had tossed them into a Dumpster that hadn't been emptied yet. Tad had pictures, an ash sample and the cans stashed safely away.

A half hour later, Deck entered the station. Suze's eyes went wide and she took a jerky breath.

"It'll be fine," he said to reassure her. "I'm set." He patted the small recorder in his pocket. "Leave the intercom on, okay?"

She nodded, then said loudly, "He's busy, Mr. O'Neill. He doesn't want to be disturbed."

"Wish me luck," Deck said, then marched to Loft's office and shoved open the door.

Loft was on the phone. He looked up, angry, then told his caller he would call him back.

"I'm busy, cowboy." He tried to sound fierce, but his eyes jerked around. "What's so damn urgent?"

"It's over," he said flatly. "You were seen."

"Seen where?" The man's face went utterly still and his eyes went cold. He knew exactly what Deck meant.

"It turns out we had a wandering guest the night of the fire. He happened to see you take the cans out of the rubble and put them in your trunk."

"I don't know what you're talking about."

"Oh, I think you do. He's been in Europe since then. He called back the investigators who wanted to interview him and they were quite interested in what happened to those cans."

"That's insane," Loft said, his jaw jutting forward. He stood. "Get out of my office, O'Neill."

"Soon enough. I thought I'd give you a chance to clear this up before I take it to the sheriff. If you turn yourself in, settle this now, you could keep from racking up more charges."

"You're full of shit."

"At first I thought maybe you set the fire yourself and were taking the cans to cover your tracks. You were on the scene pretty damn fast, after all."

Loft was staring, fiddling with paper on his desk.

"But then I realized you wouldn't be that stupid. You knew they'd notice the scene had been disturbed, that something had been taken. There would be burn patterns around the varnish cans, but no cans. Why would you do something so obvious?"

"That's enough. Get out. I don't have to listen to this." Loft leaned across his desk, trying to be menacing.

"Then I figured it out," Deck said. "You were framing Callie. You knew she'd handled the varnish cans. You knew she'd tell the investigators the truth. You tried to scare her by claiming she was a suspect before she was, but even if she didn't get charged, you would have slowed the investigation long enough to put her in financial crisis. Either way, you'd get the river acres for a song. Maybe even be a hero in her eyes."

"I would never hurt Callie. My offer was generous."

"Not with a major land deal in the offing."

"Just what do you think you know?" Now Loft's eyes grew cunning and he hunkered down, like a cornered predator ready to claw his way out.

"Thank God you're such a braggart. You made it easy. You must have found out from your developer friends that Callie's land would be in line for a major trade for pricey real estate."

"You've been drinking beer in the sun too long, O'Neill. You're having delusions."

"We've got a witness who's happy to testify about the cans. Other people are sick of your blackmail and your big mouth and they'll say what they know. I'm not sure what the charges are for fraudulent use of a federal grant, but I'm sure Homeland Security will be eager to see the gold faucets they paid for."

"Now you sound crazy." But Loft's breathing was shallow, and his body seemed poised to take action. "What do you want?"

"I told you. Turn yourself in. You could say you thought Callie had set the fire and you wanted to help her. Maybe you can cut a deal." Deck shrugged. "Not that you deserve one."

"Never going to happen."

"Do the right thing, Taylor. Save yourself a drawn-out investigation and all that public shame. Think of your father. He's a good guy. He doesn't deserve to be humiliated this way."

"You leave my father out of your horseshit." Loft sneered. "You don't know who you're dealing with," he said lowly.

"Because you have *friends?* Not anymore. What's paying for strippers at a convention compared to years of extortion from a greedy, small-time blowhard like you?" Deck had no idea whether that was true, but his words made fear flicker in Loft's face.

"Turn yourself in or expect to be arrested," Deck said. "I am sorry this will hurt your dad. In this case, the bad apple fell nowhere near the tree."

Taylor stood like a statue, his face stony, but the tremor in his hands told the truth. He was scared.

"I go from here to the sheriff's office. Last chance."

Taylor didn't move.

Deck took one of Loft's business cards from its holder, then used the man's gold pen to scribble Deck's cell number on the back. He pushed the card toward Loft. "I'll keep my phone on."

Damn. Loft was more stubborn than Deck had hoped, but he'd do something incriminating soon. Deck would have to leave the next steps to Suze and Tad.

"You hear all that?" he murmured to Suze as he left.

She nodded nervously.

"Watch him close. Keep Tad on speed dial. If anything scares you, get out, no questions asked."

Down the block, he met up with Tad as previously agreed and took the envelope with the evidence Tad and Suze had gathered. "He's scared, but he didn't fold," Deck said. "Stay on him. I'm heading to the sheriff." He lifted the envelope. "We'll get him. Don't worry." With any luck, by nightfall Taylor Loft would be under arrest.

IT WAS AFTER SIX and Callie was about to quit and head up to her room when Betsy at the front desk called to tell her Taylor Loft was there to see her.

"Send him in," she said, filled with dread. He wanted her decision on his deal. She might as well get this over with.

"I'm taking off if that's okay?" Betsy asked. "I have a date."

"Sure. It's time. Put the phone on night ring."

"Thanks so much."

Seconds later, the office door opened and Taylor entered. He looked odd. He was walking crookedly and his smile was off. Then the smell of booze hit her. Taylor was drunk. And in uniform.

"Are you okay?" she said.

"Jus' wannada see you," he slurred, holding himself in the oddly stiff way of a drunk person trying to pretend he wasn't.

"Come and sit down," she said, motioning toward her father's sofa, wishing fleetingly that she'd asked Betsy to stick around for a bit. She sat at the far end.

"I need you to sign the paper," Taylor said. He dragged the contract, now crumpled, from his back pocket and stepped in front of her. "Now'sa time."

"I'm sorry, Taylor, but it's too soon for me to sell."

"What?" His words went hard and his eyes glittered with anger. On the rare times she'd seen Taylor drunk in high school, he'd been cheerful, not mean. "You owe me this," he growled.

"I appreciate all your help, Taylor," she said slowly, "but I have to do what's best for my father and me."

"This is a damn good offer. Better than you'll get." Something in his expression scared her. He loomed over her. He was a powerful man and she realized he was armed.

She tried to get up, but he pushed her down and sat close. He seemed to switch gears. Sexual interest sparked in his eyes, scaring her. "Give me a chance," he said in a voice tight with threat. "I can be what you want." He took her arm and squeezed.

"Let go of me," she said sternly, her heart racing.

He looked down at his hand, as if noticing for the first time that he had hold of her. "Sorry." He let go. "Don't run." His voice took on a pleading tone. "I won't hurt you."

"I'm right here," she said, but she tensed, ready to spring away the first chance she got.

"Why him?" he said, his voice bitter, his eyes puppy sad. "He's got nothing. No ambition. He's a freaking ranch hand. I've improved myself. I'm moving forward. I'm better than I was in high school. Give me a chance to prove it."

"You're not yourself right now. Please leave before you do something you'll regret." She started to rise, ready to get the door, but his hand snaked out with surprising force and yanked her down again, pinning her flat on the cushions.

"You don't know what I did for you."

"Yes I do. You did a lot. I appreciate everything—"

"I got rid of that varnish to save you. I risked everything for you." He squeezed her wrists for emphasis and jabbed her stomach with a knee.

"You're hurting me. You don't want to do this, Taylor. Let me go. We can talk when you're feeling better."

He didn't speak, didn't move and he didn't let go. Instead his gaze seemed to turn inward. He wasn't listening anymore. He was gone. *Get away, get out.* She lunged upward and twisted her wrists with all her might to free herself.

For a second she thought she'd made it. He released her and she scrambled to a sitting position so she could run away.

"Stay right there." His voice was cold and his eyes were as dead and black as the muzzle of the gun she stared into.

Terror washed like a wave of ice water down her body.

"I've been nothing but nice to you," he said in a wheedling voice. "Now it's your turn to be nice to me. That land is mine. I've offered a fair price, so you need to do the right thing."

He put the paper on the table, took a pen from his pocket with the hand not holding a gun. "I'm not spending the rest of my life handing out parking tickets and hassling drunks, only to retire to a golf-cart ghetto like my dad. The Lofts owned half this county. One bad year and my great-great-granddad was robbed of it all. You owe me that land. Now sign."

"Leave her alone, Loft." Deck's voice was steady and low. "Put your weapon away."

Taylor swung the gun in Deck's direction, holding Callie down with his body. "Stay there. Hands on your head."

"This is not what you want," Deck said, still moving forward, hands up slightly. "Think this through. Be smart."

Taylor's hand twitched around the gun. "Stop telling me what I want. I know what I want."

She had to stop Deck from risking his life.

"I'll sign, Taylor. It's only fair. I was being greedy." Her throat was so dry she had to force the words.

"Good," he said, his tone like the old Taylor. "I'm glad you understand. I knew you would come around." He seemed to have to look at her, tugged by his feelings for her.

His hesitation, his focus on her gave Deck the chance he needed to lunge for Taylor's gun arm, yanking it upward. The men struggled for a few frightening seconds until abruptly, Taylor sagged, giving up.

Deck took the gun. "Call 911, Callie. Let the sheriff's office know Loft is here. They're waiting for him at his place. Then you stay out in the lobby. I want you safe."

She glanced at Taylor, who sat with his elbows on his knees, head in his hands, then left the room to make the call.

In a half hour, Callie watched as Taylor was helped into the back of a Pima County Sheriff car like a criminal. With a start, she realized that was exactly what he was.

As soon as they drove Loft away, Deck turned to Callie. She looked small and scared standing there, so he pulled her into his arms to comfort her, sick to death that he'd risked her life. "I'm sorry we left you so exposed," he said into her hair, then pulled back to explain. "Loft didn't crack when I confronted him. Tad tailed him to his house, then he ducked out for gas. By the time he got back, Loft was gone. I would have been here before Loft, except I was coming from the sheriff's office."

"What did you say to him? He acted so crazy."

Deck explained what he'd learned and suspected.

She looked up at him. "You think he was framing me? He told me he took the cans to protect me."

"With his twisted thinking, maybe he was." Where was the harm in letting her believe that?

"He wasn't like that in high school. How did he get so bitter?" Callie gave everyone too much credit. "You saved me, Deck. Again."

"I also put you in danger." Looking into her face, something gave way inside him and he realized he was in love with her. Hopelessly and pointlessly, but there wasn't a damn thing he could think of to stop it.

"You've done so much for me," she said. "To the end of my days I'll be grateful." She stopped as if she feared she might cry. Her eyes were shiny with tears.

"I'm glad we had time together," he said gruffly, though nothing in his life had ever hurt more. He wasn't quite saint enough to believe it had been worth it.

Callie had awakened him. He'd been in some kind of Van Winkle sleepfest and now he was fully, painfully awake.

A WEEK LATER, Callie took the steps from the porch headed for the barn. She needed to talk to Deck, and he'd suggested they go for a horseback ride. It would be their last one and she wore her comfortable Wranglers, her old scuffed boots and her Stetson. The red leather jacket and boots were packed away where they belonged. They were for show, not for riding.

She watched Deck emerge from the barn with Brandy, his long legs strong and sure, his shoulders broad, his dove-gray Stetson firmly on his head, so handsome and manly her throat tightened.

She would miss him so much. She would miss the ranch, too. For all the stress and trouble, enjoying it again had been a gift. All due to the man who now smiled at her.

"Hey, Callie. You okay?"

She pushed back her emotion, managing a smile, wishing she was better at hiding her feelings. Deck didn't miss a twitch or a blink. She had good news, so she focused on that. "I'm fine. Very fine, actually."

"Yeah?" He lifted the saddle onto Brandy, then held the pommel, looking at her across the horse.

"I got the word from the investigators. The fire has been declared accidental. Electrical, complicated by accelerants. They found no evidence of deliberate ignition. It looks like Taylor didn't start it. He just covered it up."

"So you're cleared. That's great, Callie." He sounded as relieved as she felt.

"Yeah. It is. Now the insurance companies will wrangle over who pays what. It'll be a while before a check appears, but at least the money is coming."

"And my loan will tide you over until then?"

She nodded. "But we should be able to pay you back sooner than I thought. Valhalla's supposed to send a check, Finn says. A lawsuit got settled in their favor, freeing up some cash. I can't believe I ever thought they might have started the fire. Taylor made me suspect everyone."

"You were scared. And under pressure. It's understandable."

"I'm not sure what we'll do about the back acres. If the ballot measure passes we might sell. From what I've gathered, a complicated purchase/swap with Tucson puts the river acres into the state preserve. The point is there will be far more money than Taylor offered me. I can't believe he was that greedy." She glanced at Deck. "Yeah, yeah, I know you told me so, but he wasn't like that in high school."

"People change."

"He did, that's for sure. Anita's going to work with me on the river issue. I like that the acres would stay wild."

"Me, too, Callie. That's all to the good."

"Yeah. Have you heard what's going to happen to Taylor?"

"So far, he's been charged with tampering with evidence. There might be more charges, certainly about the misuse of the federal grant, depending on who decides to come clean."

"He'll go to prison?" The idea sounded terrible, even though he'd done bad things. She'd declined to press charges for his assault on her.

"Who knows? He's been stopped. That's the main thing. Tad Renner's been appointed interim police chief. I made sure the mayor did that. If I have any say, he'll get the job for good."

"That's great." She hesitated. "Are you thinking about running for mayor yourself?"

He shrugged. "I've got some decisions to make, I guess." For a moment he looked completely lost, and she wanted to hug him and tell him it would be all right, though that was stupid. How could she know anything would be all right?

The look was gone as quickly as it appeared. Deck had always been self-contained. It made her sad for him.

"You ready? Horses are set." He looked her up and down. "You look good." She got the thrill she always got when he looked at her. Would it ever go away?

He adjusted the cinch on Brandy. Ranger lifted his head up and down, as if to hurry them on.

Soon, they were riding side by side toward the river to enjoy their last sunset together. As they traveled, Deck filled her in on practical issues about the cattle and the upcoming sales.

Soon they headed up the narrow trail up the hill, Callie in front. At the top, their horses stood shoulder to shoulder and Callie looked out over her family's land. "It's so beautiful."

"Yeah."

She turned and saw Deck had been looking at her.

He cleared his throat and shifted his gaze. "How's your dad?" he asked.

"Better, now that he's only taking one set of meds." She paused. "You know, you were right about us protecting each other. Around him, I'm the eternal cheerleader. It's like I never stopped trying to keep him from crying after Mom died."

He nodded.

"We have to quit it. We're missing too much about each other's lives. We're both adults. Like you said, we're sturdier than we think."

"Sounds wise of you."

"You realize, don't you, that if I'd known Dad was willing to sell the ranch, you'd have the Triple C right now and I'd never have come out here?"

"But we'd have missed all this." Deck moved his hand between them, trying to joke, but she saw pain in his eyes.

She fought her own sadness. "We may still sell, depending on how the next year goes, so, if you're interested…"

He laughed. "You're out of my price range now. I wanted a ranch, not a resort. After that, I wanted to help you and Cal."

"You've had our backs all the way." She swallowed. "You're a good person, Deck. You deserve…so much."

"When do you leave?" he asked, shaking off her praise.

"As soon as I can. We're at a standstill until we start the rebuild. I'll fly out when I'm needed, but I should get back. Stefan's impatient to buy me out, and I need to jump on that opportunity I was telling you about."

"Jessica's taking over?"

"For now. If it's too much for her, I've talked with the manager of a Palm Springs resort, who would be great."

"Sounds like you've got it handled. You need to start looking for a field manager to replace me. I'd like to move on."

"Sure. That makes sense." Her throat closed, so she looked away, out over the Triple C. "I'll miss this place." The sunset was now deep purple and gold. Surrounded by this wild beauty, she couldn't help but feel so alive.

"Will you?" He steadied his gaze on her face.

"Yes. Very much." She would miss him, too, which was the question in his eyes. "Are you sorry, Deck?"

He waited a long moment before he answered. "No. It hurts like hell, but it was worth a try." A muscle jumped in his jaw. He cleared his throat. "You?"

"Not sorry at all." She'd never hurt so much in her life.

"I know you think I'm hiding," he added, "that I'm settling for less, but—"

"That wasn't fair of me. We chose different lives."

"And what I said about you running away—"

"Sometimes I do. But not this time. And you're right about missing things when you go too fast. From now on, I'll take my time—smell the roses, check out the sunset or at least the skyline. I liked seeing the world through your eyes, Deck. I just…" She had to say it. "I wish you would let yourself want more."

"And I wish you would want less." His smile was so sad.

"That sums it up, huh?"

"It does." They were silent, pondering the truth that kept them apart. "Listen," Deck said in a tone signaling a business topic. "I'll be taking down that sold painting when we get back to the house. The buyer's picking it up tonight."

"Sure. And if you want to take the rest down, Deck, we'll replace them with something. I shouldn't have forced you."

He shrugged. "It didn't bother me as much as I thought it would." He looked away. "So, I bet you're looking forward to getting back to the city." Another subject change.

"Yeah. Sure." So why did she feel so empty? From the moment she realized she'd be able to leave, she'd felt hollowed out.

Was it her father? He was still in turmoil about Dahlia, but his health was stable and Callie would be out often.

Was it Deck? Sure. She already missed him. But there was no point in that. Even if they weren't miles apart in both geography and attitudes, she couldn't love him enough. She didn't have it in her. "I guess we should go," she said finally. "The light's fading."

Without a word they turned away from the sunset and made their way down the hill and toward their separate futures.

16

DECK PUT THE HORSES AWAY and waited until he was certain Callie would be upstairs before he went into the ranch house to get his painting.

Once she left, he'd probably feel better. Seeing her every day had him in constant turmoil. He was lonely and miserable. He felt—shit—discontented. Which was stupid. The grass was always greener, didn't he know that?

He entered the ranch house, nodded at the guests in the great room, then went to the hall lined with his canvases. He'd shipped the other two when the checks came, too preoccupied with Callie and the ranch to notice how he felt about the sales.

He took down the last sold piece, then surveyed the remaining canvases: parts of a horse, a cactus study, a sunset, a distant rider. Not badly rendered, either.

He didn't cringe anymore. At first, he'd hated his art on display. He'd felt exposed, like one of those dreams where you found yourself in public stark naked with everyone laughing.

His paintings had always been his pain on canvas and he didn't care for strangers staring at that. But that had passed. His pieces were merely his take on subjects that caught his eye, interested him or moved him. Nothing more.

The buyer wasn't due for a couple of hours, so he dropped the painting off at his studio and headed into town for some rhubarb pie and company.

The diner was nearly empty. Ruby met him at the counter.

"Well, bless me, the town hero has placed his regal behind on my humble stool."

"Cut it out, Ruby."

The few diners smiled. Someone laughed. There was applause.

"People can't stop talking about what you did," she said more softly. Half a dozen people had privately thanked him for stopping Loft for one reason or another.

"You really need to run for mayor, Deck."

He sighed. "Could I have my pie without politics?"

"Whatever you say." She turned for the pie rack, and the piece she brought him held a scoop of vanilla ice cream. "You've got that à la mode look on your face," she explained. "Is it Callie?"

He shot her a glance, then went at his pie.

"Can't you work things out?"

"Nothing to work out. She's going back to New York." What the hell was wrong with this pie? It tasted like cardboard.

"Not if she has a reason to stay. Did you give her one?"

He put his fork down. "I'm not begging her, Ruby." He'd done that once already. "I won't humiliate myself." He picked up his fork again and dug at the pie.

"Since when is telling someone you want them in your life humiliating?"

"When it's done, it's done. Besides, she's the one leaving."

"So go to New York. Chase her down."

"I don't belong there any more than she belongs here."

"For a smart man, you can be stone dumb, Declan O'Neill. You ever heard of compromise? Frequent flier miles? It doesn't have to be either or. It can be both."

"It's more than where we live," he said. "We want different things." She wanted too much and he wanted too little.

"If you love each other, you work it out." She paused. "Does she even know you love her?"

He thought about that. He'd never said the words, but she had to know. Didn't she?

"What are you afraid of?" she asked.

"Nothing." Losing her, of course. People left, they died, they went away. You protected yourself any way you could. Callie did it with forward motion. He stuck with things he could count on. "Could I just eat my pie, here?"

"You already did." She nodded at his empty plate.

"Then I guess I need another piece," he groused.

She brought it to him. "Think it over, Deck. And the next time you come in here, you'd better ask me to be your campaign manager or we'll be permanently out of raspberry rhubarb, I swear." He half believed she was serious.

CALLIE BROUGHT a glass of pomegranate iced tea to her father and sat on the rocking chair beside him on the porch.

"Thanks," he said.

She rocked for a few seconds, her gaze sliding from the ranch yard up to the sky, where the stars were white specks in the velvety blackness.

"Good tea," her father said, licking his lips.

"It's store-bought. Don't tell Dahlia."

"She's not ready to joke about tea yet, I'm afraid."

"What's happening with you two?" She wanted the best for her father, but she wasn't sure Dahlia was the right woman.

"We're taking it slow. I guess I was so happy to find someone I could love, that I let her run me around a little too much. She knows she was too bossy, so we're being careful with each other right now."

"It's not my business, Dad, but maybe she's just too sensitive for someone as kind and compassionate as you are."

"We love each other, Callie. We'll work it out."

She could let that go, but she'd promised she'd be more honest. "Are you sure? Because while you were protecting her feelings, I almost lost you."

"I won't let that happen again."

"You mean you won't *tell me* if it happens." She paused, then turned to him. "We have to stop tiptoeing around each other, pretending we're not sick or scared or lonely or upset just to protect the other person. We end up strangers to each other." She stopped, waiting for his response, her heart in her throat. Was he mad? Disappointed? Hurt?

He sipped his tea, taking his time before he answered. "The truth can be painful," he said. "When you told me you didn't want the ranch, that hurt me."

"I'm sorry, Dad. I just—"

"You were upset. We both were. But I needed to know. I can see that now. You're right, Callie."

"I want us to be more honest with each other."

He studied her. "It's a habit, you know—telling the people I love what I think they want to hear. That's what happened with Dahlia and it almost killed me. You'd think that would be enough of a lesson, wouldn't you?"

She laughed. "I'm a grown-up, Dad. I can handle the truth."

"I'm not sure I can." He gave a sheepish smile.

"So we'll ease into it, how's that? I'll try not to shock you right off the bat."

"Sounds fair enough," he said, then sipped his tea, looking out over the yard, lost in thought. He turned to her. "Okay, in the spirit of honesty, I have some news you might not like. I'm going to see a doctor who specializes in alternative medicine. It's Dahlia's physician. She's been trained tradition- ally, too. I read up on her, and she's well respected. If I like her and trust her, I'm going to do what she says. That might mean herbs instead of pills, Callie."

Callie swallowed hard. Her dad was doing what she'd asked him to do, being honest. She had to show him it was okay. "I can't say that doesn't worry me, but it's your decision to make and I respect that." She paused. "And I'm glad you told me."

"Okay. Glad to hear it." He grinned out at the yard.

"That didn't hurt so bad, did it? Discussing that?"

Her father laughed. "I'll need practice, I can tell."

"We both will."

He turned to her. "Here's one for you. Tell me what's going on between you and Deck."

"Okay." She took a breath. "We were seeing each other, but we broke up. We're on good terms and I'm fine."

"I'm a grown-up. I can take the truth."

She smiled. "That is the truth. We couldn't work it out. We're just too different from each other."

"But that's what makes life interesting."

"It's too hard." She shook her head.

"You have to compromise, Callie. You know that, right?"

"Compromise, sure. But you don't stop being who you are or going after what you want."

"Is that what Deck's asking of you? Or you of him?"

"In a way. I don't know. It just won't work."

"I never wanted you to be afraid," her father said softly.

"What do you mean? I'm not afraid."

"Losing your mom was scary. If she could disappear just like that—" he snapped his fingers "—what in the world was safe anyway? I felt the same way, you know."

"I grew out of that," she said, but his words plowed into her. He'd never been so frank with her before.

"What I did was tuck into the ranch and work hard. Year after year. It took your dating club and Dahlia phoning me day after day to get me to start living again."

"Yeah, and that almost got you killed."

"You have a point." He smiled, but then got serious. "You have to take a chance on people, Callie. On love. Yeah, it's risky. You can get hurt. But don't let love go because you're scared. What's that saying? A ship at harbor's safe, but that's not what ships are for."

"I don't know, Dad." Sweat sprang out all over her body.

His words made sense, but she wanted to stiff-arm them away. "It's not that simple. I can't give up my life."

"Don't give it up, Callie. Share it." Her father wouldn't let her look away. "I'll say one more thing and then I'll leave you be. When you're with Deck, you light up like Christmas morning. Around him, you seem…I don't know…settled in your skin. Content. Easy. Maybe that sounds nutty to you."

"A little." She tried to laugh it off.

"I mean you stop acting like you're about to fly off any second after God knows what all."

"My charging, New-York style?"

"Don't let geography be your excuse to give up on love."

She didn't speak. Her throat had closed off.

"Wow," her father said with a deep breath, "all this honesty is exhausting. I hope I didn't hurt your feelings. I don't mean to tell you what to do. I just want you to be happy."

"I know you do, Dad."

He stood and leaned down to give her a hug. "I'm off to bed. Think about what I said."

"I will. And you take your time with Dahlia."

"Fair enough."

Her father left and she looked out into the dark. She could hear crickets, river toads and just plain quiet. Through the mesquites, she saw that Deck's trailer was dark. Had he gone into town? She wished she could wander over with a bottle of wine and sort this out with him. Laugh and talk and be easy together, like they'd been for those weeks of limbo.

Her dad was right. Deck did make her feel settled. Her life in New York was jam-packed. She'd always loved it, thrived on it. Lately…maybe not so much.

What did she want now? Truly? The ranch and Deck? New York and Deck? Or just plain Deck, however she could have him? Maybe she was using geography as an excuse. Why couldn't they share their lives?

She needed to think about this. And the best place to

think was the hot springs. She donned her robe, grabbed a towel and headed out. Turning on the path to look back at the ranch house, she saw how pretty the pool looked in the moonlight. A couple was enjoying the hot tub. Through the window she could see two guests working out in the gym. Music from the bar was soft and pleasant. Bookings were already up, she knew.

She'd accomplished a lot so far and there was so much more to do. Of course she'd be out to track the progress, but that wasn't the same as being here every day, enjoying the moment-to-moment pleasures of managing a place you've built.

It was the kind of thing Deck loved. To him the land, the animals he worked with, the desert he lived in, offered plenty of satisfaction. She understood that, but had never considered it for herself, just as Deck had never let moving to New York enter his mind. Maybe they'd both been unfair.

She rounded the bend to the hot springs. No guests were in the open pools, but Callie went to the private spring anyway. It was her favorite. She removed her robe and slipped naked into the dark water, which was lovely as always.

She thought about making love. Here and everywhere else they'd been together. She'd been able to let herself go with him. She'd trusted him. Wasn't that what she wanted in the end?

But she loved her career, her friends, the pace and the city. Leaving the ranch wasn't running away, as Deck had said. It was running *to* something good and rewarding.

Not exactly the whole truth. She was always running—to the next task, conversation, client, job, challenge. Because if she stopped…what?

She'd be stuck with herself and her own thoughts and feelings. And that was to be avoided because for a long time all she felt were pain and sadness and guilt and regret. She'd learned to protect herself by staying busy.

Nearly losing her father had reminded her that she could lose someone she loved in one terrible moment. Had she given Deck up out of that same fear? Was she running away from him?

And what about her capacity for deep love? Was her heart really crippled? Or just guarded? Could she change?

Maybe she already had. A little, anyway. Thanks to Deck.

Deck had helped her take back her past, replace painful memories with happy ones. Even thinking of her mother hurt less. She no longer clung to that terrible mental picture of party favors floating to the tarmac of the highway near her mother's crushed car.

Deck had given her back her mother. Even her birthday. His sweet celebration had healed the old hurt. Deck had been there for her however she needed him to be.

He would keep being there. He was that kind of guy. If anyone could help Callie heal her damaged heart, it was Deck.

If he wanted to try.

They'd both been afraid, backing away at the first bit of trouble like they'd touched a hot stove.

Why couldn't they share their lives? Geography was a challenge, but Callie loved challenges. If they loved each other, if they wanted to be together, they could work it out.

It was worth a try, Deck had said.

And this time Callie wasn't going to run.

DECK HEARD THE CAR pull up and stepped out of his studio to meet his buyer. A pretty woman, midtwenties, bounded toward him, grinning. "I'm so excited," she said, introducing herself and violently shaking his hand.

He led her into the studio where he'd leaned her painting—it was a sunset over the river—against the packing case he'd prepared.

"Oh, thank God, I love it just as much!" She beamed at him. "You know how you have something in your mind and you think it can't possibly be as good as you remembered, but it is?" She studied it with shining eyes. "Looking at this gives me this feeling. Peace and *joy*. Does that sound goofy? You hear that all the time, I bet. Such a cliché. I don't care."

He didn't get a chance to reply.

"This is my first original art, you know. I've been saving for the right one. And this is it. I can't wait to show my friends. They'll probably want to know where you're showing. Did you say you're in a gallery?"

"No," he said. "Not yet." *Not yet?*

"There's a place in Scottsdale where you'd be great." She pulled out a business card and wrote down the name. "Call them. Really. You should. So my friends won't have to drive all the way down here."

"Thanks," he said. "Let me get this ready." He boxed up the painting, while she kept talking about the place in her house she'd hang the work, her job in PR, how much she loved the current show at the Phoenix Art Museum and on and on.

Finally he put the box in her back seat, then turned to say goodbye.

"I feel like I know you from your painting, so I want to give you a hug or something…"

"Sure," he said, hugging her lightly.

She grinned at him afterward.

"So, great. Drive safe," he said, motioning at her open door, uncomfortable with her adoration.

She drove off still waving.

He realized he was still grinning. His art had made her happy. He liked that. A lot. He felt…proud. Callie was right. Selling his work could be rewarding.

Why had he held back? Like Callie with her birthday, he'd never questioned his old beliefs. When she'd dragged his art out of his studio, she'd exposed his excuses to the light.

He would call that gallery, dammit. The idea felt good, freeing. A little scary, but right.

He'd held back with Callie, too. Ruby was right. He hadn't even told he loved her. What the hell was he afraid of?

The pain, of course. The agony of losing too much. His father's death had been harder on him than he'd ever acknowledged. He'd clung to the old pain, just as Callie had done.

They'd been protecting themselves in their separate ways—him by closing himself in, her by running off. Why couldn't they stop that, trust each other, take the chance?

He'd said it was worth a try, but he hadn't tried. How could he let her go so easily? Hell, he should chase her to Manhattan. Ruby was right about that, too.

He had to talk to Callie. Galvanized, he started toward the ranch house. Then he spotted her on the path to the hot springs wearing that black robe and those silly flip-flops.

The perfect place to talk to her. He got what he needed, then he set off to chase down the woman he loved.

CALLIE WAS FLOATING, staring up at the stars, planning her speech to Deck when she heard him say her name. She sat up, not sure she hadn't imagined it.

There he stood in a terrycloth robe, holding a bottle of champagne with two mason jar glasses.

"Deck," she said, her heart full of hope.

He set down his burden, dropped his robe and slipped naked into the water. "Don't go, Callie," he blurted, then slapped the water. "Damn, that's not what I was going to say." He shook his head. "I was going to be logical and thoughtful, list options and choices, pros and cons and excuses, but that's the essence of it. I love you. I want us to be together."

He took hold of her arms, his hands warm and strong. "I never stopped loving you. I didn't realize it until I had you back. And I'm not letting you go this time. Not again. Even if I have to chase you to New York."

She chewed her lip, nervous again. "I love you, too, Deck. I want us to be together, too. I'm just…scared."

"Me, too. We've both been hurt. We've lost someone close. That did change our lives."

"But love is worth the risk, right?" she said, her heart filling with the truth of that.

"Absolutely," Deck said.

"I've blocked my feelings for so long…." She swallowed. "But you'll help me, right? You always have. You gave me back the ranch, my mother, even my birthday." She stopped. "I bet you can give me back my heart."

"Whatever you need," he said. "I'm there for you." He kissed her softly and she melted against him.

"You were right, Callie. I did hold back. My heart. My art. You make me want more."

"Deck…"

"If I have to move to New York, I'll do it. I'll buy one of those horse-drawn coaches and drive people around Central Park if that's what it takes."

Callie laughed. "No need to go insane, Deck. I can see myself here. Eventually. I need to go back and see what's what, but I think I could be happy here. With you."

"And we can live our lives with relish—"

"And mustard. Yeah."

Deck pulled her into his arms, serious now, and they kissed for a long, lovely moment.

All their past times together swirled in Callie's head like the hot, healing water sweeping around their bodies. She stepped back into the hollow place in the stone and looked into Deck's warm and steady eyes. "We've got a lot to work out," she warned.

"I'm a patient man," Deck said.

"You'll have to be."

"Don't I know it." He kissed her again, pulling her body tight against his. "Whatever it takes. You're worth everything." He looked into her face.

In the desert night, all she saw were the stars reflected in

Deck's eyes. Her heart, crippled as it was, seemed to be full of love now. Full and spilling over and she knew Deck would be there to catch every drop.

* * * * *

*Celebrate 60 years of pure reading pleasure
with Harlequin®!*
*Silhouette® Romantic Suspense is celebrating with the
glamour-filled, adrenaline-charged series*
LOVE IN 60 SECONDS
starting in April 2009.
*Six stories that promise to bring the glitz of Las Vegas,
the danger of revenge, the mystery of a missing diamond,
family scandals and ripped-from-the-headlines intrigue.
Get your heart racing as love happens in sixty seconds!*

Enjoy a sneak peek of
USA TODAY *bestselling author Marie Ferrarella's*
THE HEIRESS'S 2-WEEK AFFAIR
*Available April 2009
from Silhouette® Romantic Suspense.*

Eight years ago Matt Shaffer had vanished out of Natalie Rothchild's life, leaving behind a one-line note tucked under a pillow that had grown cold: *I'm sorry, but this just isn't going to work.*

That was it. No explanation, no real indication of remorse. The note had been as clinical and compassionless as an eviction notice, which, in effect, it had been, Natalie thought as she navigated through the morning traffic. Matt had written the note to evict her from his life.

She'd spent the next two weeks crying, breaking down without warning as she walked down the street, or as she sat staring at a meal she couldn't bring herself to eat.

Candace, she remembered with a bittersweet pang, had tried to get her to go clubbing in order to get her to forget about Matt.

She'd turned her twin down, but she did get her act together. If Matt didn't think enough of their relationship to try to contact her, to try to make her understand why he'd changed so radically from lover to stranger, then to hell with him. He was dead to her, she resolved. And he'd remained that way.

Until twenty minutes ago.

The adrenaline in her veins kept mounting.

Natalie focused on her driving. Vegas in the daylight wasn't nearly as alluring, as magical and glitzy as it was after dark. Like an aging woman best seen in soft lighting, Vegas's imperfections were all visible in the daylight. Natalie supposed that was why people like her sister didn't like to get up until noon. They lived for the night.

Except that Candace could no longer do that.

The thought brought a fresh, sharp ache with it.

"Damn it, Candy, what a waste," Natalie murmured under her breath.

She pulled up before the Janus casino. One of the three valets currently on duty came to life and made a beeline for her vehicle.

"Welcome to the Janus," the young attendant said cheerfully as he opened her door with a flourish.

"We'll see," she replied solemnly.

As he pulled away with her car, Natalie looked up at the casino's logo. Janus was the Roman god with two faces, one pointed toward the past, the other facing the future. It struck her as rather ironic, given what she was doing here, seeking out someone from her past in order to get answers so that the future could be settled.

The moment she entered the casino, the Vegas phenomenon took hold. It was like stepping into a world where time did not matter or even make an appearance. There was only a sense of "now."

Because in Natalie's experience she'd discovered that bartenders knew the inner workings of any establishment they worked for better than anyone else, she made her way to the first bar she saw within the casino.

The bartender in attendance was a gregarious man in his early forties. He had a quick, sexy smile, which was probably one of the main reasons he'd been hired. His name tag identified him as Kevin.

Moving to her end of the bar, Kevin asked, "What'll it be, pretty lady?"

"Information." She saw a dubious look cross his brow. To counter that, she took out her badge. Granted she wasn't here in an official capacity, but Kevin didn't need to know that. "Were you on duty last night?"

Kevin began to wipe the gleaming black surface of the bar. "You mean during the gala?"

"Yes."

The smile gracing his lips was a satisfied one. Last night had obviously been profitable for him, she judged. "I caught an extra shift."

She took out Candace's photograph and carefully placed it on the bar. "Did you happen to see this woman there?"

The bartender glanced at the picture. Mild interest turned to recognition. "You mean Candace Rothchild? Yeah, she was here, loud and brassy as always. But not for long," he added, looking rather disappointed. There was always a circus when Candace was around, Natalie thought. "She and the boss had at it and then he had our head of security escort her out."

She latched on to the first part of his statement. "They argued? About what?"

He shook his head. "Couldn't tell you. Too far away for anything but body language," he confessed.

"And the head of security?" she asked.

"He got her to leave."

She leaned in over the bar. "Tell me about him."

"Don't know much," the bartender admitted. "Just that his name's Matt Shaffer. Boss flew him in from L.A., where he was head of security for Montgomery Enterprises."

There was no avoiding it, she thought darkly. She was going to have to talk to Matt. The thought left her cold. "Do you know where I can find him right now?"

Kevin glanced at his watch. "He should be in his office. On the second floor, toward the rear." He gave her the numbers of the rooms where the monitors that kept watch over the casino guests as they tried their luck against the house were located.

Taking out a twenty, she placed it on the bar. "Thanks for your help."

Kevin slipped the bill into his vest pocket. "Any time, lovely lady," he called after her. "Any time."

She debated going up the stairs, then decided on the elevator. The car that took her up to the second floor was empty. Natalie stepped out of the elevator, looked around to get her bearings and then walked toward the rear of the floor.

"Into the Valley of Death rode the six hundred," she silently recited, digging deep for a line from a poem by Tennyson. Wrapping her hand around a brass handle, she opened one of the glass doors and walked in.

The woman whose desk was closest to the door looked up. "You can't come in here. This is a restricted area."

Natalie already had her ID in her hand and held it up. "I'm looking for Matt Shaffer," she told the woman.

God, even saying his name made her mouth go dry. She was supposed to be over him, to have moved on with her life. What happened?

The woman began to answer her. "He's—"

"Right here."

The deep voice came from behind her. Natalie felt every single nerve ending go on tactical alert at the same moment that all the hairs at the back of her neck stood up. Eight years had passed, but she would have recognized his voice anywhere.

* * * * *

Why did Matt Shaffer leave heiress-turned-cop
Natalie Rothchild?
What does he know about the death of Natalie's twin sister?
Come and meet these two reunited lovers and learn the
secrets of the Rothchild family in
THE HEIRESS'S 2-WEEK AFFAIR
by USA TODAY bestselling author
Marie Ferrarella.
The first book in Silhouette® Romantic Suspense's
wildly romantic new continuity,
LOVE IN 60 SECONDS!
Available April 2009.

You're invited to join our Tell Harlequin Reader Panel!

By joining our new reader panel you will:

- Receive Harlequin® books—they are FREE and yours to keep with no obligation to purchase anything!
- Participate in fun online surveys
- Exchange opinions and ideas with women just like you
- Have a say in our new book ideas and help us publish the best in women's fiction

In addition, you will have a chance to win great prizes and receive special gifts! See Web site for details. Some conditions apply. Space is limited.

To join, visit us at
www.TellHarlequin.com.

The Inside Romance newsletter has a NEW look for the new year!

Same great content, brand-new look!

The Inside Romance newsletter is a FREE quarterly newsletter highlighting our upcoming series releases and promotions!

Click on the Inside Romance link on the front page of
www.eHarlequin.com or e-mail us at
insideromance@harlequin.ca to sign up
to receive your FREE newsletter today!

You can also subscribe by writing to us at: HARLEQUIN BOOKS
Attention: Customer Service Department
P.O. Box 9057, Buffalo, NY 14269-9057

Please allow 4-6 weeks for delivery of the first issue by mail.

REQUEST YOUR FREE BOOKS!

2 FREE NOVELS
PLUS 2
FREE GIFTS!

HARLEQUIN®

Blaze™

Red-hot reads!

HARLEQUIN® *Blaze*™

COMING NEXT MONTH

Available March 31, 2009

#459 OUT OF CONTROL Julie Miller
From 0–60
Detective Jack Riley is determined to uncover who's behind the movement of drugs through Dahlia Speedway. And he'll do whatever it takes to find out—even go undercover as a driver. But can he keep his hands off sexy mechanic Alex Morgan?

#460 NAKED ATTRACTION Jule McBride
Robby Robriquet's breathtaking looks and chiseled bod just can't be denied. But complications ensue for Ellie Lee and Robby when his dad wants Ellie's business skills for a sneaky scheme that jeopardizes their love all over again....

#461 ONCE A GAMBLER Carrie Hudson
Stolen from Time, Bk. 2
Riverboat gambler Jake Gannon's runnin', cheatin' ways may have come to an end when he aids the sweet Ellie Winslow in her search for her sister. Ellie claims she's been sent back in time, but Jake's bettin' he'll be able to convince her to stay!

#462 COMING ON STRONG Tawny Weber
Paybacks can be hell. That's what Belle Forsham finds out when she looks up former fiancé Mitch Carter. So she left him at the altar six years ago? But she needs his help now. What else can she do but show him what he's been missing?

#463 THE RIGHT STUFF Lori Wilde
Uniformly Hot!
Taylor Milton is researching her next planned fantasy adventure resort—Out of This World Lovemaking—featuring sexy air force high fliers. Volunteering for duty is Lieutenant Colonel Dr. Daniel Corben, who's ready and able to take the glam heiress to the moon and back!

#464 SHE'S GOT IT BAD Sarah Mayberry
Zoe Ford can't believe that Liam Masters has walked into her tattoo parlor. After all this time he's still an irresistible bad boy. But she's no longer sweet and innocent. And she has a score to settle with him. One that won't be paid until he's hot, bothered and begging for more.

HBCNMBPA0309